The Panama Affair

Melissa Darnay

ISBN 9781705904343

To Kleriston,
For giving me my own Panama Affair

Prologue

The interrogation room reeked of urine and mold. Brianna Morgan perched on the edge of a plastic chair, trying to take up as little space as possible on its grimy surface. Alone in the room, she breathed through her mouth, gagging as the taste of human waste settled in the back of her throat.

A man cried out in Spanish. Although she didn't understand the words, she felt his fear and wished the walls weren't so thin. Panic blossomed in her chest like toxic algae, narrowing her vision and making her limbs feel numb.

She brushed a tear away with the back of her hand. She needed to steel herself against the smells and sounds of this third-world interrogation room. Swallowing hard to shut off her gag reflex, she closed her eyes and focused on her yoga breathing. If she was going to survive this, she didn't have time for a panic attack.

Brianna was a rising star at the All-Day News Network, known as ADN, based in Dallas. They'd even given her a show of her own, The Morgan Report, a little more than a year ago. Even though it was a late-night weekend spot, she had developed a cult following among the insomniacs for exposing injustice and fighting for the underdog.

At thirty-four, she was a rising star in television news, on her way to becoming the new Christiane Amanpour.

How had she ended up in this hellhole?

It all started when she met a man.

She should have known it was too good to be true. She should have known paradise always comes with a price.

Chapter 1

Some fathers teach their daughters how to play softball or grill hamburgers. My dad taught me how to play chess, which is really the ability to think five steps ahead of everyone else. — Brianna Morgan

Brianna Morgan lifted her face to the sun, letting its warmth seep into her skin. This was her first time in Panama, and she couldn't wait to explore the BonitaMar Hotel, a luxurious beachfront resort just outside of Panama City.

In five days, she would be covering La Cumbre Económica, a global banking summit. She'd checked into the posh resort early for a much-needed vacation. She had dropped her bags and her wine store purchases in her room, wanting as much outdoor time as possible. Mid-January temperatures in Dallas bounced between cold and icy, and she planned to enjoy every sundrenched moment of her preconference schedule in this tropical Central American paradise—no agenda, no cell phone—just a good novel, long walks on the beach, and an endless glass of wine.

Her lead cameraman, Mike Kowalski, was arriving early the next morning to get background video. He didn't need four days to get B-roll, but she owed him a boondoggle. They'd crisscrossed the globe over the past year, telling stories for victims who had no voice. She'd reported human rights violations that hadn't made the mainstream news, from the horrific honor killings in Afghanistan to mass murders in Zimbabwe. She and Mike were both exhausted—physically from their non-stop travel, and emotionally from the toll the atrocities had taken on their psyches.

The weather was a perfect seventy-eight degrees. Like all the tourists who came to Panama in January, she was ready to ditch her life in Dallas and start a new life in paradise.

The breeze flirted with the hem of her gem-green sundress as she sauntered to the outdoor terrace bar. It looked like a tropical bar should, with plump rattan couches, an abundance of overgrown ferns, and palm trees framing the shimmering blue ocean. She spotted an empty seating area at the far end of the verandah and sashayed her way through the other guests.

She ignored the head-swivels as people snapped their necks to catch a glimpse of her. Working in television, Brianna had grown immune to people's stares. She was taller than most men, athletically lean, and possessed a thick mane of wavy auburn hair. The halter top of her dress showed off her long neck and full cleavage, and her four-inch heels enabled her to move with grace of a 1940s movie star.

Halfway to the empty couch, Brianna's gaze flitted to a Latin man who looked like a Roman god. His high cheekbones, sharp jawline, and full lips set him apart from the rounder-faced Panamanians she'd seen. He looked unruffled by the humidity—his skin dry and smooth, his black slacks sharply creased, his lavender shirt sleeves held together at the wrist with gold cufflinks.

Although he was facing her, he was immersed in a tense conversation with the woman sitting across from him, a voluptuous Latina dressed in a tight yellow sundress with matching yellow stilettos. Her long hair had been blown out to look like black silk billowing in the breeze. They spoke Spanish in low voices, but their body language radiated tension. As Brianna approached, the bronzed-skin man glanced at her then did a double take. He stopped talking midsentence and stared at her through long thick lashes.

Thrilled that he'd noticed her, Brianna flashed him her most brilliant light-a-stadium smile, the one that had gotten her noticed at the network. As Brianna walked past, she glanced at his female companion, whose face had contorted with jealousy into a cartoonlike mask.

Brianna blinked. Whoa. That level of hatred was usually reserved for the woman who had just been caught in flagrante with a married man.

He reminded her of someone she'd met long ago. She brushed away the memory as she kept walking, not wanting to get tangled in a love triangle on her first day in paradise.

She sunk into the sofa's thick cushions. She kicked off her sandals and tucked her pedicured toes under her long legs. She signaled a waiter and ordered a glass of Albarino, a dry white wine from Spain. When the waiter brought it a few minutes later with a bowl of house-made yucca chips, her mouth curved into a smile.

She was already in love with Panama.

Relaxing for the first time in weeks, Brianna listened to the rhythmic crashing of the waves against the shore. Even though she was on vacation, she couldn't help thinking about where she would put the camera to tell the story of Panama. The commentary ran unedited in her head.

Paradise is an overused word, but this portion of Panama which borders the Panama Canal is a slice of heaven. The air is so clear that the intense colors hurt my eyes. The ocean sparkles like a field of blue diamonds, alive with dancing sunbeams. In the distance, mega ships glide over the deep-blue water toward the mouth of the canal. Not only am I experiencing one of the engineering marvels of the world, but I'm also in one of the most beautiful spots on earth.

Brianna would have been content to enjoy the view for hours, but she felt someone behind her. She glanced over her bare shoulder at the gorgeous Latin man. She appraised him with her moss-green eyes.

He smiled, crinkles appearing around his eyes. The laugh lines humanized him, making him even more appealing. She took in his thick wavy hair, his straight white teeth, and his powerful physique. In his late thirties, he was even more spectacular up close.

"I am sorry to disturb you, but I had to meet the most beautiful woman in Panama." His Spanish accent made the words sound like poetry. "My name is Lorenzo Silva."

She rose from the couch, stepped into her strappy sandals, and held out her hand. "Brianna Morgan," she said, using her on-camera voice to hide the fact that she felt like a freshman with a crush on the high school quarterback.

"It is a pleasure to meet you." Lorenzo lifted the back of her hand to his mouth and brushed his lips against her skin. When he raised his head from her hand, his liquid-brown eyes drank in the features of her face.

At five-foot ten, Brianna rarely met men who were taller than her, especially when she wore four-inch heels. He had her by an inch.

Brianna's heart felt like it had been injected with a syringe of adrenaline.

She glanced over to where he had been sitting. "Where's your friend?"

He released her hand. "Our meeting was over, and she left."

Brianna arched an eyebrow. "What a relief. I would hate to become the other woman in the space of time it takes to use the bathroom."

"Ana Maria is just a friend." Lorenzo's eyes twinkled. "And you could only ever be *the* woman. Never the *other* woman."

She crossed her arms in front of her chest. "That's quite a declaration. You just met me."

"I believe in being direct."

"Would you like to join me?" Brianna waved her hand, indicating the couch across from her.

"I was hoping you would ask." He ignored the seat she had pointed to and took a seat next to her on the sofa where she'd been sitting. "Let me take you to dinner tonight."

Studying him over her glass, Brianna sipped her wine to buy time. His broad cheek bones and muscular jaw made her heart beat faster. She needed to look past his physical perfection and discover what made him tick. "I'll have dinner with you on one condition."

He looked at her as if she were the only woman in the world. "Just ask, and it is yours."

She reached into her beach bag and pulled out her business card. "I'm a journalist. Let me interview you while I'm here. On camera."

She didn't know anything about this man, but he was intriguing— tall, sexy, smart, and from the looks of him, prosperous. But he also had a tenderness about him that was missing from most rich men.

"What will the interview be about?"

She studied his twinkling eyes, noticing they were the exact color of liquid milk chocolate. "I don't know yet, but I know you have a story to tell."

"You are very perceptive." He held out his hand to shake. "I have always been wary of reporters, but I want to get to know you. I agree to your interview, and I promise you honesty."

She put her hand out to seal the deal. Instead of shaking her hand, he pulled her toward him and placed her palm flat on his chest over his heart. Then he leaned down and kissed her on the cheek, his musky scent kicking her pheromones into high gear.

Brianna smiled. If things kept going, she wouldn't need the smutty book in her beach bag.

Chapter 2

There is nothing more exciting than meeting someone who could be the one. It is more thrilling than your biggest win, and it produces the same surge of dopamine that cocaine generates. — Brianna Morgan

Brianna slid into a booth at the back of El Filete Ardiente, the steakhouse restaurant at the hotel. They had talked all afternoon, sharing a bottle of Dom Perignon, chitchatting as they enjoyed the sunset. She'd wanted to go freshen up before dinner, but he'd told her she looked beautiful enough, so they went straight from cocktails to dinner, holding hands as they sauntered through the resort.

She'd expected Lorenzo to sit next to her on the banquette, but he surprised her by taking a seat at a ninety-degree angle from her.

He noticed her puzzled expression. "I want to see your face when we talk."

She put her napkin on her lap and leaned forward, studying him, from his dark wavy hair to his chiseled chin. "You are an enigma, Lorenzo Silva."

"I hope that is a compliment, mi amor."

"It is." She pulled her eyes away from his face and looked around the restaurant, inhaling. "It smells divine in here."

"Grilled steak and sizzling butter. Two of the best smells in the world."

The waiter, a short dark-skinned Panamanian with a round face and happy eyes, handed him the wine list. "Would you like me to recommend a wine to go with your dinner?"

Lorenzo turned to Brianna. "Do you prefer French, Italian, or Californian?"

She thought for a moment. "Let's drink a Napa Cab, if they have one."

Lorenzo glanced at the wine list then handed it back to the waiter. "We will have a bottle of Silver Oak."

She raised an eyebrow. The wine cost more than a hundred dollars a bottle in the wine store, and it was probably three times that in a restaurant. "Are we celebrating?"

As the waiter scurried away, Lorenzo leaned into her, taking her hand in his. "I have been very blessed in life. There is only one thing I am missing."

Brianna could smell the cologne on his neck, a unique smell of floral and woodsy male that increased her pulse. "What's that?"

"A woman to share my life with. Someone beautiful and compassionate, someone intelligent and strong." He stared into her eyes as he stroked her palm with his thumb. "Someone like you. Latin America is full of attractive women, but they are insecure and jealous. They want me because I have money. But if disaster were to strike, their love would fade as soon as my bank account was empty." He brought her palm to his lips and kissed it.

The intimacy of it sent jolts of electricity through her body.

He traced a finger down the right side of her face. "I do not know if you and I are meant for each other, but you seem to be everything I am looking for. Since I could be on the first date with my future wife, I want tonight to be perfect."

Brianna blinked, a journalist without words.

Lorenzo touched her chin with a feather-light caress. "I do not mean to scare you. I may look like Casanova, but my intentions are honorable."

Brianna winked at him. "At least you admit you're above average in the looks department."

He shrugged. "Being handsome is both a blessing and a curse. I have no problem getting women, but I often attract the wrong type of woman. Like I said, I am looking for a woman of substance. You might be looking for a vacation romance, but I am looking for a life partner."

Brianna leaned back, staring at his chiseled features. The waiter reappeared, uncorking and decanting their wine, giving her time to absorb his words.

Once the server left, Lorenzo picked up his glass of wine. "To the future. I do not know what it holds, but right now I hope it holds you."

She should be freaked out, but she wasn't. The reality was that she yearned for a life partner, but she had not been willing to settle. Meeting successful men was easy, but finding a tall, straight, single, intelligent man who loved his mother and would put her first was harder than it seemed. For the first time in her life, she felt like she'd met someone who would understand her desire to help those who couldn't help themselves, yet still be willing to splurge on expensive wine or designer clothes.

She'd kept people at arm's length for most of her adult life. Was she ready to put her faith in this man? She studied his face, looking for an answer. His sharp cheek bones threw a shadow over his muscular cheeks in the low light, making him look like a Roman warrior. Even though his face had hard planes of masculinity, his eyes displayed a vulnerability that made her want to open up to him.

She took a deep breath and met his gaze. "Lorenzo, I'm in. Let's see where this goes."

They clinked glasses and sipped their wine, ignoring the other diners in the busy restaurant. He leaned back in his chair, a playful gleam in his dark eyes. "Tell me a secret, something other people do not know."

"Okay, I'll play." Brianna thought for a moment. "I have an incredible sense of direction. At any time, I can tell you which way is north." She pointed north.

"That is very good. Many people have trouble with direction in Panama because the sun rises over the Pacific Ocean."

"It's not something I've worked at—it's just something I can do." She toyed with the stem of her wineglass. "It's like I can create a map in my head."

"You would make a good Boy Scout." Lorenzo reached out and fondled her hand. His hand was strong, his skin as soft as butter. "Tell me something else."

She sipped her wine with her free hand, thinking for a moment. "My dad was a naval officer. He used to say, 'Strong body, strong mind.' He taught our whole family to love physical fitness. I've been doing push-ups and sit-ups all my life." She patted her lean torso. "I do five hundred sit-ups a day. One hundred for each muscle group."

He placed a hand on her flat stomach. "Very impressive, Miss Morgan. Remind me to thank your father when I meet him."

The waiter reappeared, and Lorenzo ordered in Spanish.

After he left, Brianna asked, "Why was he smiling?"

"Because I promised to tip him more than he makes in a week if the food is perfect."

Brianna chuckled. "What did you order?"

He glanced at her through his thick lashes. "One of everything."

She gasped. "You ordered everything on the menu?"

He nodded.

"Why would you do that?"

He smiled, his straight white teeth gleaming in the candlelight. "I told you. I want everything to be perfect. What kind of first-date story will we tell our children if the shrimp is bad?" He clucked his tongue as he shook his head. "If the shrimp is not perfect, I will not allow you to eat it."

She threw her head back, laughing. "I have my own food taster. I feel like royalty."

"As you should, mi amor. You are my queen."

A moment later, the waiter brought two appetizers: shrimp cocktail and beef Carpaccio.

Lorenzo took a bite of each. "The shrimp is good, but the Carpaccio is better. They both have my approval."

Brianna dipped a large shrimp into the spicy cocktail sauce and ate it while he watched. "Delicious."

"Now the Carpaccio." He skewered a piece of meat with a shaving of Parmesan and held it to her mouth.

She ate what he offered, closing her eyes as she tasted the delicate beef and the pungent cheese. "That's incredible." She wiped her mouth with her linen napkin. "Do you know where Carpaccio originated?"

He thought for a moment. "In Italy, I assume."

Brianna grinned. "Excellent guess. The chef at Harry's Bar in Venice invented it."

"I've been to Harry's a few times, although I cannot remember ordering the Carpaccio."

"As the story goes," Brianna said, "Vittore Carpaccio was a famous painter in Venice, known for using vivid reds and whites in his art. Cipriani, who owned Harry's Bar, thought the red shaved meat and white Parmesan sauce looked like a Carpaccio painting. Thus, Carpaccio was born."

Lorenzo's eyes lit up. "Where did you learn that?"

9

"At Harry's Bar. We traveled a lot as kids. My parents taught us to love history by letting us experience it firsthand."

He fingered a lock of her auburn hair. "What other interesting tidbits do you know?"

She laughed as she scooped more of the Carpaccio onto her plate. "I have thousands of factoids swimming around in my brain. You think they're cute and clever now, but you might get tired of them one day."

His fingers whispered over the top of her head. "I could never get tired of that lovely brain of yours."

They chatted throughout their many courses. Lorenzo talked about his business in Panama as a real estate developer of luxury beachfront condos. He reminisced about his childhood, when he was poor but happy in Northern Spain, and how he and his brother spent every afternoon playing soccer—what he called fútbol—until it was too dark to see.

She snapped her fingers. "That's how I know you."

His brow pinched together. "You watch fútbol?"

"I did once. My freshman year at UCLA. My roommate and I went to a game in Indiana. I might have met you at a party."

His face lit up. "I remember you. We talked for a while, but I think I was on such a high from our win that I was not rational enough to ask for your phone number."

She blushed. "I've thought about you from time to time, wondering what happened to you."

He pulled a business card from his wallet and handed it to her. "No more missed opportunities. Here is my number."

She tucked his card in her bag and lifted her glass for a toast.

"That was our last college game," Lorenzo said. "My brother and I both played professionally after that."

"I don't remember meeting him. Was he at the party too?"

Lorenzo shook his head. "Marcio did not want to attend a silly college party. He had dinner with a recruiter that night and signed a contract a few weeks later. It was the start of his professional career."

"Are you and your brother close?"

"Yes and no. We are two sides of the same coin, two halves of the same person." Lorenzo sat back, a pensive look on his face. "I am the rock and he is the water. I am the yin and he is the yang. We are brothers, but we are also rivals."

"Isn't that normal for sibling relationships?"

Lorenzo shrugged. "He is the only brother I have, so I cannot compare. In business, we are unbeatable. In our personal lives, it is not always easy."

"So why did you stop playing professionally?"

"We had a deal. When one of us quit, the other would too." He pushed away the grilled scallops. "I hate to admit it, but I cannot eat another bite."

Brianna smirked. "I've been eating for sport for the past three courses. How about we cancel the rest of the food and get an after-dinner drink?"

"Great idea." He motioned for the waiter and explained what they wanted in Spanish.

Lorenzo turned to her. "What is your poison?"

She turned to the waiter, "Disaronno on the rocks."

Lorenzo held up two fingers. "Make that two."

She waited to continue their conversation until the waiter left. "That seems like a crazy deal to make. What if your brother wanted to quit when you were at the pinnacle of your career?"

"Before we went pro, we promised Mamá we would end our careers at the same time. As brothers, we were always very competitive. She worried that if one of our careers lasted longer than the other, jealousy would cause a rift between us, one we would not be able to mend." He shook his head. "Marcio got the losing end of our bet. I blew out my knee, and my team cut me at the end of my first season with FC Barcelona, my dream team."

"You got injured and he had to quit. Was he upset?"

"You have no idea how upset he was." Lorenzo laughed, a dry sound that didn't reach his eyes. "He was angry at the world. That is why we left Spain and came to Panama. He blamed Mamá for making him keep his promise to quit, and he wanted to punish her by moving far away. It broke her heart to see us go."

She patted his leg. She meant it to be a show of empathy, but once she touched his stone-hard leg, her pulse quickened. She put both hands on her wine glass, trying not to show how flustered she was. by his stone-hard legs. "Why didn't you stay in Spain?"

"That was part of the promise. We had to stick together. Mamá is an exceptional woman, very wise. When she dies, it will just be the two of us. It was more important to her that we stay together than stay with her."

"Did Marcio forgive her?"

He lifted one shoulder in a Gallic shrug. "Of course. She is our mother." He played with his unused spoon, worrying it between his fingers. "It took time for him to forgive me, but things were better between us after we arrived in Panama. Since we came here, we have been able to build something together. We are partners now instead of competitors. It gave us a fresh start."

There was something Lorenzo was hiding—Brianna was sure of it—but she didn't want to push too hard. This is a date, not an interview, she reminded herself.

"How long have you been in Panama?" she asked, wanting to lighten the mood.

"Seven years. We started a real estate development company called Grupo SilCasa. We have a couple projects in the Coronado beach area, known as the Panama Riviera. Our flagship project will be here, though." He pointed north. "We bought a tract of beachfront land in the next cove over for luxury condos. We start construction in two months."

"How exciting for you."

His eyes lit up, a little boy excited to open his Christmas presents. "You have no idea how hard the permits were to obtain. This is premium land, a culmination of jungle, ocean and city. It will be our legacy."

"You should be very proud of yourselves."

"We are. It is something that has brought my brother and I together."

"Is your brother married?"

"Marcio?" Lorenzo crossed himself, a Catholic to the end. "He will never marry. His version of a long-term commitment is making it through a weekend with the same woman."

She gave him a questioning look, wondering if she'd been played this whole time. "Are you alike? Should you come with a warning label as well?"

He reached for her hand. "Brianna, I told you. My brother and I are opposite sides of a coin. I want one woman, not twenty."

Brianna's eyes gleamed. "That's good to hear, because I've never seen a bed that could hold twenty-one people."

He struggled to suppress his laughter as the waiter brought their drinks.

He held up his glass. "To the start of something special."

They clinked glasses and sipped the Disaronno, enjoying the easy camaraderie that had formed between them.

"You are a good reporter. We have been talking about me all evening. How did you get into journalism?"

She brushed her hair over one shoulder. "It was an accident. When I was a junior in high school, a group of rich kids were bullying a girl named Sonya Goodwin, a girl from the wrong side of the tracks. She wore the same pair of patched jeans to school almost every day. The rich kids taunted her, calling her horrible names and treating her like a servant because she was poor. I knew it was wrong, but I was too scared to say anything. One day, they went too far and made her cry in front of everyone in the cafeteria. Not little tears but mascara dripping, snotty tears." Brianna took a deep ragged breath. "Sonya committed suicide that night."

He squeezed her hand.

Brianna's eyes filled with tears at the memory. "When I told my dad what had happened, I thought he'd hug me and tell me it would be alright." She shook her head. "But he didn't. He lectured me for thirty minutes. I'd been given strength and intelligence and the support of a loving family; I had to use those gifts to help others who couldn't help themselves."

She dabbed at her eyes. "I was so ashamed of myself. If I'd had the courage to stand up to the bullies, Sonya would still be alive. That night, I wrote an article for our weekly school paper. I called out the mean kids for their bullying. I praised Sonya for her tenacity, for the fact she'd wanted to better her life by staying in school. And then I challenged all the other kids, the ones like me who'd stood silent on the sidelines. I likened our silence to the Germans who'd stood by and allowed Hitler to annihilate the Jews."

He touched her chin. "That was very brave of you."

13

She gave him a sad smile. "Too little, too late, but I found my voice. When my article was published, the other kids rallied around me. I realized the power of the pen, and I started using it to fight for people who couldn't fight for themselves. By the time I went to college, I knew that I had to be a journalist. I had to use the media's power to help the other Sonya Goodwin's of the world."

He rubbed her shoulder. "That is a heavy burden for one pair of shoulders."

She shrugged. "Sometimes. But I owe it to Sonya to help others."

He kissed her on each hand. "Let's take a stroll on the beach."

Brianna peeked under the table at his Ferragamo shoes, wanting to bring some lightness back to their evening. "You want to walk on the beach in your python loafers? Those must have set you back at least a grand."

He looked down at his shoes as if seeing them for the first time. "You noticed my shoes?"

"I'm a reporter. I notice everything."

"I will remember that."

After paying the bill, he pulled her out of the booth. He dipped his head as if he was going to kiss her, but he brushed his lips against the tip of her nose instead. "Cute nose." He winked. "Come on. Let's walk." He put his hand on the small of her back and led her out of the restaurant.

She inhaled deeply as they meandered through the deserted resort. Jasmine and honeysuckle were fragrant in the night air. "It smells delicious out here."

He picked a yellow Lady Slipper and handed the flower to her. "You are delicious."

Brianna took the flower, squeezing his hand as they walked together in the moonlight, a Mona Lisa smile playing at the corners of her mouth. It was breezier than before, and the heavy salt air hung like a sweater on her shoulders. They wound their way through the beachfront pools toward the beach. She leaned into him for warmth.

He wrapped his arm around her. "Cold?"

She looked up at him. "Not anymore."

When they reached the edge of the sand, he let go of her hand and kicked off his shoes. "Want to race?"

Brianna laughed. "After that big dinner?"

He grinned as he rolled up his pant legs.

She stretched her arms like a lazy hotel cat as she stepped out of her sandals, and then, without warning, she pushed him over into the sand. "You're on!"

Brianna leaped past him and ran as fast as she could. She'd made it a few yards before Lorenzo rocketed to his feet and powered past her, exploding into the surf.

She waded after him, laughing as water splashed onto the hem of her sundress and up her leg.

"No fair." She laughed, giving Lorenzo a playful bump on the arm. "You're a professional athlete, and I'm just a weekend warrior."

He smiled down at her. "I was a professional athlete, but I am an old man now. I just turned thirty-seven last month."

"You don't run like an old man. Look at me," she wheezed. "I'm three years younger, and I'm breathing like I just ran a marathon. You're not even out of breath."

He laughed, his eyes flashing in the moonlight. "You are in great shape." He ran his fingers lightly up her arm. "Besides, I like you out of breath."

Lorenzo turned in the surf and opened his arms. Without a word, she collapsed into him. As the cool water lapped at their ankles, he tilted her face toward him and kissed her. He tasted of amaretto and salt spray, his lips soft and warm.

When he deepened the kiss, she pulled away. "I've had a great evening, Lorenzo."

"Uh-oh." He pulled her back into him, nibbling her lip as a wave crashed and the sand shifted under their feet. "That sounds like an exit line."

"It is." Brianna forced herself out of his arms but kept hold of his hands. "It's late. I need my beauty sleep."

"You are already beautiful enough. The night is young. Stay with me a little longer."

"I'd love to stay out and play, but I forgot to lock my chastity belt."

He smiled, his eyes crinkling at the corners. "Did I mention I am great at picking locks?"

"Of course, you are." She nudged his arm with her shoulder. "I bet you're great at just about everything."

"Brianna, Brianna." Lorenzo sighed. "Let me walk you to your room before I forget I am a gentleman."

He led her back to where they had left their shoes, holding her hand in his and massaging her fingers individually. She felt like her body had lost its bones and would melt into a puddle of jelly.

They were quiet on the way to her room, the easy banter of the previous few hours overshadowed by the sexual tension crackling between them.

When they were near her room on the nineteenth floor, Lorenzo nudged her into the alcove in front of the door. "We do not want the cameras to see." He nodded toward the ceiling camera at the end of the hall. "Some things are meant to be private."

He kissed her, a gentle meeting of their lips, heat radiating off his body. "I will call you in the morning. Tomorrow will take you to lunch and show you the beauty of Panama."

Brianna noticed that he didn't ask. She might have argued, but she didn't have the strength. She needed her energy to resist his charm.

"I'll bring my appetite," she said, turning to insert the key card into the lock.

As soon as the lock clicked open, the power in the hallway flickered off.

Lorenzo wrapped his arms around her from behind, pressing his body against her back. "Do not be afraid," he whispered. "I will protect you from the dark."

She leaned into him. "But who will protect me from you?"

Lorenzo moved his lips to her ear, so close that she felt the heat from his breath. "You do not need protection from me. I am here to give you pleasure."

The generator powered on, sounding like a 757 about to take off after the quietness of the power outage. The lights flickered on, a bright reminder of reality.

Unsure whether she should be grateful or upset that their intimate interlude was over, Brianna forced herself to step away from him. "Does the power go out a lot?"

"Not as often as one might think, but it happens." He traced a lock of her hair that had curled in the humidity. "After all, this is Panama."

She turned and gave him a chaste kiss on the lips before slipping into her room. "Until mañana." She swung the door closed before she could change her mind.

Then she did what any modern woman would do when she was nuts for a guy. She Googled him. She read about how he had played soccer for several minor teams in Europe before being picked up by FC Barcelona, the brass ring in his sport. Then she read about Grupo SilCasa, the business he owned with his brother. He'd been modest. The company was well-funded, met deadlines, and had been voted one of the best companies to work for in Panama.

When Brianna fell into bed hours later, she dreamed of a beautiful Spanish soccer player with expensive taste in shoes.

Chapter 3

Think about the worst day you've ever had. My second day in Panama was worse than that. — Brianna Morgan

Brianna jumped out of bed at six in the morning, excited to spend sunrise on the beach. She'd left the sliding glass door open, wanting to hear the crash of the waves as she slept. She pulled a slinky white robe on and stepped out onto her balcony. To her right, the trees in the jungle were still bathed in darkness, but in front of her, the ocean glowed as if lit from within. Dozens of ships dotted the horizon, their lights twinkling in pre-dawn.

She inhaled deeply, reveling in the tropical scent. What made it smell like that? she wondered. Was it the salt from the sea? The abundance of flowers? The proximity to the jungle? Or the negative ions generated by the ocean? She'd have to investigate that for a story.

She changed into a navy one-piece bathing suit and twisted her hair into a messy bun. She didn't want to miss one moment of her time in this lush wonderland.

After tying a multi-color sarong around her waist, she stepped into a pair of beach shoes. She took a moment to gloss her lips with a hint of color. After all, she might run into Lorenzo. Their date wasn't until noon, but Brianna had learned to always be prepared.

The thought of Lorenzo Silva quickened her pulse. He had knocked Brianna's equilibrium out of whack as soon as he had approached her at the terrace bar. She'd never met anyone quite like him. He was suave yet genuine, aggressive yet warm, intelligent yet sexier than any man deserved to be.

The thing she liked the most about him was the fact that he had been open and direct with her. He opened his heart and gave it to her like a gift. Successful men didn't do that. They hid their emotions behind their corporate spreadsheets, wanting to dazzle her with private jets and expensive gifts.

She tucked her room key and some sunscreen into a fun black plastic beach bag she'd picked up at duty free. She walked briskly through the hotel, and once outside, skipped to the sand. The sun was just rising, and she had the ocean to herself.

Hundreds of birds sang in the nearby jungle canopy. A flock of green parrots swooped from branch to branch at the edge of the water, chattering noisily. A toucan flew by, its oversized colorful beak making it top-heavy in flight. Brianna inhaled, enjoying the heavy scent of tropical flowers, mesmerized by the jungle activity just a few feet from the ocean. She laughed out loud, giddy with the joy of a tropical paradise and the fresh bloom of new love.

She walked along the beach for a bit, following an iguana until it skittered under some rocks. After untying her sarong, she tucked it in her beach bag and dropped it on the sand. As she moved into the surf, she kicked at the foam, thinking of Lorenzo and last night's kiss. She needed to burn off the sexual energy before she saw him again. She didn't want a vacation romance; she wanted a lasting love.

She'd had her share of boyfriends, and had been engaged to her college sweetheart, Pierce Huntley. He was the most handsome boy in school—and was still the nicest guy she knew—but he'd left her for another man when he came to the realization that he was gay. It took her a long time to trust another man after that.

By the time her career had taken off, she was dating moguls and executives. They were intelligent and exciting and showered her with gifts, but they all had narcissistic tendencies, not to mention trust issues of their own and wandering eyes. She'd rather be single forever than end up in jail for murdering an unfaithful husband. Ending up in jail was one of those unfounded fears that come from reading too many crime novels, but it had become her one true phobia.

Wading farther out, she dove under a wave. Brianna was a strong swimmer and still tried to swim at her health club a few times a week whenever she wasn't on location. With every stroke, she felt Lorenzo's touch against her skin. She'd have to swim harder if she was going to get him out of her head this morning. She swam along the shoreline until she saw the kayaks on the beach, a perk for vacationers at the resort. Kayaking was exactly what she needed to burn some energy.

She swam back to shore and dragged a kayak into the shallow water. Then she pulled herself into the boat and kayaked along the coastline. After a half hour of hard paddling, she had rowed out of the bay. Just around the first curve, she spotted a small, secluded cove in the distance and thought it would be a good place to rest.

She paddled to the shore and hopped out when her kayak hit sand. She waded onto the tiny beach, dragging the kayak onto the beach with her. She wondered if Lorenzo knew about this hidden cove. It would be a great place for them to go with a picnic lunch and a bottle of wine. The beach scene in From Here to Eternity flashed in her mind. She'd never been a fan of sand and sex, but Lorenzo might be able to tempt her into anything.

She walked around the cove, stepping up onto large rocks to give her calves a workout. At the far end of the cove, she saw what looked like a cave. She wandered over, excited by the thought of spelunking on her first morning on the beach. It had a low opening, but she didn't hesitate to drop to her knees and duck inside. It was much darker than she'd thought it would be, and it smelled pungent, like spoiled meat.

Once inside the cave, she stood up, blinking as she moved forward so her eyes could get accustomed to the lack of light. Tripping on something in the sand, she looked down and saw a man's shoe. She bent down touched it, then shuddered as her fingers skimmed what felt like snakeskin.

Bile shot to Brianna's throat as she realized the shoe was attached to a man's body. Even worse, she recognized those lips—they had kissed her just a few hours before.

A primal instinct screamed at her to run. She scrambled out of the cave and ran at full throttle to the kayak. She could paddle back to the resort, pack her things, and be on her way to the airport in less than an hour.

She'd interviewed people in third-world jails. Once they were behind bars, guilt or innocence didn't matter. She'd once confided to her best friend, Katherine, that her greatest fear was being jailed in a foreign country. Her phobia became so intense that she had to tell her producer no more prison interviews outside of the States. She couldn't stand being in jail, even as a visitor. Just the thought made her tremble with fear.

Brianna ran through the surf, pulling the kayak with her. She wanted to get as far away from the body as possible.

She was having a difficult time getting her limbs to do what she wanted. Her movements were clumsy and out of sync. She tried to paddle, but it felt like moving through Jell-O. Her vision had narrowed, and she realized she was having a panic attack. She forced herself to stop paddling and breathe. After she took a few deep breaths, her brain switched gears from flight to fight.

Something had happened to Lorenzo last night. When Brianna had left him, he was warm and vibrant and pulsing with masculinity. Now he was dead. She could barely think the word.

She stopped paddling and closed her eyes, thinking of the body she'd just seen. Healthy, virile men don't just drop dead. Even though she didn't know him well, she couldn't fathom that he would commit suicide. He seemed to be too much in love with life for that.

"What happened to you, Lorenzo?" she asked aloud.

Someone had killed him. She didn't know how yet, but she knew it in the roots of her hair.

She took a deep breath and allowed her inner fighter to emerge. "I'll find out who did this to you." She switched directions and paddled back to the cove. "I promise I'll find out, even if I have to go to jail to do it."

She secured the kayak again and walked slowly back to the cave. She ducked back in, not wanting to disturb anything. She let her eyes grow accustomed to the dark before she turned her gaze toward Lorenzo's body.

Brianna shut off her emotions, going into reporter mode and focusing on the scene. Lorenzo was curled on his side in a fetal position, his eyes wide open. His shirt and face were stained with what smelled like vomit. Even though it was dark inside, his face and neck were cherry red, as if he'd been severely sunburned. Or boiled in a lobster pot.

There was no blood around the body that she could see, but the air was rank with urine, feces, and vomit. Brianna breathed through her mouth as the dank, fetid space closed in on her. The scent of death was strong, and it threatened to overpower her senses. She forced herself to ignore it as she moved around the tiny cave.

She ran the different scenarios through her head. He could have had a heart attack, or maybe a poisonous snake had bitten him. But if either of those had happened, how had he ended up in this cove? As far as she could tell, it was accessible only by kayak or boat.

Something didn't add up.

She peered around the small cave with a critical eye, looking for insects, snakes, weapons, anything out of place. The only thing that seemed odd was a bottle of Disaronno liqueur tipped onto its side within reach of the body. The cap was off, and it was empty.

Disaronno was Brianna's favorite after-dinner drink. They'd each had a glass last night.

Why would he bring a bottle of her favorite liqueur to this secluded spot, especially after their perfect date? It was hard to believe he would have come out here in the middle of the night just to drink. He ran a big company. They'd had a full day planned today. Drinking by himself didn't make sense.

Brianna knew she had to alert the authorities, but she had to be smart about it. She was a tourist in Panama, she didn't speak Spanish, and she didn't know Panama's laws.

She shivered even though it was warm. Shock was starting to set in. She needed a plan, but she felt her brain shutting down. She always thought best when she exercised, so she'd make her plan in the kayak on her way back to the resort.

She left the cave and headed back to the kayak, taking her time to get back in. She hadn't put a lifejacket on when she had left the resort, and the last thing she needed was to have an accident.

By the time she was back onshore, she'd formulated her plan. She would summon the police and alert the American embassy. But first she'd call Babs Whittaker, her producer in Dallas at ADN. The best way to get out in front of this thing was to be in front of it with a camera.

Chapter 4

Detective John Bethancourt was born in Panama to an American father and a Panamanian mother who had worked as an executive assistant in the American Zone of the Panama Canal. His father had been stationed in Panama with the US Army, one of thousands of people assigned to protect the Panama Canal in the seventies. His father had fallen in love with the country first, followed by the woman who would become his wife shortly after that. He had shared both loves with his three children.

Detective Bethancourt was known as a Zonian, a class of people with dual citizenship and multi-cultural roots. He was tall like his father, had dark features like his mother, and spoke Panamanian Spanish, as well as American English without an accent.

He had gone to college in Syracuse, New York, where his father's family lived, but he detested the cold and moved back to Panama before he developed any roots in his father's country. Because he had dual passports, he was the one chosen to attend training courses in the US He'd been trained by the NYPD, the Secret Service, and the FBI.

At forty-two, he was happily married to another Zonian and had three kids under ten. He was the top homicide investigator for Panama's Policia Nacional, and he typically caught the high-profile cases. From the moment he got the call about a possible murder near the BonitaMar Hotel, he knew every move would be scrutinized. Not only was there a questionable death at a tourist resort, but the dead man was also one of Panama's elite.

Panama is a small country of less than four million people, but the circle of people with power and influence is miniscule. Everyone who was anyone had met the famous Silva brothers, or at least knew who they were.

A fútbol fanatic, Detective Bethancourt had followed the careers of Lorenzo and Marcio Silva even before they had come to Panama. He had met them on three occasions over the past seven years, always feeling like a shy kid meeting his boyhood heroes, especially when the Silva brothers were together.

This wasn't just another case to him. It was personal.

He worked his cell phone on the drive to the exclusive BonitaMar Hotel. He called Eric Pinto, the hotel's security chief, someone he knew and trusted. Before arriving at the resort's front gate, he'd already gotten an update on Lorenzo Silva's last known location the previous night. Silva had been seen with an American journalist named Brianna Morgan. They looked like they were about to go into her room when the power went out. Pinto's team was still working to find out when Lorenzo Silva had left the hotel.

Brianna Morgan was also the one who found the body. That was a big coincidence. Except Detective Bethancourt didn't believe in coincidences.

He needed to interview the American journalist first thing, but he didn't want to go into the interview blind. He called Moses Souza, a young computer geek in the police department. "Moses, it's Bethancourt. I need a bio on an American: last name Morgan, first name Brianna."

"When do you need it?" Moses asked.

"Now. I'm driving but I'll stay on the phone."

Moses clicked his computer keys as he accessed an international database. "Brianna Lynne Morgan is thirty-four years old with a bachelor's degree from UCLA and a master's in journalism from Columbia. Never married. She has a news show called The Morgan Report on ADN, one of the biggest news networks in the States. It's on Sunday nights at ten."

Detective Bethancourt exited the Pan-American Highway. He tapped the steering wheel, knowing he only had three minutes left before he hit the dead spot and lost cell reception. "Tell me about her family. Give me the thirty-second version."

Moses pounded on his keyboard, typing and talking at the same time. "Her father was career navy, so they moved around a lot when she was a kid. Her dad is retired now and lives in Naples, Florida. She has one brother Jack Morgan, two years older. He was a Navy SEAL and now works for ARGON, a defense contractor with offices all over the world."

"No other siblings?"

"Another brother, James, who died when he was sixteen."

"Why is she in Panama?"

"My guess is she's here for that big banking conference that starts next week, La Cumbre Económica."

"Great start, Moses. Keep digging. Call me if you get anything good."

Detective Bethancourt didn't wait for Moses to say goodbye; he just clicked the phone off. He absorbed the information as he navigated through a mountainous jungle area impervious to cell signals.

Brianna Morgan had attended good schools, so she was no dummy. She wasn't married and had no kids, so work was her life. She had her own national show at thirty-four, which meant she was important to the network. She'd have their backing if things got messy.

If she had murdered Lorenzo Silva, she would be a worthy adversary.

Detective Bethancourt redialed Eric Pinto at the BonitaMar as soon as he got through the dead zone. "Eric, do you have eyes on the American journalist, Brianna Morgan?"

"Sure do. We've had cameras on her since you first called." He mumbled something to someone else. "John, I've got you set up in a conference room, the Sunset Room on the main level. It's ready for you whenever you need it."

"Thanks. I'll check in with you after I catch up with Miss Morgan. Do you know where she is right now?"

Pinto snorted. "She's hard to miss. Go down to the pool bar and follow the crowd. I've never seen so many people taking selfies."

Detective Bethancourt showed his badge at the gates of the swanky resort. His name was on a list, and security waved him through. He parked in an unloading zone and headed to where Brianna was taping a segment to air later. He stood off to the side and watched her as she put on a show for the camera.

She wore a white pencil skirt that was so tight he could see every curve of her body. Her red sleeveless blouse had a plunging ruffled neckline. Any more cleavage and it would have been tasteless, but it was sexier than if she'd been wearing a bikini. He could see the creamy tops of her breasts and the silhouette of her long legs. His imagination painted the rest of the picture.

"This is Brianna Morgan, coming to you from Panama City, Panama. Welcome to The Morgan Report. Just days before La Cumbre Económica, the banking summit that could change financial laws around the world, I discovered the dead body of Lorenzo Silva, a prominent local real estate developer and a former professional soccer player for FC Barcelona. I found his body in a small cove near the BonitaMar Hotel, a five-star resort on the outskirts of Panama City."

A beach ball bounced into the frame, followed by children's laughter.

"Cut," she waved her arms at her cameraman. "I want to do that part again. But this time let's change the background. Start with the ocean and the ships in the background." She pointed at the view she wanted. "Pan across the resort next. I want people to see how luxurious this place is."

The cameraman nodded. "Got it."

Brianna never looked directly at him, but Detective Bethancourt saw her register his presence out of the corner of her eye. He was dressed in street clothes—slacks, a dress shirt and a blazer—but she blinked once when he came into her peripheral vision. It was a tiny tell, but to a trained professional, she could have announced it on camera.

"Let's show people this is the last place a murder should take place," she said, a decibel louder than she'd been speaking before. Yes, she knew he was here, and she knew he was a cop.

Brianna turned and faced the opposite direction, her back to Detective Bethancourt. The cameraman readjusted the camera on one shoulder and used his other hand to count down with his fingers: Three…two…one.

Detective Bethancourt could watch her all day. She sparkled with charisma, and he could see why people loved her. He had to break her rhythm and catch her off guard.

"This is Brianna Morgan, reporting from Panama…"

He stepped into her line of sight, and she stopped talking mid-sentence. She made a slicing motion with her hand to indicate she wanted to stop filming.

"Can I help you?" Brianna's voice dripped with irritation, adopting a slight Southern accent that hadn't been there a moment before.

Detective Bethancourt studied her without speaking, as if reading her thoughts. He did this to make suspects uncomfortable. Brianna wasn't a suspect yet, but he assumed everyone was guilty. That was what made him so good at his job.

"I'm Detective John Bethancourt from the Policia Nacional. I'm investigating the death of Lorenzo Silva. Are you Brianna Morgan?"

Her face went blank. "Yes."

"You found the body?"

"Yes."

"I'd like to ask you a few questions. Please come inside where we can speak in private."

He wasn't asking.

"Of course," she said, blasting him with her thousand-watt, on-camera smile.

She turned to her cameraman. "Mike, get some B-roll of the area while I'm speaking to the detective. I won't be long."

"Sure thing." Mike looked thrilled to have a front-row seat to a scandal.

Detective Bethancourt indicated the direction of the conference room. She flung her Prada handbag over her shoulder, trailing a red silk scarf that matched her blouse and shoes. She kept her back ramrod straight as she walked beside him, her gait long despite her six-inch platform heels.

Detective Bethancourt was tall for a Latin. At six feet, he was usually the tallest person in the room. With her power shoes on, Brianna had him by four inches. No, this woman wasn't dumb. She knew that height equals power, and she wore supersized shoes to exploit that power. He wouldn't make the mistake of underestimating her.

As they entered the hotel lobby, the cool air washed over them. He would have preferred less air conditioning so he could see her sweat when he asked her tough questions, but police work was always a tradeoff. More than seeing her sweat, he needed her indoors, in a quiet place, where she couldn't hide her eyes behind sunglasses or get distracted by tourists wanting to get close to the TV camera.

"In here." Detective Bethancourt indicated a small room at the end of the hallway.

The generic conference room held a medium-size conference table with eight chairs—three on each side and one at each end. A long skinny table stood against the wall, probably meant for beverage service. Other than that, the room was barren. No doughnuts, no coffee, no water. This wasn't a social visit.

Brianna walked ahead of him and took the chair at the head of the table. Her chair choice told him she was used to being in charge.

Detective Bethancourt set a piece of paper and a pen in front of her.

"Please write your name at the top," he said, standing over her.

She seemed to think for a moment, trying to figure out what this was about, before pulling a Mont Blanc fountain pen out of her handbag and writing her name with an elegant flourish. She handed it to him in an off-handed manner, as if she had just autographed a glossy headshot for a fan.

After he had confirmed she was right-handed and didn't like to give up control, he walked to the other side of the table and sat across from her at the other head chair.

He stared at her without speaking.

The long silence combined with intense eye contact was meant to make her uncomfortable, but he was the one off his game. He was used to interviewing bad guys. He'd never interviewed a woman as beautiful as Brianna Morgan before. It was hard to look away from her intense green eyes and her Slavic cheekbones.

This could be the one of the more difficult interviews he'd done because he was used to interrogating ugly men with low IQs. As a reporter, she also would be a trained interrogator.

"Miss Morgan, what are you doing in Panama?"

"I'm here for La Cumbre Económica."

"That doesn't start until next week."

"I came early to spend some time in Panama." She leaned back as if they were having a friendly cocktail conversation. "I've been to seventy-four countries, but I'd never been here before."

"What were you doing when you found the body this morning?"

"Exercising."

"Can you be more specific?"

She looked up and to the right, as if remembering something. "I had dinner with Lorenzo Silva last night. I was going to interview him for my TV show, The Morgan Report. During our conversation, he told me about the little cove between this property and the one next door, where he's

28

going to build luxury condos. When I saw the kayaks, I thought it would be fun to explore the place he told me about." She leaned forward, exposing some cleavage. "I found his body in a small cave and came back to shore to call the police."

Her answer sounded rehearsed. He needed to shake her up.

"Did Lorenzo tell you about the cave?"

"No, but it wasn't hard to find since the cove is so small."

Detective Bethancourt tapped his pen on the table. "I've lived in Panama most of my life. I didn't know about that little beach."

"Perhaps I'm more curious than you are." She gave him a flirtatious smile, showing off her straight white teeth. "It's a prerequisite for being a journalist."

"You just happened to find a hidden cave in a cove that no one knows about. And in that cave, you just happened to find the dead body of the man you had dinner with last night. Is that correct?"

Brianna nodded. "Yes. Truth is stranger than fiction." She used her right hand to move her thick made of auburn hair from one shoulder to the other.

The subtle floral scent of her perfume wafted toward him, and desire flashed through his body. He looked down and took a breath. He wasn't a pubescent teenager. He had to get his body under control. He thought about the smell of his children's hair before bedtime.

When he looked up again, his face was a mask. "When did you first meet Mr. Silva?"

"Late yesterday afternoon."

"Did you have an appointment with him before you met?"

Brianna uncrossed her legs and crossed them the other way, dangling one long leg over the other, looking like she was on a beach chair by the pool rather than in an interview with a detective. "When I met Mr. Silva yesterday, I asked him if I could interview him for my show."

"Ah, your show," Detective Bethancourt said as he tapped his pen against the table. "What's a human rights journalist like you doing in Panama for a banking conference?"

"I covered the Panama Papers scandal the moment it broke in 2016," she said, unruffled by his poking. "And I've covered the fallout ever since."

"If you came to Panama to cover the banking conference, why did you want to interview Mr. Silva?"

"It's a summit," she said.

"Excuse me?"

"It's a summit. Not a conference. There's a difference."

He bit the inside of his cheek to avoid rolling his eyes. "What's the difference?"

"At a summit, important talks happen between high-level people. For example, when presidents meet, they always attend a summit. A conference is for everyday people who are sent somewhere to discuss something or learn something. The meeting that's about to take place is a summit between real power players in the banking industry."

"If you were coming to Panama for a banking *summit*," Detective Bethancourt said, "why were you planning to interview Mr. Silva? He's not a banker."

"It was a human-interest angle. People don't care about banks half a world away, but they do care about where they could potentially retire. As I'm sure you're aware, Panama is a retirement haven for many Americans. Since Mr. Silva sold real estate to Americans, his rags-to-riches story was intriguing. Plus, a handsome face always plays well to audiences."

Another prepared sound bite, Detective Bethancourt thought.

"Were you involved with Mr. Silva romantically?" he asked.

"I just met him yesterday."

Detective Bethancourt noticed that Brianna didn't fidget, play with her hands, or scratch at phantom itches like most people did when they were under scrutiny. She was used to being watched and was perfectly in control of her body.

"I didn't ask when you met him. I asked if you were romantically involved with him."

She leaned forward, her eyes narrowing. "What are you getting at?"

"It's a simple question, Miss Morgan," Detective Bethancourt said, a touch of annoyance in his voice. "Were you involved romantically with the deceased man, Lorenzo Silva?"

"I didn't have sex with him, if that's what you want to know."

"If I pull up the hotel's security footage from last night, I won't see him leaving your room?"

"He was never in my room last night, so it would be impossible for your tapes to show Lorenzo Silva walking out of my room."

She didn't look like she was lying.

Everyone has a tell, that little thing they do when they're lying. Some people cough, others look away. When Detective Bethancourt had caught her by surprise outside, she'd blinked. That was the only tell he'd seen. He didn't know what she did when she was lying, so he'd have to push harder.

"Lorenzo never went near your room?" he asked

She smiled, as if she knew something he didn't. "He's a Latin gentleman. At the end of the evening, he walked me to my door, but he never went inside."

She sounded sure of herself, but he wouldn't know the truth until he saw the tape.

"Did you have dinner with him last night?"

She nodded. "Yes."

"Where did you eat?"

"At El Filete Ardiente, the steakhouse here at the resort."

"What was he like during dinner?" Detective Bethancourt asked.

"What do you mean?"

"Was he happy? Sad? Preoccupied? Angry?"

"He was happy."

"What was he happy about?"

"He said business was great. He was excited about his new project on the property next door." She waved her hand toward the beach next to the BonitaMar.

"What else did he talk about?

"He spoke about his childhood and his time as a professional soccer player. That seemed like a very happy time in his life. He also talked about his brother, Marcio. I haven't met him, but they seemed to be close."

"Did he talk about his ex-wife?"

She blinked. Yes, that was her tell. She hadn't known about the ex-wife.

She recovered quickly with a practiced professional smile. "I wasn't having dinner with him to sort through his dirty laundry."

He scoffed. "I thought you were an investigative reporter. Isn't it your job to dig up the dirt on your subjects?"

She shrugged. "He wasn't a target."

"Did he mention any enemies?"

"No."

"Any former girlfriends with a grudge?"

"Only the one he was with."

It was Detective Bethancourt's turn to be surprised. "He brought a girlfriend to dinner?"

She shook her head. "No. He was with her earlier. I only got a glimpse of her. I think her name was Ana Maria. I don't know her last name."

"Why do you think she had a grudge?"

Brianna steepled her fingers and thought for a moment. "When I walked past them at the hotel's terrace bar yesterday afternoon, they were having a tense conversation. They were speaking in Spanish, so I didn't understand what they were saying, but it seemed personal. I could be wrong, but I make my living reading people, Detective. It wasn't a happy conversation."

Detective Bethancourt jotted something down in his notebook. "What does she look like?"

"Late thirties, Latin, on the short side, with long dark hair and big boobs."

"You've just described half of the women in Panama."

Brianna smirked. "Guess you don't have too many blondes here."

"Nor redheads." He rapped his knuckles twice on the table. "Anything else that made her stand out?"

She nodded. "She was wearing a bright-yellow dress with matching yellow stilettos. If you look at the security footage, I'm sure she won't be hard to find."

Of course, a journalist would know about security tapes. He narrowed his eyes. "Let's go back to when you found the body. Walk me through it."

"The cave was dark," Brianna said. "It has a small opening very low to the ground, so not much light gets in. When I first went in, I couldn't see right away because it was so bright outside and so dark inside." She put her hands out, as if re-creating her actions. "I think I pressed my hands against the wall of the cave. Then I tripped over his shoe."

"How did you know it was his shoe?"

"When I tripped on it, I reached down to touch it. It was obviously a man's shoe."

"Did you touch anything else in the cave?"

Brianna shook her head. "Not that I can remember."

"Did you touch his body?"

"No."

"You didn't check his pulse?"

"No."

"Then how did you know he was dead?"

Brianna's mask slid, and he saw sadness in her eyes for the first time. "I just knew."

"Please be specific."

Brianna looked up and to the right, typical body language for a right-handed person who was recalling a memory, although she was smart and could be faking it, Detective Bethancourt thought.

She frowned. "His expression was frozen in place. His eyes were different. Flat. And he didn't blink. Plus, his body seemed stiff. Rigor mortis had set in."

Detective Bethancourt cursed American television. Thanks to shows like CSI and Law and Order, everyone talked like a detective.

"And there was that smell," she said. "I've never been around a dead person before, but it smelled exactly like I thought death would smell like."

"How long did you stay in the cave?"

"A few seconds. I ran out right away because I thought I was going to be sick." Her voice trembled, and she looked down at her hands to compose herself. "But I made myself go back in after the shock wore off."

"Why?"

She looked up at him, her moss green eyes as wide as those of a frightened child. "I wanted to figure out what happened. I'd just seen him a few hours before, and his death didn't make sense."

"How long did you spend in the cave the second time?"

"A minute. Maybe two."

"Was he wearing the same clothes you'd seen him in the night before?"

"Yes."

"Did you notice anything unusual?"

Her forehead furrowed. "You mean, besides the dead body?"

"I'm sorry. Sometimes I forget that not everyone looks at corpses for a living."

She sighed and looked away. "There was a bottle of Disaronno liqueur next to the body. It seemed out of place."

Detective Bethancourt leaned forward. "Why?"

She pursed her full lips as she pondered the question. "Lorenzo didn't seem to be that guy—you know, the one whose best friend is a bottle. The empty bottle in an isolated location didn't mesh with the successful extrovert I'd had dinner with. We had wine with dinner, but he never seemed intoxicated."

"Is there anything else you can think to tell me about your time with Mr. Silva?"

She frowned, curling a tendril of hair around her finger. "I didn't know him well, but he seemed on top of the world." She stilled, studying him a moment. "Detective, how did he die?"

She seemed earnest, her face about to crumble. He hoped it wasn't an act.

"I can't tell you that," he said. "It's an open investigation."

She nodded. "I understand. I just wish I could have prevented it. Maybe if I'd…"

He opened his palms to encourage her. "Maybe if you'd what?"

She shrugged and then looked at him with a vulnerability he hadn't seen before. "Maybe if I'd slept with him, he'd still be alive."

He gave her an X-ray stare. "You'll be staying here at the hotel during the summit?"

"Yes."

"You can go then," he said, standing to indicate that the interview was over. "For now."

Chapter 5

The smell of death clings to your nasal passages. Even when you're breathing fresh air, it's still there. Years from now—if I'm still alive—I'll remember every nuance of that smell — Brianna Morgan

Brianna's stomach grumbled as she left the conference room. She looked at her watch. It was only ten o'clock, but she hadn't eaten anything since last night. She stopped at the hotel's coffee kiosk to get coffee and a bagel. She usually ate egg whites and fruit for breakfast, but she didn't have time for a sit-down meal. Plus, after the morning she'd had, she needed carbs to keep her brain sharp.

As she ate, Brianna thought about her interview with Detective Bethancourt. He'd only lobbed softballs, but the investigation was just starting. She knew there'd be a second interview with harder questions. She'd come across as strong, but the adrenaline was wearing off. Her hands shook as she picked up her coffee cup. She'd seen plenty of people rotting in third-world prisons for less. She hadn't dodged a bullet yet.

She set the coffee cup down and shook her hands as if they were wet, trying to get rid of the shakes. She closed her eyes and inhaled, using her yoga training to calm her body as she formulated a plan. She needed to interview people close to Lorenzo, starting with his brother. The detective might be good, but she was better.

She pulled her press badge out of her bag and hung it around her neck. It was surprising how many doors opened when people saw she worked in the media. She'd made a promise to Lorenzo that she'd find his killer, and she intended to keep it.

She tugged her iPad out of her bag. Searching her notes program, she found the information she'd put together that morning on Lorenzo's brother, Marcio. She found the number for their office. It was Saturday morning, but she'd discovered in her research that Panamanians worked until noon on Saturday. She'd start at his office.

Brianna's Spanish wasn't good enough to fumble with a receptionist at Grupo SilCasa who might not speak English, but she remembered how helpful the concierge had been when she had checked into the BonitaMar hotel. She tucked her iPad back into her shoulder bag and headed toward the concierge desk, intent on asking him to act as an interpreter.

Then she saw him.

She halted mid-stride, rooted to the floor in the middle of the lobby.

Her brain said it was a mirage, but her eyes said it was Lorenzo.

It couldn't be him. He was dead. She'd seen his body.

She rubbed her eyes with her fingers like a little girl wiping away the sleep. When she opened them again, he was still there, looking as handsome as ever, wearing a button-down black shirt and pressed black slacks. His high cheekbones and generous mouth were the same. His broad physique and flat stomach were the same. His erect carriage and wavy hair were the same.

"Lorenzo," she breathed, her legs releasing her from where she'd been frozen. She propelled forward, striding toward him as fast as her platform heels would allow.

When she got within a foot of him, he turned and looked at her. His eyes locked onto hers, but when they dipped to the press credentials dangling around her neck, he looked away.

He put out his hand to stop her from getting any closer. "I am not talking to the press right now."

"Lorenzo," she started, her voice little more than a whisper. "I thought—"

"And I definitely am not talking to the press about the death of my brother."

Brianna blinked, feeling like she was in a wormhole. And then it dawned on her. "You're...twins?"

Lorenzo had said he had a brother, but he didn't mention they were twins.

Identical twins.

Marcio nodded.

Why didn't Lorenzo tell her he had a twin? And why didn't she discover that in her research? It seemed unfathomable that there would be two men as beautiful as Lorenzo. Brianna's brain usually processed information with lightning speed, but somehow it had short-circuited.

For the first time in her life, Brianna Morgan was speechless.

Marcio looked at her with concern. "Are you okay?"

Too little sleep and too much adrenaline had made her brain foggy. Brianna fiddled with her press badge. She decided to go with honesty.

"I'm sorry," she said. "I didn't realize you were Lorenzo's twin."

His face softened. "Most people cannot tell us apart. Could not tell us apart."

His voice had the same musical lilt his brother's voice had had.

"I thought you were Lorenzo when I saw you."

He opened his mouth to speak, but no words came out. His brow pulled together in a V.

"I'm so sorry," Brianna said. "It's hard enough to lose a brother, but a twin…"

"Only Mamá can tell the difference all the time." He pronounced "Mamá" the Spanish way, with the emphasis on the last syllable. "How am I going to tell her?"

Without thinking, Brianna pulled him into a hug. "I know it hurts," she whispered in his ear. "I lost my brother too." She blinked back her tears, partly for this man's pain, partly for her own loss of Lorenzo, and partly because the loss of her brother, James, when she was a teenager. "You'll find the strength to tell your mother, and she'll find the strength to hear it. And then you'll somehow find the strength to go on."

He hugged her tighter, burying his face in her hair. Holding on, one survivor to another. He felt familiar, his body so much like Lorenzo's body. He even smelled the same.

"Gracias." He pulled away abruptly, embarrassed by the emotion.

Brianna needed Marcio to be an ally. For that, he needed to hear the truth.

"My name is Brianna Morgan. I'm a reporter from the United States, but I also had dinner with Lorenzo last night."

He looked at her, his brown eyes roving up and down her face, as if he were looking for something. Then his eyes shuttered. Whatever he was about to share was gone.

He held out his hand to her. "I am Marcio Silva."

They shook with the formality of strangers, an awkward moment after the intimacy of their hug. He made no attempt to kiss her hand like his brother had the night before, but he did hold on to her hand for a moment too long.

"There's something else you need to know." She took a deep breath. "I was the one who found Lorenzo's body this morning."

He looked at her, surprise widening his eyes. "You found his body? How? Where?"

"In a cave, on a small beach between the hotel and your property."

"Did he look like he had been…murdered?" Marcio choked on the last word.

Brianna hesitated. "I don't know for sure, but my gut says yes."

Marcio cocked his head back and looked at her. "I thought the same thing. My brother was too healthy for a heart attack, and there's no way he would take his own life."

"Can we go somewhere and talk?" Brianna asked. "I didn't know Lorenzo very well, but since I got to know him a bit yesterday, I want to find out what happened to him."

"I would like that," he said. "I came to the hotel because I didn't want to be alone. My brother and I have been connected our whole lives. We have done everything together. We both went to the States for university; we both played professional fútbol; and then we started our business together in Panama. We were two halves of the same person."

She studied him, trying to reconcile the fact that the lips, the eyes, the hair, the body, and the voice in front of her belonged to someone other than Lorenzo. "Those are the same words he used."

Marcio scraped his palm over the stubble on his cheek. "I need to know everything you saw this morning, no matter how awful it was."

"Are you sure you want to know?" she asked. "Everyone has secrets they don't want uncovered. We might find out something about Lorenzo that you would prefer not to know."

He pulled back his mouth into what he thought was a smile, but it ended up looking like a snarl. "Trust me, I know everything about him— the good and the not-so good."

She wouldn't bet her career on that being true, but if he wanted to know, she would help him.

She scanned the lobby, sensing the frenetic energy that comes when people are involved in someone else's crisis. People were buzzing about, trying to be a part of the sordid affair without getting dirt under their nails.

She touched his arm. "This place is turning into a zoo. We need to find someplace quiet to talk."

"Of course. Follow me."

Marcio led her down the back stairs toward the pool area, where she saw her cameraman, Mike, getting video. She didn't try to catch his eye. Mike was a technology geek at heart; he could keep himself busy for hours.

They walked by five swimming pools and two restaurants. Brianna had to concentrate to keep up with Marcio's long strides. They didn't speak as they walked. She assumed he wanted to wait until they had some privacy, just like she did.

At the far end of one of the pool areas, they passed a tall set of hedges that separated the resort area from a service street.

"Where are we going?" she asked, wondering how long she'd have to march in her six-inch heels with the sun beating down on her.

"My apartment in Casa Bonita," he said, pointing to a tall white building.

She studied the Greco-Roman edifice, rising like a white phoenix out of the green jungle canopy. She'd noticed the residential tower when she arrived yesterday.

"Is this one of your buildings?"

He shook his head. "No, it belongs to our biggest competitor. But it is also the closest place to live to our new project. I wanted to see what it was like to live in this developer's building. They are good at some things and not-so-good at others. We want to be fantastic at everything."

Spoken like a champion, Brianna thought.

They walked up a slight hill to the front of the building. A uniformed doorman greeted them, one arm held at a ninety-degree angle behind his back.

"Buenos dias, Senor Silva," he said with a big smile. "Como está?"

The doorman clearly hadn't heard about Lorenzo's death or he wouldn't have asked such a dumb question.

"Buenos dias, Luis," Marcio said, ignoring the question.

When they entered the air-conditioned lobby, Brianna looked around in awe. Italian marble covered the floors and walls of the expansive lobby, while heavy teak furniture formed intimate seating vignettes in the cavernous space.

Three other employees saw Marcio, all of them lighting up with genuine affection as they wished him a good morning.

Brianna followed Marcio to the elevator bank. The walls around the elevators were decorated with thousands of rounded abalone shell pieces, bringing the spaces alive with color and light.

After Marcio pressed the button for the top floor, the elevator shot up. When it stopped at the twenty-fourth floor, he led her through a thick mahogany door.

Polished marble extended as far as she could see. A great room with twelve-foot ceilings connected with a large open-plan kitchen. Huge slabs of white quartz counters dominated the kitchen. In the center stood a huge commercial side-by-side refrigerator and freezer that looked large enough to keep Marcio fed for months.

But the best part of the apartment was the view.

"Wow, this is unbelievable." Brianna said, looking out the floor-to-ceiling windows as a massive container ship cruised into the Panama Canal. "That's the biggest ship I've ever seen."

"It is a super ship and can hold thirteen thousand shipping containers. Now that the new shipping lane is open in the canal, we see them every day. It costs the super ships almost a million dollars in fees to get through the canal, but it is much cheaper than if they had to go around South America."

Brianna knew it was easier to talk about mundane things than for Marcio to address the pain of his brother's death head on. Even after all the years, she still remembered doing the same when she discovered her brother had drowned.

"You've done a beautiful job decorating."

A hint of amusement flashed in his eyes. "What did you expect?"

She shrugged, a smile tugging at the corners of her mouth. "A bachelor pad with black leather couches and chrome side tables."

"The most important thing I learned about decorating is the importance of hiring a decorator." He smiled, but there was no happiness in his eyes. "Please have a seat." He indicated the granite dining table. "Would you like some coffee? I make a great cappuccino."

"Sure." She dropped her bag on one of the chairs. "Sugar too, please. I like it sweet."

From experience, Brianna knew he would find a small amount of solace in the normal act of making coffee and providing hospitality. It would keep his grief at bay for a few moments longer.

She reached into her bag and pulled out her iPad, a notebook, a pencil, a yellow highlighter, and three pens—black, blue, and red.

Marcio glanced at her impromptu workspace as he set a cup of steaming cappuccino in front of her. "Are you always this organized?"

She nodded. "Tools of the trade."

"I should hire you. My office staff could use some organization."

"You couldn't afford me." She kept her voice light.

He leaned into her, so close she could feel his warm breath on her face. "You would be surprised at what I can afford."

Brianna turned away from him, lifting the cup to her lips to hide her surprise. Was he flirting with her? Or was that pride in his voice? She decided to let it go for now. Grief does funny things to people, she told herself. It turns some into nymphomaniacs and others into nuns, some into raging alcoholics and others into teetotalers. Having survived the death of her brother, she knew better than most how topsy-turvy Marcio's emotions were right now.

Instead of sitting down across from her at the round table, which seated six, he chose a chair next to her. "Brianna, I need something from you."

She waited in silence as he collected himself. Whatever he was about to ask, it seemed difficult for him.

"I need to know everything about Lorenzo. Where you found him, how his body was positioned, everything." He looked down at his hands and then back up at her, his eyes imploring her to agree. "I need you to be more honest with me than you have ever been. Do not try to spare my feelings. Do not leave anything out."

Brianna sipped her cappuccino, savoring the intense coffee flavor, buying herself a few moments. She set the cup down and faced him. "Are you sure you want to know?"

"I am sure."

"Once you hear it, you won't ever be able to forget it."

Marcio leaned forward, taking her hands into his. "I need to know. Please do this for me. Tell me every detail."

"Can I ask you something first?"

"Anything."

"How did you find out?"

He released her hands and picked up his spoon to stir his own cappuccino. "A good friend works for the Policia Nacional. As soon as he heard, he came over to tell me. He wanted me to hear it from him."

"Was it an official visit?"

"No."

"I don't know how it works in Panama, but I assume you'll be getting another visit today when they do the official notification. You might even need to identify Lorenzo's body."

He nodded. "I expect they will come here soon."

"When they do, it might not be a good idea for me to be here."

Marcio frowned. "What do you mean?"

"I was with your brother last night. I discovered his body this morning. And yet I'm a stranger. I'm not Panamanian, and I don't speak Spanish. Plus, I was interviewed this morning by the lead detective, a man named Bethancourt. I don't know if I'm a suspect, but I'd be surprised if I weren't. I just want to give you the option to be alone when they come. After we talk, I can go."

"I do not want to be alone right now." He reached for her hand again. "Thank you for being here."

She squeezed his fingers before withdrawing her hand. "I have an odd question for you, Marcio. Why did I not know that you and Lorenzo were identical twins?"

He leaned back and crossed his ankles, resting his folded hands on his taut abdomen. "When you're an identical twin, it becomes your whole identity. We were good at the same things, went to the same university, even followed the same career path. When we were boys, we realized we needed more individuality. We wanted to not always be referred to as the Silva twins. Once we were famous enough to give interviews, we made the reporters sign an affidavit promising not to mention the fact that we were twins. It is something we insisted on, and the media complied."

"That makes sense." Brianna picked up a pencil and tapped it on the pad in front of her as she thought. "Okay. I'll tell you about Lorenzo because I would want to know as well." She studied him, looking to see if he was strong enough to hear the sordid details. "Are you ready?"

He leaned back in his chair. "Yes."

She closed her eyes so she could focus on the details. "Do you know the cove between the BonitaMar and the property where your new project is happening?"

"Yes, of course."

"I went kayaking this morning and found the cove by accident. In the back of the little beach area, there's a cave with a small opening."

He raised an eyebrow. "A cave?"

"A small cave, probably only big enough for three or four people. Lorenzo's body was near the wall, as if he'd been sitting on the sand with his back against the rock wall before he died. He was curled into a fetal position, wearing the same clothes he had on last night. He was still very buttoned up."

A muscle ticked in Marcio's jaw. "What do you mean by 'buttoned up'?"

She struggled to find the right words. "He was still dressed like he was when we had dinner. He hadn't rolled up his shirt sleeves or taken off his shoes." She paused, closing her eyes to focus on the details. "I didn't see any blood, and it didn't look like his body was at an odd angle, which would have been the case if any bones were broken."

Brianna opened her eyes and looked at Marcio. She wanted to watch him when she told him the rest of the story.

"His mouth and shirt were covered with dried vomit. I might have thought a poisonous snake had bit him, but his face and neck were cherry red."

Marcio knitted his brows together. "What does that mean?"

"I did a story once on cyanide poisoning. Victims convulse, foam at the mouth, and turn bright red."

"Cyanide?"

"There was also a bottle of Disaronno next to him. It's an almond liqueur. It could have masked the bitter almond taste of the cyanide. Especially since he'd had wine and Disaronno with me earlier. His taste buds weren't fresh."

Marcio continued to frown.

"I didn't know your brother well, but I don't think he committed suicide for two reasons. First," she said, using her fingers to tick off her points, "when I was with him, he was exuberant and happy, excited about the future."

Marcio's eyes flashed. "My brother was not depressed for even one moment in his life. He was a fighter. When life was hard, he always fought back."

She nodded. "Second, from what I could tell, there's no way to walk to the cove. You need to get there by boat. Is that correct?"

"You can walk there, but that part of the jungle is full of sinkholes that can snap your leg. Lorenzo never would have taken that risk at night."

"And if he had walked through the jungle for some reason, his shoes would have been caked in mud. But they were clean."

Marcio nodded. "He had to get there by boat."

"But there was no boat or kayak onshore or floating nearby. If he did go by himself and the boat drifted away—or if he pushed it away—the police eventually will find it."

Marcio rubbed his chin, his stubble making a light scratching sound. "We have a yacht, but I have already called the harbormaster. It is in the marina where we last left it."

She scribbled down a note to remind herself to check the yacht.

"There is a third reason why he did not commit suicide." Marcio leaned back in his chair. "We were raised in Santiago de Compostela in Spain. I do not know if this town means anything to you, but it is where the apostle Saint James is buried. It is the most famous pilgrimage destination for Christians after Rome and Jerusalem. Hundreds of thousands of people flock there every year, and for many, it represents the highest, most profound moment of their faith in God."

Brianna nodded. "I've been there. I did a story on the pilgrimage about a year ago. It's a beautiful town. I remember how peaceful I felt when I was there."

"Growing up there was like having God looking over our shoulder. We were sure if we lied, we would get caught. We thought if we cheated, God would strike us dead. There is no way my brother took his own life. Not only because we believe suicide is a sin, but also because he knew it would devastate Mamá."

Brianna reached over and pressed her hand against his. "Suicide is out then. Unless he had a seizure or a stroke, that leaves murder."

The cloud passed from Marcio's eyes, replaced by something hard. She saw the idea of murder gave him something—or someone—to fight.

"Now we need to figure out who would want Lorenzo dead," she said. "And once we do—"

Brianna cut him off. "Let's get to work." She wasn't going to fuel Marcio's revenge fantasies.

She powered up her tablet and pulled up an Excel spreadsheet. "You've heard of walking a grid to look for something?"

Marcio nodded.

"We'll do the same thing with the people Lorenzo knew. We'll create a grid of every person in Lorenzo's life and then figure out who would want him dead."

"I like it."

"Let's start with categories of people Lorenzo knew. For example, employees are one category and neighbors are another. Once we know the categories, we can go back and fill in names." Her fingers flew over the keyboard as she typed. "Give me some other categories."

Marcio moved his chair closer so he could look over her shoulder at the iPad screen. "Family, politicians, competitors, real estate brokers, ex-girlfriends."

Brianna winced when Marcio said, "ex-girlfriends." There must have been a lot of them if they deserved their own category.

"I have some competitors' names to add," he said, leaning over her to type on her iPad.

He kept his elbows up as he typed, the back of his arm brushing against Brianna's left breast. Did he realize he was touching her breast? she thought.

Marcio pulled away. "I will call my office and get the names you need."

He made one call after another, his rapid Spanish washing over her, as he spoke to one person after another.

Once they had delegated all they could, there was only one category left.

"We just need to fill in the 'ex-girlfriend' category."

Brianna kept her face neutral. She didn't want Marcio to know she had been one of Lorenzo's girlfriends, even for an evening. It had been such an intense interlude that she could barely wrap her mind around it. There was no way she could get someone else to understand what she and Lorenzo had both known within a short time—they could have been soulmates. It was too precious to share, so she kept it to herself.

"What about his ex-wife? What did you think of her?"

Marcio leaned back in his chair. "Valentina Arias Silva. Now there is a piece of work."

Brianna knitted her brows. "What do you mean?"

"She was born rich and entitled. The only time she has ever been nice is when Lorenzo courted her. He was smitten. She was on her best behavior because she wanted to snare a handsome husband. I knew she was a bitch the first time I met her, but he would not listen to me. She represented everything he wanted—a strong family, a beautiful face, and unlimited money."

"How long were they married?"

"Three years. He knew it was a mistake about two weeks after they returned from their honeymoon, but he stuck it out. He wanted to make it work and thought she could change. The problem is that money had spoiled her. She was so far removed from reality that she couldn't help being a bitch."

"How so?"

Marcio thought for a moment. "Their wedding was a production. Two thousand guests, live music, lobster, champagne, open bar, entertainers, fireworks…no cost was spared. Her father spent almost a million dollars. Instead of being grateful, the wicked girl pouted at every little thing that went wrong."

"Bridezilla."

"That is the understatement of the decade. Two wedding planners quit, and her father had to pay the third one a small fortune to keep from

47

quitting. Lorenzo should have known better. He assumed she was reacting to the stress of the wedding. He thought things would get better once they were married."

He shook his head. "No. The glow wore off as soon as they got back from their honeymoon. Lorenzo threw himself into work, and Valentina threw herself into the open arms of every handsome gigolo who showed interest." He sighed. "I told my brother that she was a bad wife, but he did not believe me. I had to hire a private investigator to get photos. Once he had the proof, he filed for divorce."

"How did her family take it?"

He toyed with his water bottle. "Her father threatened us. Said if Lorenzo divorced his darling daughter that he would ruin us. But then I showed him the photos of his daughter doing nasty things, images no father wants of his daughter." He shrugged. "We came to an agreement. The photos would stay buried, and Valentina would sign the divorce papers."

Brianna wanted to know more, but she needed to move on. "What about his other girlfriends?"

Marcio picked up his empty water bottle and headed to the kitchen. "All his girlfriends' names should be in his phone. He never deleted anyone. It was one of his quirks."

"Do you know where his phone is?"

Marcio put the empty bottle in the trash and pulled two cold bottles of water from the fridge. "He must have had it when he died. We will need to get that from the police."

Brianna closed her eyes.

"Are you tired?" he asked, setting a bottle of water in front of her.

"No, I'm just trying to remember where Lorenzo kept his phone."

Marcio snorted. "That is easy. He kept it in his hand. He never let his phone out of his sight. If he was in a meeting, it was sitting next to him. If he was with a woman, it was also next to him, but upside down so she could not see if another woman called."

So much for wanting one woman instead of twenty, she thought, clenching her jaw to shield herself from the unexpected pain.

"I don't remember seeing it last night at dinner." She used too much force to twist the cap off bottle, and water spurted out of the top.

Marcio went to the kitchen and came back with a hand towel. "Maybe you were special."

She gave him a sharp look as she accepted the towel. "And I don't remember seeing it this morning when I found him." She used the towel to soak up the water, and then she jerked her head up. "Although it could have been underneath him."

He plopped down next to her. "I will call his phone. Maybe he left it here."

"He was here last night?"

Marcio wrinkled his brow. "Of course. He lives here."

Brianna's eyes widened in surprise. "Lorenzo told me he spent most of his time at his place on the beach. I assumed he meant the beach town of Coronado, since he said your company has a couple of projects there."

"We have a place there too." Marcio punched in Lorenzo's cell number and put the phone to his ear. "He spent most of his time there overseeing the beach project. I stayed here so I could work on the new project. But we share both places."

Marcio put his phone down. "The call went to voicemail."

"Have you been in his room since he left?" she asked.

"No. We shared everything, but we respected each other's privacy."

"We need to look in his room. I don't know what we'll be looking for, but maybe he left something that can help us figure out what happened."

Marcio nodded. "Good idea."

"We shouldn't touch anything, just in case the police need to preserve evidence." Brianna pushed back from the table and stood up. "Do you have any dishwashing gloves?"

He gave her a questioning look.

"So we won't leave fingerprints."

The corner of his mouth twitched. Was he amused?

"I think my maid keeps gloves with the cleaning supplies," he said as he disappeared through the kitchen to the laundry room.

Brianna rummaged in her bag for something to tie back her hair and found two hair bands. She pulled her hair into a ponytail, then braided the ponytail. As she secured the second rubber band at the end of the braid, Marcio returned.

He offered her the yellow gloves. "I could only find one pair."

"That's okay," she said, pulling on the gloves. "You live here so your fingerprints are everywhere already. Lead the way."

They left the great room and entered a den that had been turned into a home office. It had an antique partners desk with a chair on each side, an armoire, a floor lamp, and a few surprising decorative touches, including a globe inlaid with semiprecious stones.

Brianna longed to run her bare fingers around the globe, but she'd watched enough crime shows to know that she needed to be careful. They were already suspicious of her; she didn't need to add fingerprints or DNA to fuel Detective Bethancourt's fire.

A flat-screen TV dominated one wall, showing a soccer game with the volume muted. There was only one window in the office, which made the room darker without the infusion of bright tropical light.

"We share the office." Marcio flicked on the overhead light. "He gets one side of the desk, and I get the other."

Each side of the desk had a well for their legs, as well as a set of drawers. A laptop sat on the opposite side of the desk, facing away from them.

"Is that Lorenzo's computer or yours?" Brianna asked.

"Lorenzo's."

"The police will take it, so make sure you get anything you need as soon as possible."

"Noted."

"Do you think he backed up his contacts to his laptop?"

Marcio nodded. "Yes. He was very careful that way."

Brianna poked her head into one of the two bedrooms that opened to the den. "Is this his bedroom?"

"Yes. The other room is our guest room. While you look, I will check his laptop."

Brianna turned on the light as she entered Lorenzo's bedroom. It was eerie to go into a dead man's room, especially one she had wanted to get to know intimately just hours before. It felt invasive, as if she were snooping, but it also felt oddly intimate. This was the personal space of the man who could have shared his life with her.

She went into the bathroom. Everything was in perfect order. The towels were uniformly folded; the sink was clean; and the toilet seat was down. Either this man was a neat freak, or his maid came every day. Or both.

Brianna picked up his cologne, Invictus. She inhaled it, and her insides turned to liquid. It smelled like him. Her eyes welled with tears of what could have been. She dashed the wetness from her eyes with the back of her arm. She had to focus on finding out what had happened to Lorenzo.

For the sake of thoroughness, she looked under the sink and in the toilet tank. Nothing out of the ordinary.

She moved into his bedroom, which also offered a spectacular view. A glass wall opened to a private balcony overlooking the ocean. Lorenzo's Tommy Bahama bed butted against a picture window that showcased a golf course against mountains and jungle. In the corner, a brown leather recliner faced the flat screen TV on the wall. These boys loved their televisions.

The entire back wall was a built-in closet. When Brianna opened the closet door, she saw his clothes were so organized that it looked like a high-end boutique rather than a man's closet. Long-sleeve button-down shirts were in one area, polo shirts in another; everything was arranged by color and pressed to perfection.

Brianna felt like a voyeur and blushed when she saw that Lorenzo's underwear drawer was full of colored underwear, folded into tight balls and lined up like cloth soldiers. She looked over her shoulder to see if she if Marcio was nearby. When she was sure she was alone, she unrolled a pair of his underwear. The fact that he wore boxer briefs didn't surprise her. Ultra-fit men seemed to prefer those.

Her mind wandered to what he had looked like wearing these. I need to stop this, she told herself. She hurriedly re-rolled them and pushed the drawer shut. She couldn't let herself go there.

She finally found a drawer that was less organized. It was full of old T-shirts and soccer shorts. The clothes weren't as crisply folded, so perhaps he had folded them himself. She held a shirt up to her nose. It smelled like him, a warm citrus mixed with something utterly male. She stuffed the shirt back into the drawer, not wanting Marcio to catch her smelling his brother's clothes.

She walked through the bedroom to the balcony. Two white wooden Adirondack chairs faced the ocean with a side table between them. There was no place to hide anything, so she came back into his room and looked around.

The bed was the only thing she hadn't inspected. She felt under the pillows, but from the sheets' military-like stretch, it was obvious the maid had been the last one to make the bed. On an impulse, she felt between the edge of the mattress and the box spring. Directly under where his pillow would be, she felt something. She pulled it out and held it in her gloved hand. It was a lock of shiny black hair, about six inches long, tied with a yellow ribbon and encased in a cellophane bag.

Why would Lorenzo have a lock of hair under his bed? She turned it over in her hands. This was not what she'd expected to find.

Brianna went back to the office, where Marcio was typing commands on Lorenzo's laptop. "Do you know what this is?" she asked, holding up the lock of hair.

"It looks like hair."

"Do you know who it belongs to?"

Marcio reached for it, but Brianna pulled it out of his reach. "Not without gloves."

He put his hands behind his back. "I will not touch it. I promise."

She set it in front of him.

He studied it for a moment. "I have no idea where he got this, but it looks like Latin hair. Where did you find it?"

"Under his mattress, in the exact spot beneath his pillow." She picked up the bag. "Any guesses where it came from?"

"No. Lorenzo has not been in love with a woman since Valentina Arias."

"It will be your job to make sure the police find this." She picked up the hair and headed back to Lorenzo's room. "I'm going to put it back where I found it," she called over her shoulder. "I think where I found it is just as significant as what it is."

Chapter 6

Detective Bethancourt surveyed the beach where Lorenzo Silva's body had been discovered. It was hard enough investigating a crime scene in a house or hotel, but the cove could only be safely accessed by boat. Everyone—and everything—had to be shuttled back and forth on fishing boats: investigators, photographers, and equipment. On top of that, the tide was going out, which made getting to the cove more difficult.

The mid-day sun beat down on him. His face was shielded by a Panama hat, but he felt sweat dripping down his back. He took off his blazer and rolled up his shirtsleeves. Several things bothered him about the crime scene. First, he couldn't find the victim's cell phone. In today's world, people were never far from their phones. Had this been an accident, the phone probably would have been on or near the body. When one of his detectives looked up Lorenzo's number and tried to call it, it went straight to voicemail. The phone was either turned off or at the bottom of the ocean.

The second thing that troubled him was the trace amounts of candle wax found in the cave. What was the significance? Had Lorenzo been here for a romantic liaison or was he part of a satanic cult?

The third thing niggling at his brain was the fact that the scene had been cleaned. A murder scene usually was littered with evidence. He and his team only had the bottle of Disaronno and the candle wax. There was no boat left behind or any other means or transport, and no footprints in the sand, aside from the ones left by Brianna Morgan when she had found him. If indeed her story was true.

Even though the tide had come in, they should have found Lorenzo's footprints higher on the beach and in the cave. The fact that they weren't there meant that someone had wiped all the footprints clean, pointing to the involvement of someone else. And that meant murder.

With the sun high in the sky, Detective Bethancourt left the scene and took a fishing boat back to shore. As lead detective, he had to notify the family. Panama being what it was, he was certain Marcio Silva already had heard the news, but he still had to make a formal notification.

The stink of death clung to his clothes, but he didn't want to take the time to go home and shower, especially since Marcio Silva lived on the same property as the BonitaMar. He kept extra clothes in his car for times like this. He would use the employee locker room at the resort to shower and change.

Rather than call first, he walked from the BonitaMar to Casa Bonita and flashed his badge at the concierge. The man's eyes grew wide; everyone in the building knew something was going on at the beach, but they didn't know one of the residents was involved.

Detective Bethancourt rode the high-speed elevator to the twenty-fourth floor and exited to the posh penthouse level. He rang the doorbell to Marcio Silva's penthouse. He heard voices inside—a man's and a woman's—and then footsteps approaching the door.

When the door opened, Detective Bethancourt held up his badge and spoke Spanish to Marcio. "I am Detective Bethancourt with the Policia Nacional. I need to speak with you. May I come inside for a few minutes?"

"Si," Marcio said, opening the door for him.

Detective Bethancourt had only taken a few steps Brianna Morgan emerged from the kitchen. He stopped and stared. What was she doing here?

Before Marcio could introduce them, Brianna stepped forward but didn't extend her hand. "Hello. Detective Bethancourt. It's good to see you again." She sounded as sincere as a vacuum salesman.

Detective Bethancourt switched seamlessly to English. "I didn't think I would see you again so soon, Miss Morgan."

"I told you I wanted to solve this case as much as you do."

Rather than spar with her, he looked her up and down. She still had on those ridiculously high shoes that allowed her to look down at him.

When his eyes made it back up to her face, Brianna was smirking at him. He'd just given her a once-over, and she'd caught him in the act. It's not that he was interested in her—he was happily married—but she was a gorgeous woman.

He noticed her hair was different. Instead of the thick waves he'd noticed earlier, she had pulled her hair tightly into a braid. She would be beautiful with any hairstyle, but this one was far less flattering, he thought.

Why had she changed her hairstyle to one so austere?

Brianna Morgan was inserting herself into this investigation, and Detective Bethancourt wanted to know why. But first he had to make the official notification.

He turned to Marcio Silva and spoke to him in Spanish. As he'd assumed, Marcio already knew about his brother's death; he could do a formal identification at the morgue once the body had been transferred.

While he was talking to Marcio in Spanish, he kept Brianna in his peripheral vision. She seemed to be following their conversation, nodding at appropriate times. She'd said she didn't speak much Spanish, but he would need to figure out if she'd told him the truth.

She might be beautiful, but if she had murdered Lorenzo Silva, he would lock her up just as fast as he would a fat, toothless man from Panama's seediest ghetto.

Chapter 7

After Detective Bethancourt left, Marcio's phone kept buzzing with calls and texts as people heard the news, but he ignored his phone. There was no one he wanted to talk to right now.

He cracked his neck from side to side. "We have four suspects so far. Santiago Ruiz, a fútbol player from Lorenzo's time at Real Madrid. Ana Maria Lopes, who is—how do you Americans say— a jilted lover. Lorenzo's ex-wife, Valentina. And Laura Mareno worked for SilCasa, but we were about to fire her."

Brianna touched his arm with the lightness of a butterfly. "It's after two. You need to eat lunch, Marcio."

He responded without looking up. "I am not hungry."

"I didn't ask if you were hungry." She poked him in the bicep to get his attention. "You need to eat because your body needs fuel. If you won't do it for yourself, do it for Lorenzo."

"You are right." He scratched the stubble on his cheeks. "I do not feel like cooking. How about room service?"

Brianna lifted her eyebrows in surprise. "You have room service? I thought this was a condo."

"A full-service condo, perfect for two bachelors." He stretched. "Sandwich, fish, soup, or a hot fudge sundae? Just name it."

"Grilled fish would be great."

Marcio punched a number into his phone and gave instructions in rapid-fire Spanish. "I ordered us both chipotle salmon, quinoa, and a salad," he told her once he hung up.

"Brain food." Brianna nodded in approval. "Perfect."

Marcio handed her the list of four potential suspects. "Now what?"

Brianna bounced the eraser tip of her pencil against the table as she studied the list. "We should go talk to them. But I don't want to overlook the others on our list just because they don't stand out. Do you have anyone who can help us check out the rest of the names so we can concentrate on these four? Perhaps look at the social media accounts of everyone who was connected to Lorenzo?"

He nodded. "Jose Mendoza handles all the IT for my company. I can have him work on it with my assistant. I will send him the file and see what he can find."

He stepped closer to her and touched the top of her arm where her skin peeked out from the red ruffles of her blouse. "Brianna, I do not know if I could have gotten through this day without you. Thank you for being here."

She looked up at him and squeezed his hand. "No thanks are needed. I know what you're going through."

Brianna pulled her hand away. "While you talk to your computer guy, I'll see if my cameraman can hook us up with some hidden cameras. When we go knocking on doors, I want proof of what's been said."

He watched her walk out to the balcony to make her call. She moved with the grace of a model yet had the brain of a neurosurgeon. A rare combination.

By the time their food was delivered, they had finished their calls. Marcio pulled two white porcelain plates from the cupboard and transferred the food from the Styrofoam containers.

Brianna leaned against the quartz kitchen counter. "I'm impressed. Most men would just hand me a to-go container and a plastic fork. Are you always so civilized?"

"We grew up poor," Marcio said, carrying the plates to the dining table. "Because of that, Mamá worked extra hard to teach us how to be proper. We did not have a lot of clothes, but they were always cleaned and pressed. We did not have fancy food, but our stomachs were always full." He set the plates on the dining table. "Mamá never approved of eating in front of the television. We always ate together as a family at the kitchen table. When Lorenzo and I were teenagers and wanted to gulp our food like street dogs, she made us put our silverware down between each bite to slow us down."

Brianna giggled. "Your mother sounds like a force to be reckoned with."

"You have no idea."

He brought two glasses of iced tea to the table and sat next to her. "I know this might sound odd, but I would like to toast my brother."

She smiled. "It's not odd at all. I'd like that."

He held his iced tea in his left hand and took hold of her hand with his right. He looked directly into Brianna's eyes as he toasted with his tea. "To my brother. I hope he is looking down on us right now."

"And smiling," Brianna said, clinking her glass with Marcio's.

Brianna sipped her tea then took a bite of salmon. "This is delicious. Thanks for suggesting it."

"Mamá taught us both how to cook, but we do not always have time. Room service saves us."

"Is your mother in Spain?" she asked, before taking a bite of quinoa.

"Yes. She will not leave our home while my grandmother Nani is still alive. She comes to visit for short periods, but my grandmother cannot travel." He sipped his tea. "Latins do not drink iced tea like Americans do, but I fell in love with it at university. Lorenzo and I both got scholarships to the University of North Carolina in Chapel Hill."

"UNC is a good school. Lorenzo told me you played soccer."

"Yes. That is also where we learned to call it soccer. In Europe, we call it fútbol." He looked up from his food, the first smile of the day toying with the corners of his mouth. "In the United States, soccer is just another activity that a mother organizes for her kids. In Europe, it is a religion."

Brianna laughed. "True, but it's changing."

"Soccer is becoming more respected in the States. I would like to think Lorenzo and I played a small part in that. We were the national champions two out of the four years we spent at UNC."

"That's amazing," Brianna said. "Lorenzo said you played professionally as well."

He nodded. "We were both drafted right out of university, but we never played for the same team."

"How long did you play?"

"Six years." Marcio used his knife to push a piece of salmon onto his fork, European style. "Do you follow fútbol?"

"No. Sorry." Brianna ate her last bite of salmon, put her fork down, and leaned forward in journalist mode. "How did you become a real estate developer?"

"We made a decent amount of money playing fútbol, but we wanted to invest it in Latin America, since there is so much more opportunity here than in Europe. When we were looking for the right place start a business,

Lorenzo fell hard for Valentina Arias. She comes from a wealthy Panamanian family. We moved to Panama seven years ago and have been here ever since."

Brianna's cell phone rang. She looked at the caller ID. "I need to get this."

While Brianna went to the balcony to answer her phone, Marcio cleared the table, watching her through the glass walls.

When she returned, Marcio was packing his computer bag.

"That was my cameraman, Mike," she said. "He found some spy cams from a local distributor. He's going to buy a few different types for us to use when we talk to the people on the list. Then we can have proof if anyone says something odd or incriminating."

"Great idea." Marcio zipped up his laptop case.

"I think we need to prioritize, talk to the most likely suspects first."

"Agreed. We can take one person off our list right away. Jose just sent me a text. Santiago Ruiz, the fútbol player who hated Lorenzo, was in Spain last night, playing a game. It was televised."

"One less person to interview." Brianna gathered her pens and notebooks and put them into her Prada bag. "He wasn't my favorite suspect anyway. Athletes have a lot of testosterone. If he killed Lorenzo, it would have been very physical. He would have used a knife, a tire iron, a hammer, maybe even his fists. Poisoning—if that's how Lorenzo indeed died—is very female. I think the person who murdered him is a woman."

Marcio studied her, and then slowly nodded. "I agree."

Brianna closed her bag and set it on a dining room chair. "We also need look at all of Lorenzo's spaces—houses, cars, boats, office—any place he spent time. Since we found something here, we might find something somewhere else that'll give us a clue as to what was going on. I'm not familiar with police procedures in Panama, so I'm not sure how quickly they'll check these places. We can't assume they'll be slow, so we should do that first. Did Lorenzo keep a car here?"

"Yes."

"Let's go look at it."

They took the elevator to the parking garage. Marcio led her to his brother's car, a fully loaded black Porsche Cayenne Turbo S.

Brianna whistled softly. "Nice car."

"My brother loved beautiful things."

"This car would give sticker shock to anyone who doesn't make at least a million a year."

"I don't drive anything nearly as flashy," Marcio said, pointing to the late-model metallic-blue Range Rover parked next to the Porsche. "That's my car."

"Yeah, that's a real beater," she said, sarcasm dripping from her words.

Marcio clicked the Cayenne open. "It might not be a beater, as you say, but my SUV cost far less than Lorenzo's Porsche."

Brianna rolled her eyes and pulled on the yellow dish gloves she'd brought from Marcio's apartment before opening the front passenger door. "I'll check the front; you check the back." She searched both front seats. "This is the cleanest car I've ever seen. No gum wrappers, no napkins, no ketchup packets. I doubt your brother ever ate in his car."

Marcio chuckled. "Never. Lorenzo was a neat freak, almost germophobic."

With the back of her gloved hand, she pushed a tendril of hair out of her face. "Did you find anything back there?"

"Nothing." He shut the back hatch. "I will look under the hood."

She closed the front driver door. "I'll look in the wheel wells."

"Nothing here," Marcio said a few moments later, closing the hood.

"I've got something." Brianna pulled a magnetic hide-a-key box from the driver's-side front wheel well and slid the top of it open. It was empty except for a bright-green feather.

"That's strange," she said. "Why would Lorenzo keep a feather in this box instead of a key?"

"He would never keep a key to his car in a box like that. It would have been too much of a security risk." Marcio walked around the car to look at the feather.

"Does this mean anything to you?"

He looked at it closely without touching it. "No. I have no idea why it was there."

Brianna snapped a picture of it with her phone. "It's interesting that it was in the wheel well closest to Lorenzo's seat. It reminds me how that lock of hair was under his pillow."

He cocked his head. "They are both feminine items—hair and a feather. Lorenzo would never have put them there." He jangled his keys. "Do you think the same woman who hid these charms killed him?"

"It's possible. Whoever she is." Brianna closed the lid on the hide-a-key box and replaced it under the wheel well. She took another picture of where it was hidden. "Is your yacht nearby?"

"Yes. At the marina, about fifteen minutes from here."

"Can we go look at it?"

Marcio smiled. "I will drive." He pulled out another set of keys and clicked his Range Rover open. He motioned for Brianna to get in.

She stepped up into the SUV, looking every bit as elegant as Grace Kelly, despite her high heels and tight skirt.

Marcio drove Andretti style around the windy road that followed the ocean.

Twelve minutes later, they pulled into the marina. Marcio hopped out and ran around the vehicle to help Brianna out of the SUV. Leading her down the ramp toward the marina entrance, he pointed toward the biggest yacht there. "Our boat is at the end."

As he led her down the walkway, the yachts got bigger. The one on the end was sleek and glossy. The name on the side read, El Gemini, Malaga, Spain.

"The Gemini," she said aloud. "The Twin."

"Mamá named her. She always said Lorenzo and I were two halves of the same person."

Brianna looked at him sharply. "Yes, those are the exact words he used when he told me about you."

Marcio caressed the side of the yacht, rubbing it as if it were a beloved pet instead of an inanimate object. "From the time we were young, Mamá encouraged us to do everything together, to share everything."

"Your mother sounds like a smart woman."

He turned back to look at her. "She is. In fact, you remind me of her."

Chapter 8

The instinct to survive is stronger than any of your learned behaviors. One minute you're opening a door for a stranger, and the next you're stomping on a child's head while fleeing a crowded concert. You think you're not that person—the one who will push, shove, and trip someone else in your race for survival—until it happens to you. — Brianna Morgan

Being compared to a man's mother was a double-edged sword. Brianna, however, smiled at the compliment.

"I should have changed my shoes before gallivanting around the marina," she said, wanting to lighten the mood.

Marcio grinned down at her. "Do not worry. I will help you."

"That's what I'm afraid of," she said under her breath, as he stepped onto the yacht with the grace of a ballet dancer.

Marcio reached out to steady her, his touch searing her skin. Why did he have to look exactly like his brother?

Although Lorenzo's death was still fresh, there was something about getting on a yacht with a handsome man that made her feel like she was on a mini vacation. She half expected a uniformed waiter to bring them champagne.

"Tell me about the yacht," Brianna said, trying to stay focused on something—anything—other than how handsome Marcio was in the sunlight.

"She is a Hatteras 72, which means she is seventy-two feet long," he said proudly. "Lorenzo and I wanted something comfortable, but we also wanted a boat we could take out by ourselves, without a captain or crew. She has four staterooms and a separate berth for the crew. We have a first mate, Charlie, who spends twenty hours a week here, cleaning, doing maintenance, and keeping her in top shape, so our time on El Gemini is all pleasure. Charlie goes out with us sometimes, but most of the time it is just my brother and me."

Marcio was bouncing back and forth between present and past tense when referring to his brother. Brianna realized his brain hadn't fully accepted the loss of his twin yet.

"We should start in the sky lounge," he said, leading the way past the outdoor teak table and up a flight of stairs.

The sky lounge reminded Brianna of a bar on a cruise ship. Behind the captain's helm, barstools curved around a granite bar. Unlike the fishing boats she'd been on, the entire area was enclosed. She knew nothing about yachts, but she guessed the futuristic helm station was home to a state-of-the-art electronics system.

She looked out the front windows. "How often do you take her out?"

"Once or twice a week. We like to go out on Sundays, just the two of us. We occasionally take clients out during the week, but only if we really like them. El Gemini is sacred to us."

Brianna pulled the latex gloves out of her handbag. "I'm afraid to touch anything." She snapped the gloves into place. "Why don't you look in the helm, and I'll look in the bar."

They each searched without finding anything unusual. Just like Lorenzo's home and car, the yacht was sparkling clean and uncluttered.

"There's nothing here," she said. "Where next?"

"The main salon. Follow me."

Marcio led her down the stairs and through a sliding glass door. The salon looked like a luxury apartment, with gleaming mahogany walls, a large round dining table that seated eight, and a sunken wet bar.

"Wow, another bar," Brianna said, awestruck by the two-tier granite bar. "I guess yacht owners don't want to be too far from their adult beverages."

Marcio chuckled. "I am not an alcoholic, I promise. I did not design it; I just paid for it."

They divided the room in half, searching every cabinet and under every cushion. Brianna paid attention to the brands of liquor. The bar had almost every type of rum, vodka, gin, and liqueur she had ever seen, including an unopened bottle of Disaronno.

"Who buys the liquor for the yacht?" she asked.

"Charlie keeps everything stocked. Is something wrong?"

She shook her head. "Just curious."

"Follow me to the galley," Marcio said, leading her into the most un-galley-like kitchen she'd ever seen. It looked more "French country" than "boat kitchen," with its tall mahogany cabinets, an oversize built-in side-by-side refrigerator, and polished beige-and-brown granite counters that gleamed under strategically placed spotlights.

"What a gorgeous kitchen," Brianna said, her eyes lighting up.

Marcio ran his hands over the polished granite. "Yes, it is beautiful."

"I'll take this half," she said, as they got into the rhythm of their search.

"Do you cook?" he asked, as he opened a cabinet door.

"I love to cook." She closed one drawer and opened another. "I don't always have time, but cooking relaxes me. I love the gratification of doing work then getting quick results. I can go into the kitchen, and in an hour, I have something tangible that I created."

"I like to cook too, but mostly because I like to eat." Marcio grinned.

"What's your favorite food?" As soon as she asked it, she mentally kicked herself. This wasn't a date. But asking questions was who she was.

"You would not believe me if I told you," he said, looking up from one of the cabinets.

Brianna opened the freezer, just to be thorough. "Let me guess. Ice cream."

He chuckled. "You are a great detective."

"That wasn't hard to guess. There are at least a dozen pints of ice cream in here."

He gave her a lopsided grin. "Some men drink beer when they are out on the water. We eat ice cream."

She giggled. And then her giggle turned into a laugh. The laughter continued until tears rolled down her face. She couldn't stop laughing, even though she knew it was inappropriate.

She slid down the island until she was sitting on the floor, her arms wrapped around her belly as she laughed, her face wet with tears.

Marcio pulled two spoons out of a drawer then took two pints of ice cream out of the freezer. He slid down next to her on the floor, his back against the island. He held up the cartons. "Triple chocolate or blueberry cheesecake?"

"Chocolate." Brianna pulled her gloves off and placed them next to her before wiping the tears from her face.

Marcio handed her a spoon and the pint of chocolate ice cream.

"I'm sorry. I don't know what got into me."

"It is the stress," he said. "It makes you do crazy things."

Brianna giggled, hiccupped, then took a bite. "Wow. This is insanely delicious." The ice cream calmed her and stopped her laughter. She took another bite. "I can't even remember the last time I had ice cream."

"Wait until you try the blueberry cheesecake. It is my favorite."

"Let me try it," she said, reaching for his carton.

Instead of giving it to her, he held up his spoon for her to taste it.

Brianna hesitated for a moment then leaned forward to take the ice cream from his spoon. Her eyes closed in bliss. "Mmm. That's so good."

Marcio smiled at her, his eyes crinkling in the corners just like Lorenzo's.

"You look cozy," a voice said from behind them.

Marcio leapt to his feet in one feline motion. He relaxed a bit once he saw who it was. "Detective Bethancourt, what are you doing here?"

"I came to post a police officer outside. We don't know what happened to your brother yet, but right now we're assuming foul play. I wanted to make sure any evidence is protected in case we need to search the yacht. I wouldn't have entered, but I heard a woman's crazy laughter and thought someone must have broken in. I never expected the laughter to be coming from you…today of all days."

Marcio's eyes narrowed and his nostrils flared at the rebuke. Brianna could see that the detective's admonition had ticked him off. Rage was an easy emotion for an athlete to feel on the best of days. During a crisis like this, Marcio's anger would be as combustible as a field of dry grass in a hot California summer. She needed to defuse the tension before it got ugly.

Detective Bethancourt was on the opposite side of the island, and Brianna wasn't sure how much of her he could see. It wouldn't be totally out of place to find latex gloves in a kitchen, but she didn't want to bring them to his attention. She inched the gloves against the side of the island, then stood up, kicking them flush with the bottom of the island.

She turned to face him. "Hello, Detective Bethancourt."

Chapter 9

Detective Bethancourt studied Brianna. She was blushing and looked guilty of something. What, he didn't know. This woman had been cozy with the dead man, and now she was getting chummy with the man's brother. He had to figure out what her game was. People didn't just insert themselves into a family who had experienced a tragic loss to be helpful. There was always another reason.

"Three times in one day. You seem to be everywhere, Miss Morgan."

"Ice cream?" she offered, holding a pint out to the detective.

"No, thanks." He continued to stare at her.

Most people withered under his stare. Or chattered to fill the uncomfortable silence. Not Brianna. She took another bite of ice cream as she stared back at him, her green eyes challenging him as though this were a game she enjoyed.

Marcio clenched his fists and took an aggressive step toward Detective Bethancourt. "Now that you can see there is no intruder on my boat, you can be on your way."

Realizing he had poked a sleeping lion, Detective Bethancourt put his hands up. "I didn't mean any disrespect. I'm just trying to find out what happened to your brother. I thought that's what you wanted as well."

Marcio looked down, shuffling his feet on the floor like a little boy. "It is."

"May I speak bluntly?" the detective asked.

Marcio nodded.

"You have known this woman less than a day." He pointed straight at Brianna. "She was the last person who saw Lorenzo alive, and then conveniently, she was also the one who discovered his body."

Brianna took another bite of ice cream, a hint of a smile on her face. "That was very melodramatic, Detective Bethancourt. You should do dinner theater."

Detective Bethancourt shifted his gaze to Marcio. "If I were you, Mr. Silva, I would stay far away from this woman. I don't know how she's involved—or even if she's involved—but if she is, your life could be in danger."

Brianna licked ice cream off her spoon. "I normally would agree with your logic, but I know something you don't know." She pointed the spoon at Detective Bethancourt. "I didn't kill Lorenzo."

"No? Then who did?"

She switched containers and took another bite, rolling her eyes in ecstasy. "Really, you have to try this. It's the best thing I've ever tasted."

Detective Bethancourt was silent.

Brianna put the ice cream container down and leaned her hip against the island; she was the picture of calm. "Here's something else I know: if you're focused on me, it's going to be harder for you to catch the real killer. Since you're wasting your time and resources, I can't leave this investigation to you." She winked. "Sorry, Detective, but you're stuck with me until we solve this."

His cheeks started to burn. "You've got that wrong. You are stuck with me. I'll be on you like stink on a diaper."

Brianna put the lid on her pint of ice cream and put it in the freezer. "I realize I'm not a detective like you, but in this age of Big Brother and the proliferation of security cameras, there has to be a better suspect than me. Especially since the security cameras will show I was in my room all night last night."

Marcio crossed his arms. "Detective, it sounds like a simple task to clear Brianna's name. Just watch the security tapes."

Brianna nodded. "The video footage will prove that Lorenzo walked me to my room at around eleven thirty last night." She shot Detective Bethancourt a hard look. "I went in alone and stayed there until six thirty this morning. Since I'm not Spider Woman, I couldn't have gone out through the window of the nineteenth floor and made it out undetected."

Marcio closed his container of ice cream and put it back in the freezer. "Lorenzo had to be on half a dozen different hotel cameras after he left Brianna. Think about it—he walked down the hall, got on the elevator, went to the lobby, and walked by the pools, at the very least."

Detective Bethancourt studied Brianna. She seemed earnest, but she was an actress. "Unfortunately, we're unable to verify your story. The power went out right as Lorenzo went into your room, and we never saw him come out."

A vein throbbed in Brianna's neck. He was getting to her; he just needed to push harder.

"Lorenzo never went into my room," she said.

"The camera shows him going into your room."

Brianna clenched her teeth for a nano-second before answering. "Does the camera show him going into the alcove where my door is? Or does it show him entering my room?"

Detective Bethancourt glared at her. "Are you arguing semantics with me?"

"Semantics is saying the same thing a different way. What you're saying is fiction, because it never happened." Brianna looked at Marcio to see how he was taking all this. He looked like a poker player, working to keep his face neutral, but a muscle twitched in his jaw. She returned her gaze to Detective Bethancourt. "I suggest you go back and watch the tapes again. Lorenzo walked me to my door, but he never entered my room."

"I'll watch the tapes again." Detective Bethancourt sucked his teeth. "It's convenient that the security system went down just as Lorenzo went into your room." He put his hands up as if to ward off an attack. "Excuse me. Went into the alcove in front of your room."

Brianna rubbed her temples. "You got me, Detective. I confess. I used my superpowers to cause a blackout and fry the electrical circuit. If you look at the security footage, you'll see me wiggle my nose and tap my heels together three times."

Marcio chuckled. "She has a point, Detective."

"It wouldn't be hard." Detective Bethancourt paused. "If she had an accomplice."

Brianna leaned into the island, getting as close to Detective Bethancourt as she could without jumping the granite. "And in this delusion of yours, what possible motive would I have? I just met the man yesterday, at four o'clock in the afternoon."

"I haven't figured that out yet." Detective Bethancourt tapped the granite island twice with his knuckles. "But I will. Have a good evening. I'll see myself out."

He started to walk away then turned back. "Oh, and Mr. Silva, be careful of spiders. I hear black widows can be deadly, especially at night."

Chapter 10

Marcio tossed in bed. He had barely slept. Sunrise was still hours away, but he'd rather be up and moving than wrestling with his covers.

He threw back the sheet and slid out of bed. El Gemini's floorboards creaked as he walked to the galley in his boxer briefs. He hadn't wanted to go back to Casa Bonita, where everyone would know what had happened.

After Detective Bethancourt left, Brianna took a taxi back to the hotel. Marcio had offered to drive her, but that redheaded vixen was as stubborn as any woman he'd ever met.

He needed to call Mamá today. He should have done it yesterday. Spain was seven hours ahead. She would be awake now, running her household like the general she was.

He made a cappuccino and sat on the sun deck watching the moon's glow on the water, listening to the rhythmic lap of the water against the hull. The breeze picked up and goosebumps appeared on his skin.

Right now, Mamá didn't know. Once he told her, it would be real. This might be the last cappuccino he would enjoy for a long time.

When his coffee cup was empty, he pushed himself out of the deck chair and returned to his stateroom. Donning a pair of swim trunks and a sweatshirt, he walked barefoot to the sky deck and plopped into the captain's chair. He took a deep breath and dialed his mother's number.

Mamá was nothing like the stereotype of a Spanish matron. She wasn't a fragile flower to be coddled. She was exceptionally beautiful, which made her look soft to those who didn't know her, but she was as tough as rebar beneath her coifed hair and flawless makeup.

Their father had been killed in a fishing accident when the boys were toddlers, and she'd raised them by herself. Being the most attractive woman in Santiago de Compostela, she could have remarried a dozen times, but she didn't want to saddle her sons with a stepfather. Instead, she lived by her wits. She worked as a tour guide during the day and a restaurant hostess in the evening. Any extra money she earned or gifts she received from hopeful suitors went to furthering her sons' educations. She took them to museums, taught them to dance, instructed them how to cook. Most of all, she instilled in them a strong desire to succeed.

When Marcio and Lorenzo began to make a little money, they showered her with gifts—designer handbags, silk scarves and trips to the spa—things she had denied herself while raising them. When they made real money, they bought her an oceanfront villa near Barcelona. They filled her closets with couture and her wine cellar with rare vintages. Unlike some women, who might be uncomfortable with such lavish gifts, Isabella Silva put on her new life like a queen's skin, knowing she had finally achieved her destiny. She had sacrificed much for her boys, and now they were taking care of her.

Marcio had expected the conversation with his mother to be hard, but he hadn't expected her to book the first flight to Panama. She would arrive the next evening, and if it was true that her firstborn son was dead, they could both fly back to Spain together for the funeral.

There would be no negotiating this. When Isabella Silva put her mind to something, no man could talk her out of it. Not even her son.

Chapter 11

Moses Souza had the small IT area to himself. That was just the way he liked it. He got more work done when other people weren't distracting him with their constant demands.

He had moved to Panama from Brazil to attend university. Aside from his native language of Portuguese, Moses was fluent in English and Spanish. Armed with a computer science degree and an IQ of 165, Moses had started working for the Policia Nacional right after graduation. Four different multinationals had offered him jobs, but he had turned them all down. He wanted to work inside the system. After that, he knew the job offers would double.

Detective Bethancourt poked his head in the door. "Haven't you gone home yet?"

Moses shook his head but didn't look away from the computer screen. "Not yet."

The detective set a steaming mug of café con leche next to Moses. "The sun's already out. It's a new day."

Moses checked the clock on one of his computer displays: 6:00 a.m. He scratched his full head of curly hair. How had he lost an entire night?

"What have you got, kid?"

Moses pointed to the center monitor. "Watch this. At eleven thirty-four, Lorenzo Silva goes with Brianna Morgan into her room. Then the power goes out. Instead of a five-second blip, which is what usually happens when the generators come on after a power outage, the entire video security system went offline for over five hours."

Moses pressed "play." They watched Lorenzo and Brianna walk from the elevator down the hall, then disappear into the alcove in front of her room. Then the security tape turned to snow.

Detective Bethancourt frowned. "Brianna Morgan said Lorenzo never went into her room. I can't tell from the video if she's lying or telling the truth."

"I thought the same thing," Moses said. "So I went to the hotel last night to run a few tests." He pointed to the third screen. "This is me last night." He typed a few keys and a new video displayed. "The security camera loses me as soon as I go into the alcove in front of the room. From the security tape, it looks like I went in the room, but I never did."

"Which means it's possible she's telling the truth."

Moses leaned back in his chair. "It's possible."

Detective Bethancourt scratched the back of his head. "If he did go in her room, any idea when he came out?"

"Can't help you there, boss." Moses picked up his coffee and slurped it. "Thanks for this. I needed a hit of caffeine."

"Thanks for your hard work." Detective Bethancourt peered over his shoulder at the monitors. "Have you looked through the tapes to see if Lorenzo Silva showed up after the cameras went back online?"

Moses nodded. "Yes, I checked. More than once. No sign of him."

"When does Brianna Morgan reappear?"

Moses checked his notes. "Six-sixteen the next morning. Just like she said."

"Have you talked to the security guard who was on duty when the power went off?"

Moses nodded so hard his head bobbled on his thin neck. He ate like a pony, but he couldn't keep weight on his lanky frame. At six feet even, he had the metabolism of a hummingbird, always eating, always in motion. "The guard didn't even know the tapes weren't recording. He saw the images on the screen and thought everything was okay. Stupid Panamanian."

Detective Bethancourt crossed his arms and glared at him.

"Sorry, boss." Moses tried to look contrite, but he didn't quite pull it off. Brazilians were like stray dogs—they had to be clever or they'd starve. Whereas Panamanians were like pampered pooches—fat, happy and lazy in paradise. He worked hard because he had to, and he resented their laidback attitude.

"The security guard's name is Pedro Gonzalez," Moses said. "He's married, with three kids. He has a bank account, but there isn't much cash in it. He makes six hundred bucks a month, and by the end of the month, he's always out of money. No unusual deposits."

"Do I want to know how you got into his bank account?"

Moses grinned showing a row of crooked teeth. "Don't ask. Don't tell."

"Did you ask Pedro what he saw on the monitors while the tapes weren't recording?"

"He said he didn't see anything unusual." Moses fiddled with a Gumby doll on his desk. The caffeine had kicked in, and his fingers needed to be in motion. "He probably wasn't even watching the monitors. The guy has three little kids at home. I bet he took a nap."

Detective Bethancourt paced in the confined space, smacking his hands behind his back. "We have a dead guy in a cave, and no apparent mode of transportation. The security guard seems clean so far, just not very smart. Brianna Morgan is our best suspect, but she has no motive—that we know of." He stopped pacing and looked over Moses's shoulder at the monitors, as if hoping an answer would appear like quarters from a slot machine. "Dig into Brianna Morgan's life. Find out everything you can about her. She's hiding something, and I want to know what it is."

"Any parameters?" Moses asked, his eyes gleaming at the opportunity to go rogue.

Detective Bethancourt thought for a moment. "Just don't do anything stupid, Moses. The last thing we need is the Americans on our back for illegal hacking."

Chapter 12

After my brother's death, people I hadn't spoken to in years called to see how I was doing. Did they think my pain would lessen, just because they called? No, of course not. They wanted a front-row seat to my grief. — Brianna Morgan

Brianna woke up five times during the night. Her brain refused to stop replaying the moment when she discovered Lorenzo's body. Unlike the previous morning, when she had bounced out of bed with excitement, this morning she wanted to pull the covers over her head and hide for as long as it took the pain and worry to subside.

What a difference a day made.

One day she's madly in lust, and the next she's a suspect in a murder investigation. She should have run. She toyed with the idea of packing her bags and fleeing the country while she still could, but then her pride kicked in. If that lazy detective wouldn't solve this case, then she would.

After leaving Marcio the night before, she'd returned to BonitaMar and finished taping the segment for The Morgan Report. It would air tonight. Babs Whittaker was thrilled that she'd landed a meaty story on her vacation, and she was already having the production team create promo videos for a follow-up segment next week.

She dragged her exhausted body out of bed and pulled back the curtains. Fuchsia, red and orange streaked the sky as the sun peeked over the horizon. Within minutes, the sky changed from a watercolor of pinks to a brilliant blue. How could anyone be murdered in a place of such spectacular beauty?

She took a military-style shower, in and out in less than three minutes. Last night, over room service, she had mapped out her plan of attack. She would talk to the three most likely suspects today. All women. All Latin. Today would be a busy day.

She needed Marcio's help.

Brianna picked up her phone, debating whether to call or text him. The phone rang in her hand. She glanced at the caller ID. "Marcio, I was just about to call you."

"I am glad you are awake," he said. "We have work to do. Mamá is flying in from Spain and will be here tomorrow night. We must find out who killed my brother before she arrives."

Brianna blinked. "Uh, okay. Find out who killed Lorenzo by tomorrow. Do you want to end world hunger too?"

He chuckled. "I took a personality test at university. I am a type A. Sometimes I want the impossible."

"You think?"

"Let me start over." He paused. "Good morning, Brianna. Did you sleep well?"

"Yes, thank you," she lied. "How are you this morning?"

"As well as can be expected." He sighed. "Mamá said she is flying to Panama because she wants to make sure the police do their job. It is going to be hard enough to shoulder her grief...but allowing her to get involved? I would like it very much if we could figure out who killed my brother before she arrives, or at least find a solid suspect, someone she can focus her energy on."

"Marcio, I will do everything I can to help you."

"I searched the rest of El Gemini this morning. I did not find anything. But we rarely took a woman on board." He paused. "In fact, I think you are the first woman who has been on our boat in a long time. At least one who was not a client or accompanied by her husband."

"Why didn't you take women on board? It seems like your yacht would be the perfect way to get women to fall for you."

"That is the point," he said. "They would have been falling for the yacht rather than the men. Plus, El Gemini was sacred; something just for us."

"Okay, I get it," she said, even though she didn't. She juggled the phone from one hand to the other as she stepped into a cobalt-blue sundress and zipped up the tight-fitting bodice with practiced dexterity. "Marcio, I have a question for you."

"Yes?"

"When we first met yesterday, you said only your mother could tell you and Lorenzo apart. Is that true?"

"Yes. There were things about us that were different, and some people could tell us apart some of the time. But for the most part, Mamá was the only one who could always tell us apart."

"What about Lorenzo's ex-wife, Valentina? Wasn't she able to tell you apart?"

Marcio scoffed. "In order to tell us apart, someone has to pay attention. The only person Valentina ever focused on was herself."

"That's sad," Brianna said, stepping into her strappy high-heeled sandals. "No wonder he divorced her." She spritzed perfume into the air and walked into the cloud of droplets. "Can you text me the phone numbers for our top three femme fatales?"

"Of course. I will do that as soon as we hang up."

"Do they all speak English?" she asked.

"Yes, I think so. The Americans controlled the canal for almost a hundred years. All educated people in Panama speak English—at least the ones who want to succeed."

"Perfect." Brianna headed to the mirror above the low dresser and brushed a coat of mascara on her eyelashes. "The hotel has a buffet restaurant on the lobby level that's open for breakfast. Do you know which one I'm talking about?"

"I do. It's called El Barco."

"Yes, that's the one. Meet me for breakfast at nine, and I'll outline my plan of action." She held the phone with her shoulder as she fastened a pair of diamond studs to her ears. "There is one thing, though."

"Yes?"

"I need you to wear Lorenzo's favorite shirt today, something people associate with him."

"Why?"

"We're going hunting."

Chapter 13

There's nothing more exhilarating than chasing down a story. I bet Wolf Blitzer cried when he left the war zone and took an anchor job. After all, you can't get an adrenaline fix from behind a desk. — Brianna Morgan

Brianna sat in the corner of the busy restaurant facing the entrance. She sipped a cappuccino and watched the bathing-suit clad vacationers as they piled their plates full of eggs, smoked salmon and fruit at the all-you-can-eat buffet, frenetic to get their money's worth. She had never been a fan of buffets, preferring a few bites of perfection to many plates of blasé.

Marcio walked in at exactly 9:00 a.m. Even though the large restaurant was crowded, his eyes found hers within seconds.

His fitted turquoise button-down shirt and crisply pleated black slacks would have made any man look good, but he looked like a piece of art, sculpted by Michelangelo himself. Brianna watched in amusement as heads swiveled to stare as he strutted by. Several women sat up straighter, arching their backs in a subconscious attempt to get his attention, their faces brightening with instant smiles. Men looked at him with envy and sucked in their guts.

Ignoring them all, he headed toward Brianna, never taking his eyes off her. When he reached her table, he leaned down to brush his lips against her cheek in the typical Latin greeting. He pulled out a chair across from her, oblivious to the commotion he'd just stirred up.

Trying to hide the effect he had on her, she made a show of looking at her watch. "Not only handsome, but punctual too. I knew you'd be on time."

"Not all Latins run late."

She used both hands to pick up her cappuccino, studying him as he sat across from her. He was in complete control of his body, sitting casually erect as only athletes could. "Are you going to eat breakfast?"

"No. Just coffee." He flagged down a waitress and waited until she poured an Americana, a normal cup of black coffee. After she left, he stirred in three packets of sugar.

Brianna chuckled. "Like sugar, do you?"

He gave a lopsided grin. "I have a horrible sweet tooth. I can eat an entire cake in one sitting."

"How do you stay so fit?"

"I have a high metabolism. And I love to work out."

"You're lucky." Brianna pushed her coffee cup away. "If I eat a slice of cake, I can't button my skirt the next day."

"You just need to exercise more."

"You think I don't exercise?" She flexed her bicep and showed off her lean muscle.

"I am not talking about jogging or going to the gym." Marcio lowered his voice, letting his eyes focus on her lips. "You need to find a pleasurable activity that burns calories." He kept his eyes on her as he lifted his cup to his mouth.

Was he flirting with her?

She looked away as her stomach flip-flopped. His pheromones were sucking the oxygen from the room. She needed to concentrate.

"What is our plan?" he asked, back to business.

Brianna gave him a slow smile. "We're going to set a trap for our killer."

His eyes sparked with curiosity. "How?"

"Television. Everyone wants their fifteen minutes of fame." She leaned forward, lowering her voice as she laid out her plan. "My cameraman, Mike, is setting up a studio in one of the penthouse suites. After I got off the phone with you, I called two of our lady suspects and invited them to be on my show. They both accepted."

"Of course, they did." Marcio leaned back in his chair and crossed his arms, his biceps bulging through the fitted shirt.

"People love the idea of being on camera, but when they're sitting under bright lights with pancake makeup cracking their faces, they get nervous. When they're nervous, they're more likely to slip up."

Marcio nodded his approval. "What do you want me to do?"

"Wait in one of the bedrooms until I give you the cue to come out. You're going to be my secret weapon."

"How is that?"

"I want them to think you're Lorenzo."

His eyes flickered.

"You said no one except your mother could tell you apart. I want to shake them up."

His jaw tightened. "You want me to play Victor Victoria."

She nodded. "You'll have an earpiece so you can hear everything that's being said. It'll help me if all the conversations are in English, so if they try to speak to you in Spanish, get them back to English."

"And once we get all their guilty little secrets on camera, what then?"

"Then we analyze the tapes. We watch them backward, forward, and in slow motion. We look for subtle body-language cues and micro-expressions. Everyone lies. We just need to find out if their lies are related to Lorenzo."

Marcio nodded again. "What about the third suspect?"

"I couldn't reach her. Her phone just rang and rang. I'll keep trying. I've saved a spot for her at the end of the day."

"Will everyone at the shoot know about your plan?"

She nodded. "Some will know more than others, but they've been told that we're there to catch a killer."

He took the last swig of his coffee. "When do we start?"

"As soon as we pay the bill."

"Are you going to eat?" he asked.

"Not now. I'll have some food sent up to the room. I want to get started."

Marcio reached into his wallet and dropped some bills on the table to pay for their coffees. "Vamenos."

As they left the restaurant, he put his hand on the small of Brianna's back to guide her out. Her spine tingled at his touch. Lorenzo had done the same thing.

They walked in silence to the elevators. Brianna waved her room key in front of the key reader in the elevator and pressed the highest floor. When the elevator opened, she led the way to the presidential suite.

Marcio winked at her. "Nice. Journalists must do well."

"Not as well as professional athletes." She swiped her key and opened the door. "But we do have good expense accounts." She pushed the door open. "And good connections."

They walked into a large living area decorated in earth tones and whites. In front of them, a wall of windows showed off the ocean view. The suite radiated casual luxury.

The room buzzed with activity. Two men were setting up portable lights, while another guy conducted a sound check. Two TV cameras sat on each side of the living area, and a third boom camera was positioned overhead. A woman scurried around, plumping pillows and rearranging furniture.

"How did you pull this together so quickly?" Marcio asked, his eyes round with wonder.

Brianna shrugged a slender shoulder. "ADN is one of the biggest TV networks in the world. They have connections everywhere. I told my producer what I needed, and she found the people."

"Hi, Brianna," Mike said, popping up from behind a camera.

"Hi, Mike. This is Marcio Silva. Marcio, this is my right-hand-cameraman, Mike Kowalski."

Mike grinned and put a beefy paw out to shake Marcio's hand. Nice to meet you, bud." He turned to Brianna. "We'll be ready in about an hour. Wanna take a look?"

"Sure." She studied the view through one of the three cameras located around the room. "Looks good. Make sure you have one camera on their faces and another on their bodies the entire time. I don't want to miss anything."

"Will do, Mister Ed."

Marcio raised his eyebrows. "Mister Ed? Like the horse on that old TV show?"

"That's the one." She blushed. "It's an inside joke. Last year, I was doing a story about men who live at their favorite bars. I walked up to a guy and started chatting with him. I didn't go in with cameras blazing because I didn't want to spook him. Of course, he thought I was trying to pick him up. He was flattered that the 'show horse' in the bar—his words, not mine—had approached him. Mike thought that was funny and was teasing me about it. I told him I was more of a talking head than a show horse, and the nickname Mister Ed became our secret way of communicating whenever I got too much unwanted male attention. Then it just became a pet name."

Wanting to get on with business, Brianna picked up an empty water glass and flicked her fingernails against it. It emitted a high frequency sound, and everyone turned to see what was going on.

"Hi, everyone," she said. "I'm Brianna Morgan. Thank you so much for coming on short notice. We are going to have a super-hectic day today, but I've been told you're all the best of the best. My network has authorized a big bonus at the end of the day, so I promise you the next eight hours will be worth it. If you have any questions, please ask. If I'm not available for any reason, then ask Mike; we've been together a long time, and he knows what we need."

She turned to Marcio. "This is our guest of honor, Mr. Silva. Please treat him better than you'd treat George Clooney."

She heard a mixture of "Yes" and "Got it."

"We start shooting in one hour. That means we have to be ready in forty minutes."

"Yes, ma'am," two of the camera operators said in unison.

She looked around. "Mike, is the makeup artist here?"

"Yeah, she's setting up in the fourth bedroom." He pointed to the far end of the hall.

Brianna motioned for Marcio to follow her. She pushed the door open. "Hi, are you Sheri?"

A tiny woman with dark curly hair and perfect makeup, waved them in. "Yes, I am. Come on in."

"I think you know my producer, Babs Whitaker. Thanks again for coming on short notice."

"Honey, I'm just so excited to be here." Sheri finished spreading out pots, brushes, and tubes on the table in front of her. "I watch your show almost every day. Wait until I tell my friends that little old me did the makeup for Brianna Morgan."

Brianna smiled, warmed by the woman's Southern charm. "Sheri, this is Mr. Silva. He'll be in the hot seat first."

"Hi, honey. You can sit here." Sheri said with a bright smile as she pointed to a desk chair in front of a makeshift vanity. Marcio's movie-star good looks brought out every woman's shiniest personality.

Brianna led Marcio to the chair. "Down you go."

He frowned. "Why do I need makeup?"

"Because you might end up on camera." She pushed him into the chair. "No arguments. I'll have the sound guys put a microphone on you too. Just in case."

He shook his head. "I do not think this is a good idea."

"Don't be nervous, honey." Sheri patted his shoulders as if he were a skittish horse. "You have amazing bone structure. You're going to look fantastic on camera."

Marcio gave her a wary look.

"I'll take good care of you, sweetie," Sheri said, poking in her makeup tool chest. "I'm from the South, and the only time I lie is when my best friend asks me if her butt looks fat in a teensy-weensy bikini made for a teenager. Bless her heart, she still thinks she's a size two, even though she's popped out four kiddos and shops at the mature-lady store."

Marcio sighed and leaned back. "Okay. I am in your hands."

Brianna hid her triumphant smile. "I'll be back in a few minutes." She went back out to the living area. "Mike, did someone order food?"

"I did." The woman who had been plumping pillows raised her hand, her posture so erect that she had to be a dancer or a yoga fanatic.

"Are you my producer?"

"Yes. I'm Cristina Espinosa." She had a hooked nose, a mannish mouth, and intelligent eyes. Brianna liked her instantly.

"Thanks so much for coming. Is there anything you need?"

Cristina pushed a curl of honey brown hair behind her ear. "I'd like to sit down with you for five minutes and go over the agenda."

"Let's do it. We need to be completely in sync."

Brianna turned to Mike. "I'm going into the other room for some strategy with Cristina. Make sure we're ready to go on time."

"I'm on it, boss."

Brianna led Cristina into another bedroom and shut the door. She walked over to the sitting area, which had a small table and two chairs. She motioned for Cristina to sit down. "Babs briefed you on my agenda?"

Cristina nodded. "We're here to get a confession and catch Lorenzo Silva's killer."

Brianna cocked her head, appraising the other woman's no-nonsense attitude. "Yes. That means doing whatever it takes. I might make them cry, I might make them mad, I might cause one of our femme fatales to snap. We need to be ready for anything." She tapped on her iPad until the files came up. "I'm going to send you my notes for the first interview."

"Do you want me in your ear?" Cristina asked, holding up an earbud.

"Absolutely." Brianna took the earbud and put it in her ear. "The cameramen know what they're doing. I've worked with Mike for years, and he hired the other two. The focus will be getting as much information out of our interviewees as possible. Once they figure out what's going on, though, they might not be very cooperative."

Brianna tapped the iPad a few more times, pulling up the email program and attaching some files. "I'm also sending you a brief dossier on each interviewee. There will be a break between interviews, so just focus on the first one for now, Valentina Arias."

"Got it."

"Oh, and one other thing." Brianna stopped typing on her iPad and leaned forward, making eye contact with Cristina. "Whatever happens, keep the cameras rolling."

Chapter 14

Detective Bethancourt rubbed Vicks VapoRub under his nostrils before entering the Morgue Judicial. He didn't like going to autopsies. Even after ten years in homicide, the sight of the ruined bodies squeezed his heart and gave him chest pains. Plus, the scent of death made him nauseous, the smell lingering for days in his clothes and hair.

He'd thrown away more than one set of clothes. Now he kept an extra set in his office, just for autopsies. Afterward, he'd wash them three times in hot water, place them in a plastic storage bag with dryer sheets, then return them to his office drawer for his next date with the morgue.

The deputy director of forensic medicine, Dr. Camila Duarte, already had started the autopsy when he walked in. While staff doctors handled most autopsies, Dr. Duarte was conducting this one herself. Her boss, the director general, had called and demanded it.

Lorenzo Silva's death had been in the Panamanian news every moment since the story had first broken. Not only had he been a wealthy businessman and a former pro athlete, but he'd also been married to an Arias, one of the richest families in Panama.

"Good morning, Camila." Detective Bethancourt gave her a genuine smile, despite his discomfort with their meeting place. "What do you have so far?"

A handsome woman in her late forties, Dr. Duarte wore hospital scrubs covered by a plastic apron. She had pulled her hair up under a paper hairnet and protected her face with a clear plastic shield. She looked more like a welder in hospital garb than a doctor.

"Good morning, John." She sounded chipper. "We have a healthy male, thirty-six years old, seventy-four inches long, one hundred ninety-two pounds. A specimen of athleticism."

Detective Bethancourt studied the corpse, his perfect body ruined with a Y-incision down his chest. "He played fútbol professionally."

"I remember reading about him. He made the papers when he married Juan Arias' daughter."

"That's him." Detective Bethancourt leaned against the stainless-steel counter farthest from the autopsy table. "Do you have time of death yet?"

"Between nine on Friday night and three on Saturday morning,"

"We have him on camera until eleven-thirty Friday night, so that narrows it down. Have you determined the cause of death?"

Dr. Duarte pointed at where the heart had been before she'd removed it. "Cardiac arrest from a lethal dose of cyanide. I ran a blood test. It came back positive."

Detective Bethancourt nodded. "That was my guess when I saw how red his skin was. I asked our crime-scene techs to test the bottle of Disaronno as well. I should know in a few hours. Now I just need to figure out if it was murder or suicide."

Dr. Duarte looked up from the corpse. "I'm not the detective, but a man doesn't keep himself in this sort of perfect physical condition if he's suicidal."

"Agreed." Detective Bethancourt knocked his knuckles twice on the stainless-steel table. "Anything else?"

"His BAC was point oh-eight. Not completely sober but not drunk enough to have consumed much more than a few ounces of amaretto, especially since he'd had red wine prior to that with dinner." She grinned. "Red wine is easy to detect in the stomach and small intestine. It turns everything a delightful shade of Merlot."

Detective Bethancourt scratched the stubble on his face. He had forgotten to shave that morning. "Point oh-eight seems low. According to sources, he had cocktails before dinner, wine with dinner, and then amaretto after dinner. Shouldn't it be higher?"

Dr. Duarte wiped her gloved hands on a towel. "There could be a few reasons. First, our boy here was in great physical shape. His metabolism worked faster than a typical person's. Second, he could have had less to drink than you thought. Or third, the lower blood alcohol could point toward a later time of death, closer to three a.m."

"What's your theory?"

"A combination of all three." Dr. Duarte picked up a needle and suture thread from her supply table and started to close the Y-incision on the corpse's torso. "An athlete with a high metabolism who had less to drink than we thought and died at the far edge of the window for time of death. That would explain it best."

Detective Bethancourt left his perch and approached the body. "Or we're missing something," he said, studying it.

She knotted the suture thread and snipped the end with scissors, before starting a new suture. "Science doesn't lie, John. It's my job to figure out the 'what.' It's your job to put the pieces together and determine the 'who' and the 'why.'" Dr. Duarte looked up from the corpse. "I have the easy job."

Chapter 15

Marcio peered at himself in the mirror of the master bathroom of the presidential suite. His face looked orange from the thick stage makeup. He grimaced, not worried about his outward appearance but nervous about all the things that could go wrong today. He had the energy of a caged lion.

He strode across the room and picked up a bottle of water, his hands shaking from adrenaline as he unscrewed the cap. Surprised by his trembling hands, he set the bottle down so fast that water spilled out the top. He flexed his fingers, focusing his energy on his breathing to calm his body. He closed his eyes, visualizing himself winning today in the match of wits. It would be the most important game of his life.

After a few deep breaths, he picked up the water bottle again and drank it down in one long gulp.

The master bedroom of the presidential suite had been turned into a control room. Cristina walked in and peered at the bank of monitors that had been set up on one wall. A couch had been moved in front of the monitors for easy viewing. He stood next to her, too nervous to sit. "What are we watching?"

"There are three TV cameras in the main room—two regular cameras and a boom camera that takes video from above. You probably saw those when you walked in."

He nodded.

"Each camera's image is shown here in real-time." She indicated three of the monitors with her left hand. "Brianna has hidden five other cameras around the suite so we can watch our subjects before they know they're on camera." She pointed to five other monitors. They will be on camera from the moment they enter until the time they leave.

The doorbell rang. They watched on the monitors as Brianna opened the door and flashed her on-camera smile.

"You must be Valentina." She sounded as if she were greeting her childhood best friend. "I'm Brianna Morgan. Come in. We've been expecting you."

"It's a pleasure to meet you." Valentina looked every inch the mid-thirties socialite, dressed in designer fashion from her earlobes to her stilettos. She wore a frilly yellow blouse with a plunging neckline and a three-quarter-length black mermaid skirt. Her Panama-blond hair looked like she had just come from the salon, straight and glossy from a professional blowout, but her skin was rough from too much sun.

"Hmm," Cristina said, more to herself than to Marcio.

"What?"

"It's nothing." She tried to hide a smirk.

Marcio looked from Cristina to the monitor and back again. "Ah, I understand. You thought she'd be more beautiful than she is."

Cristina looked embarrassed, and then shrugged one shoulder. "I've heard so much about Valentina. I thought she'd be a nine or a ten." Cristina gave the monitors an appraising glance, a wicked gleam in her eye. "She's only a seven. Maybe even a six without her team of stylists and trainers.

Marcio grunted. "I've see her without makeup. Trust me, she isn't even a five."

Cristina bit back a smile as she turned back to the screen.

Valentina clicked across the marble foyer in black stilettos, showing off Christian Louboutin's signature lacquered red soles. She looked around the suite, apparently in awe of the cameras and lights. "I didn't realize there would be so many people here."

"It takes a lot more people to create a TV news show than most people realize." Brianna led her to the kitchen and pointed to platters of bread, cheese, and fruit. "Would you like some breakfast? Or if you'd like something else, we can order it for you."

Valentina patted her flat stomach. "Gracias, no. I could not eat a thing."

"Okay, then we can get started." Brianna led her to the makeup room. "Valentina, this is Sheri. She's going to make you beautiful for the cameras." She smiled her friendliest smile. "Not that you're not already beautiful. Have you had your makeup done for TV before?"

Valentina flicked her hair off her shoulders and lifted her chin in an arrogant tilt. "Of course."

Brianna flashed her a show-business smile. "Then you know it'll look very heavy when you see it in the mirror, but you'll need every bit of it to stand up to the bright lights."

Sheri motioned to the chair. "Sit here, honey."

Valentina lowered herself into the makeup chair, keeping her spine erect. She moved deliberately, as if the cameras already were rolling.

Little did she know, they were.

Brianna poured a cup of tea from a nearby pot. "Have some tea, Valentina. It'll help calm your nerves."

"I am not nervous," Valentina squeaked.

"The tea also will help with your voice. When you're under stress, your vocal cords can contract and make you sound funny."

"What kind of tea is it?"

"Almond. It can be bitter, so I've added some sugar." Brianna handed Valentina a cup and saucer. "Have you had it before?"

Valentina blew on the liquid in the cup. "No. I usually drink green tea. Without sugar."

Brianna patted the woman's arm. "It's different than what you're used to, but trust me, it'll be good for you." She turned to go. "I'll leave you in Sheri's capable hands. Just come out to the main room when you're done."

Brianna left the room and closed the door behind her. Rather than stopping in the living room, she kept walking to the control room. After she knocked three times, Marcio opened the locked door.

They focused on the screens, watching Valentina blow on her tea, reluctant to take a sip.

"When did sugar become the devil?" Marcio asked.

Cristina chuckled. "When the elite decided it's better to be thin than happy."

"Why the almond tea?" Marcio asked.

Brianna answered without looking up from the monitors. "I wanted to see how she responded to 'bitter' and 'almond' in the same sentence."

Marcio frowned. "I do not understand."

"The person who killed Lorenzo knows that cyanide tastes like bitter almonds, which is why she probably used Disaronno to hide the taste. Guilty people project their sins onto others. If she drinks the tea without question, it's a good sign that she's innocent. If she doesn't drink the tea, then chances are higher that she's our killer."

They watched Valentina take a sip, her nose wrinkling and lips pursing as soon as she tasted it. She set the cup and saucer down hard on the table in front of her, spilling some of the tea into the saucer. "Sheri, this is too sweet. Get me tea that doesn't have any sugar in it."

Marcio pointed to Valentina on the screen. "It did not take long for the queen's imperious attitude to appear."

Cristina crossed her arms in front of her chest. "Twenty bucks says that tiny little Southern girl can hold her own."

In the makeup room, Sheri held a foundation brush in midair, looking directly at Valentina. "Honey, I think the entire pot is already sweetened."

Valentina sneered, her face contorting in rage. "I did not ask you to think. I told you to get me a new cup of tea. Now stop what you're doing and do what you're told."

Sheri forced a smile. "Honey, I'm here to do your makeup. I'm not here to wait on you."

"How dare you talk to me that way," Valentina hissed. "Do you know who I am?"

"Oh, I know exactly who you are." Sheri sprayed a cotton ball with an unknown liquid and dabbed it on Valentina's face. "You're a spoiled Latina who's trying to be an American, with your fake not-quite-blond hair and your bought-and-paid-for boobs. You think being sexy is the only thing that's important. It's not. Well, unless you're a call girl or some rich man's toy." She dusted powder over the makeup she'd just applied, her face inches from Valentina's. "American women know if you want power, you have to have more than a pretty face and a lean body."

Valentina put out her hands and pushed Sheri back a few inches. "Stop talking and make me beautiful. That's your job, isn't it?"

In the control room, Marcio chuckled. "I am surprised Valentina did not slap her. She has a nasty temper."

Brianna nodded. "I heard. That's why I asked Sheri to push her buttons."

Marcio appraised her with a long look. "I would hate to have you as an adversary."

She winked. "Good thing I'm on your side."

Cristina put her hand on her earpiece, listening. "We're all set up." She studied each monitor closely, making sure the cameras were positioned to her liking, before turning to Brianna. "Is your earpiece in?"

Brianna put the plastic receiver in her ear. "It is now."

"Testing, testing," Cristina said. "One, two, three, testing."

"Perfect." Brianna turned to Marcio. "If you catch Valentina in a lie or she says anything odd, let Cristina know. She was rude to Sheri, and I want to see her sweat."

"That is the upper-class culture in Latin America," Marcio explained. "Be deferential to those above you, be nice to those who are in your same class, but freely abuse those who are below you. Many rich Latins treat their dogs better than they treat their maids."

Brianna's eyes shone with bloodlust. "Give me good intel, Marcio. I'm itching to go after this woman and knock her down a few pegs."

Marcio opened the bedroom door for Brianna. "There is nothing I would like more than to see Valentina Arias down for the count."

Cristina waved to get their attention. "She's finished. Brianna, you're on."

Marcio reached over and squeezed Brianna's shoulder. "You do not need it, but good luck."

She smiled at him, and after hesitating for a second, gave him a return kiss on his cheek. "That's for Lorenzo." After closing the door behind her, she strutted into the living room and sat down in a plush armchair. Television was her playing field, and she oozed confidence.

Valentina walked out of the makeup room, looking like an overdone beauty contestant. Sheri had gone extra-heavy on her makeup to throw her off her game.

"Don't you look gorgeous, Valentina?" Brianna gushed. "Please stand still while Carlos gets your microphone set up."

A short Panamanian in his late twenties appeared from behind a large piece of equipment wearing jeans and a green polo shirt.

"Sorry, but I need to put my hands on you." He showed Valentina the two pieces of the wireless mike set. "I'm going to pin the mike to your blouse. Then I need to run the cord under your blouse and attach the battery pack to your skirt. Is that okay?"

Valentina held up her arms. "Do what you must."

Carlos pinned a wireless mike to the deep V in her blouse. Her breasts were pushed up in such a way that his knuckles brushed against them.

Valentina slapped his hands away. "Watch where you put your hands, moron."

"Sorry," he muttered, his face flushing crimson as he took a step back. When he came toward her again, he approached her as though she were a rabid dog—hands up, moving slowly. He tried not to touch her body as he dropped the wires down the front of her blouse. Once he had attached the battery pack to her skirt, he took two giant steps backward. "You're done," he announced, breathing out in relief.

Brianna pointed to a chair. "Just sit there, Valentina. Before we get started, we need to do a mike and camera check. Just look at me and tell me something. It can be anything." She leaned forward, as if they were friends. "Maybe tell me something about that hot hunk you're dating." Brianna winked. "And does he have a brother?"

"How did you know about Enrique?"

Brianna shrugged. "I'm a reporter. It's my job to know things other people don't. But you haven't always been discreet, have you?"

"We try not to be seen together, but Panama is so small that we always see people we know." Valentina pouted, her full lips jutting out like those of a toddler throwing a tantrum. "You can't ask me about him when the cameras are on, because his wife is a friend of mine. She'll kill me if she finds out."

Brianna turned her fingers near her lips, as if locking her mouth shut. "I won't tell a soul."

Marcio looked at Cristina with surprise. "She uncovered an illicit affair in less than a minute. How did she know?"

"I don't think she did. She guessed. Women like Valentina spend all their time and energy trying to get a man, even if it's someone else's man. They haven't learned how to be alone."

Brianna turned toward the sound equipment. "How's the sound, Carlos?"

"Perfect. We're ready to roll."

"How's the video, Mike?"

"Video's good." Mike gave her a thumbs-up. "We're spinning."

"Are you comfortable, Valentina?" Brianna asked.

Although the woman nodded, she looked like she'd just swallowed a barracuda, teeth first.

Brianna shook her hair out. "Mike, do the countdown."

"Rolling in three." He held up three fingers, then two, then one, and then he dropped his hand.

"Good evening. I'm Brianna Morgan. Welcome to The Morgan Report. I'm reporting from Panama, the gateway between North and South America. Panama is famous for its canal...and it's infamous for being a tax haven for the wealthy around the world. Panama also is home to the powerful Arias family, who've been called the Kennedys of Central America.

"With me today is Valentina Arias Silva. Valentina, welcome."

Valentina smiled, her lips quivering. "Thanks for having me, Brianna."

"What was it like growing up as an Arias?"

"It was a normal family. I was surrounded by brothers and sisters, cousins, and aunts and uncles. Holidays were loud and rowdy, with a lot of food and laughter."

She sounded stiff.

"It sounds idyllic." Brianna smiled, as if encouraging her to relax. "Where did you go to high school?"

"I went to boarding school in Switzerland," she said, lifting her chin in the same arrogant gesture she'd made before. "I learned French and Latin there, and it also was a finishing school. We were taught how to be ladies who would one day take our places in society."

"And from there you went to college in the United States."

"Yes. I went to the University of North Carolina."

"Why not an Ivy League school?"

"Because she didn't have the grades, let alone the smarts," Marcio muttered.

Valentina crossed her legs and smiled, comfortable with the question. She'd prepared for this one. "I wanted to experience the United States as a real person. I didn't feel an Ivy League university would expose me to average American students."

"Is it important for you to stay in touch with average people?" Brianna asked.

"Yes."

"She sounds sincere," Cristina said.

"All narcissists do," Marcio quipped.

"And how do you do that?" Brianna's face showed nothing by curiosity. "Your family has been in politics for generations, with two presidents in your lineage. How do you stay in touch with the average person?"

"I do volunteer work, helping the poor in Panama. Last month we collected Christmas gifts for orphans."

"There are a lot of poor people in Panama." Brianna leaned forward. "The average worker makes about six hundred dollars a month. Is that correct?"

"That's right."

"Which means your shoes would support an average family for about two months."

Valentina looked down at her Louboutins. "I never thought about it that way."

"You probably don't think about the poor very often, do you?"

Valentina opened her mouth to say something, but no words came out.

Brianna quickly changed the subject. "Let's talk about your college years. What did you study?"

Valentina looked relieved. "I loved my time at UNC. I majored in marketing and learned so much about business."

Brianna arched an eyebrow. "Did you? And how have you put that knowledge into practice?"

"Excuse me?"

"The business principals you learned at UNC." Brianna enunciated each word. "How have you used this knowledge? You've never worked, have you?"

Valentina looked puzzled. "No. Why would I work?"

"Yes, why would you work," Brianna said flatly. "Socialites don't need to work. Silly question. I'll move on." She shuffled note cards, which she didn't look at, giving the audience time to draw their own conclusions. "You met your husband at UNC, didn't you?"

"Yes, but we're divorced now."

"What was his name?" Brianna looked like she didn't know.

"Lorenza Silva. He played soccer for UNC. We got married very young."

"Really?" Brianna cocked her head. "I thought you didn't get married until five years after you graduated?"

"Yes, but we started dating at university." Valentina bounced an ankle back and forth over her crossed leg.

Marcio pointed at the screen. "She does that when she's lying. That ankle-flip thing."

"Got it." Cristina pressed her mike button. "Brianna, the fast ankle flip is a sign she's lying."

"How long were you married?" Brianna asked.

"Three years."

"Why did you divorce?"

Valentina flipped her ankle again, faster this time. "We grew apart."

Brianna went poker faced. "Rumor has it you cheated on him."

Flip, flip, flip. "Don't believe everything you hear."

"How do you feel now that he's dead?"

Valentina went still. "I thought this interview was going to be about me and my family."

"It is. Lorenzo Silva was part of your family. And now he's dead." Brianna paused. "Did you kill him?"

The color drained from Valentina's face. Then her ankle started flipping again.

"Did you murder your ex-husband?"

"How dare you?" Valentina snarled.

"Did you do it yourself or did you hire someone else to do it for you?"

Valentina shot out of her chair. "I do not have to listen to these ridiculous accusations. Do you know who I am?"

"I'm assuming that's a rhetorical question." Brianna looked unfazed. "Before you leave, there's someone I want you to meet."

Valentina tossed her hair and stomped her foot. "I don't care if you have Leonardo DiCaprio jumping out of a cake. I am through with you."

Cristina barked orders into her headset. "Cameras two and three, keep your focus on Valentina until she walks out the front door."

Valentina marched over to where she'd dropped her handbag. Just as she was about to pick it up, Marcio walked into the room. "Hello, Vali."

Valentina stopped moving and stood as still as Lot's wife after she'd been turned into a pillar of salt.

"Have you missed me?"

Valentina shook her head, her eyes wide. "No. It can't be."

"Oh, it is." He stepped forward.

"Lorenzo? I thought you were dead." Valentina's lip quivered.

He took another step forward. "You made a mistake, Vali. You killed the wrong brother."

Valentina's head continued to shake from side to side. "I didn't kill anyone. I swear."

"Marcio is dead because of you."

Her eyes widened as he stepped into her personal space.

"I would never try to kill you. Or your brother." She took a step back.

Marcio followed her like a predator. "I moved to Panama because you said you loved me. Like a fool, I believed you. And then you cheated on me with that sniveling polo player."

"I didn't mean to," she whined.

"Then, when I wanted a divorce, you hid behind your family. You wanted to ruin our business. You could not stand that we would be successful without you. Or that I could be happy without you. Is that why you wanted to kill me?" He had her backed up against the wall.

"I didn't try to kill you. I swear. I didn't kill Marcio. I didn't even know he was murdered. I thought he'd had a heart attack. That's what everyone is saying."

"Well, they're saying it wrong," Marcio said, putting his nose so close to Valentina's face that he could smell her fear. "My brother was murdered. And guess what? You are my prime suspect."

Recognition flickered in Valentina's eyes as she saw a vein throbbing in his neck. "You're not Lorenzo. You're Marcio." She pushed him in the chest to get him to back up. "You think I can't tell the difference between my ex-husband and his asshole brother? What kind of crazy game are you playing?"

Marcio shrugged. "You caught me. I'm not Lorenzo. But someone killed my brother, and my money is on you."

Chapter 16

During the Roman games, the mob cheered while blood flowed like a river into the ground. The mob doesn't care who is torn apart. They just want blood. — *Brianna Morgan*

Brianna left the presidential suite and went back to her hotel room. She flopped on the bed, closed her eyes and breathed deeply. She was bone tired. She'd been so happy just a few days before. Had it just been two days since she'd arrived in Panama? It seemed like she'd been here for weeks.

The rest of the crew had taken a break for lunch, but she needed a nap. She wanted to snatch twenty minutes of sleep so she could be on her game when the next interview started.

She opened her eyes and gazed at the minibar. Brianna was a wine fanatic and always augmented her minibar with a selection of premium wines whenever she traveled. Knowing she would be in Panama for more than a week, she had purchased a half-dozen bottles of wine, liqueur, and champagne.

A small glass of wine with some mind-numbing television would take her mind off everything and allow her to sleep.

She peeled herself off the bed, kicked off her heels, and headed to the minibar. She pulled out a bottle of chilled Argentinian Chardonnay and poured a few ounces into a wineglass. She swirled the glass and sniffed the wine. The aroma hit her brain—green apples, toasty oak, and rich butterscotch. Yes, she needed that.

Brianna sat on the edge of the bed, sipping her wine and channel-surfing until she found an old movie, Gentlemen Prefer Blondes. Perfect.

She scooted back on the bed until she was leaning against the headboard. Her mind wandered as she let the banter from the movie wash over her. A minute or two later, she finished her half glass of Chardonnay. Should she pour herself another or switch to red? From the bed, she perused the red wines she had purchased, lined up like soldiers above the minibar.

Something was missing.

Brianna stopped breathing. It couldn't be.

She jumped off the bed and ransacked the bottles of wine. It wasn't there. She opened the minibar fridge and pulled everything out.

It was gone. The Disaronno amaretto she had purchased her first day in Panama was missing.

She stood still in the middle of the room. Did she forget to buy it? She closed her eyes, trying to remember. No, she had picked up the bottle at the nearby liquor store and put it in her cart. She was sure of it.

Perhaps the clerk had forgotten to ring it up. Perhaps she had left the bottle in her cart.

She grabbed her handbag and dumped the contents onto the bed. She opened her wallet and pulled out all the receipts. Then she ruffled through them until she found the one from the liquor store. Even though the receipt was in Spanish, she saw it right away: Disaronno.

Brianna closed her eyes, remembering how she had unpacked the amaretto from the box and put it on the minibar counter.

This was bad.

The bottle she had purchased was missing.

Could her missing bottle be the same bottle that had been next to Lorenzo in the cave? If so, her fingerprints would be all over it.

Brianna trembled as she thought about the implication.

If she ran, she would look guilty. But if she didn't run, she might end up in jail.

She had to think, but first she had to sleep. She tipped the bottle of Chardonnay and poured a full glass. She gulped it down in one breath, as if it were medicine, then rested her head on the pillow.

She had to sleep. Then she would figure out if someone was trying to frame her.

Chapter 17

Detective Bethancourt walked into the police station for the second time that day. His brain buzzed. The bottle of Disaronno had tested positive for cyanide. He now had the cause of death and the murder weapon. He just needed to figure out the "who" and "why." Technically he couldn't rule out suicide yet, but it didn't fit. This was murder.

He carried a plastic sack into the IT department and handed Moses a Styrofoam container. "Hey, kid. I brought you some lunch."

Moses turned in his chair and took the container. "Great. I haven't eaten since yesterday. What's for lunch?"

"Panama special. Beans. Rice. Chicken. Salad."

"Thanks. Looks good." He used the plastic fork that came with it and took a big bite.

Detective Bethancourt opened his own takeout box, holding the Styrofoam container with one hand while using the other to eat a bite of chicken. "Anything on Brianna Morgan yet?"

Moses grinned as he chewed, looking even younger than his twenty-three years. "I hit the jackpot, boss."

"Yeah? What've you got?"

Moses expanded a screen on the center monitor. "When you told me Lorenzo Silva was poisoned with cyanide, I focused on linking the luscious Miss Morgan to cyanide. This is what I found." He pressed the "play" button and a video started.

This is Brianna Morgan, reporting from Harbor Town, Maine. With the recent Harbor Town cult committing mass suicide by drinking communion wine laced with cyanide, I'm here to bring you the science behind the poison.

Throughout history, many people have died from cyanide poisoning, both willingly and unwillingly. The serial killer Cyanide Mohan killed twenty women in India between 2005 and 2009. Adolf Hitler used cyanide gas to exterminate Jews during World War II. Not only have other cults—

such as Jonestown and Heaven's Gate—used cyanide as their one-way ticket to the hereafter, but governments also have chosen cyanide as their poison of choice. Many states use cyanide as part of the lethal injection cocktail when carrying out capital punishment on inmates who have been sentenced to death.

A fatal dose of cyanide can be as low as 1.5 milligrams per kilogram of body weight. So, for a man who weighs one hundred eight-five pounds—or eighty-four kilograms—it could take just one hundred twenty-six milligrams to render a lethal dose. That's less than half an ounce of cyanide. In fact, the suicide pills issued to US and British soldiers during World War II were about the size of a pea.

How does cyanide kill you? If prevents your cells from using oxygen. Think of it as a form of internal asphyxiation. If you're given a lethal dose, you'll immediately slip into a coma because your cells aren't getting oxygen. This is followed by seizures and finally death. Cyanide poisoning is a quick death, which is why many mass suicides choose it as their way to die.

In nature, cyanide comes in many forms. It can be found in peach pits, apple seeds, flaxseeds, almonds, lima beans, bamboo shoots, and many other food items. The amount of cyanide found in these foods is so small, however, that you'd have to eat exorbitant amounts for the poison to have an adverse effect. For example, you'd need to eat fourteen thousand cups of rice in one sitting for the cyanide in brown rice to kill you. Your gut would explode long before the cyanide killed you.

On the flip side of the cyanide equation, small amounts of this natural poison can do irreparable harm. For example, if you happen to swallow a cherry pit, the pit will pass through your system whole, and no cyanide will enter your system. But if you crush a handful of cherry pits and then eat them, that small amount of nature's toxin could result in your death.

If you happen to join a religious organization and someone asks you to take a cyanide pill or eat crushed cherry pits with your oatmeal, do what Nancy Reagan suggested during her husband's administration and "Just say no."

Moses took another bite and stopped the video. "That was four years ago, but it proves she knew how cyanide works. The second video is even better." He pressed a few buttons and a new video appeared and started to play.

This is Brianna Morgan, reporting from Beijing, China. Like many of you, I was saddened at the brutality of Tanya Everhart's rape and murder last year in Miami Beach, Florida. As a nation, we prayed for her when she went missing, and we cried for her when her body was found. After the shock of her death wore off, I became infuriated by this senseless crime.

Ever wonder how rapists and murderers get dangerous drugs, like the ones that incapacitated Tanya Everhart, allowing her to be killed by a madman? All you need to do is get on a plane and cross a border.

You've probably heard that you can get medicines without prescriptions in places like Mexico, but did you know you can get dangerous drugs—such as Rohypnol and cyanide—on the streets of China? To find out whether this was true, I went undercover in China. I knew I couldn't go unnoticed in China, so I asked one of my colleagues to go shopping with a hidden camera. What you're about to watch will give you chills.

Our undercover agent, Song, is going into an innocuous herb shop. See, there she is in the blue dress. Now she's asking the man behind the counter for one hundred fifty milligrams of cyanide. That's enough to kill an average person. Now she is asking for two milligrams of Rohypnol. He doesn't ask her any questions about why she needs either drug.

The scene changed to a modern lab with white-coated technicians. Brianna's voiceover continued.

Once Song bought the cyanide and Rohypnol, we took them to a lab to have them tested, just to make sure they were what the herbalist said they were. The test of the cyanide came back positive for sodium cyanide, a water-soluble poison that can kill within minutes. The Rohypnol tested positive for flunitrazepam, a category of drug similar to Valium or Xanax, but much more potent. Available for just a few dollars, these drugs were as easy to purchase as a pack of gum.

Moses pressed the "stop" button. "That was three years ago. I also have her back in China five weeks ago doing a story on child labor. Do you want me to play it?"

Detective Bethancourt wiped his mouth with a paper napkin and shook his head. "No. I get it. She reported on cyanide twice. She knows how it works and where to buy it. Good work. Did you find any connection between her and Lorenzo Silva before the day of his death?"

"Not yet."

Detective Bethancourt patted Moses on the shoulder. "Keep digging."

Chapter 18

Marcio looked at his watch. Brianna should have been back twenty minutes ago.

He was just picking up the hotel-suite phone to call her room when she walked in. She had dark circles under her eyes, and her skin had lost its fresh glow.

"Sorry I'm late," she said to the room at large. "Is Laura here yet?"

"Not yet." Marcio set down the receiver and walked over to her. "Are you okay?"

She didn't look at him. "Fine. Just tired."

He smelled alcohol on her breath. "Did you sleep?"

Brianna nodded. "A bit. But not enough."

"Brianna, look at me."

She hesitated then raised her eyes to meet his.

He placed his hands on her shoulders. "Cancel the other interviews. You do not need to do this."

"Thanks, Marcio, but I do need to do this. I owe it to Lorenzo." She sighed and pulled away. "Let's get started."

Brianna went into makeup. Through the open door, Marcio watched as Sheri touched up her hair and face.

Fifteen minutes later, Brianna came out, her high heels clicking in soldierly precision as she made her way across the suite.

Marcio smiled at her. "You have your glow back. Now you look like the same woman who pounced on Valentina Arias."

"I'm ready for my next victim." She curled her fingers into claws and hissed dramatically. "Any word from Laura?"

"Not yet. She is a Latina. In her mind, it is more important to make a grand entrance than to arrive on time."

Brianna crossed her arms in impatience. "Marcio, you're her boss. Please call her and have her get her butt here pronto."

"Just her butt?" Marcio winked.

Brianna flashed him a grateful smile. "And the rest of her too."

Mike poked his head out from behind his camera. "If she's anything like Valentina, her breasts will get here five minutes before her butt."

The other cameramen chuckled.

"I've been trying not to stare," Mike continued, "but the butts on these Latinas are like those Weeble toys we used to play with as kids. What's up with that?"

Cristina pulled a bottle of water out of the fridge. "Latin women like big round hoochies, so what God doesn't give them, they buy." She patted her own flat butt. "Of course, some of us don't care."

Mike grinned, the wide-eyed smile of a boy who'd just discovered his first dirty magazine. "I want to do some R and D. Find out exactly what a fake butt feels like."

Brianna leaned against the kitchen counter and shook her head. "Boys, boys, boys. Always thinking about T and A."

Marcio frowned. "T and A?"

"Dude!" Mike exclaimed. "Where have you been? 'T and A' means 'tits and...'"

The doorbell rang.

"Saved by the bell," Brianna muttered, striding across the marble floor. She shooed Marcio into the control room and waited until he had closed the door before she opened the front door. "Hi, you must be Laura. Please come in."

Laura Mareno looked up, smiling through a long curtain of honey-colored hair, highlighted to look almost blond. Just shy of five feet, she had the petite frame of a pre-pubescent girl, breasts the size of cantaloupes, and the fresh-faced look of a farm girl. The effect was sexier than if she'd been a long-legged platinum blond. She wore low-slung taupe slacks belted at the waist with a gold chain, and an off-the-shoulder paisley blouse, displaying youthful skin that glowed like stretched toffee.

"Wow!" Cristina said in the control room to Marcio. "Now she's a nine."

"Nine and a half," Marcio said. "As long as she does not speak."

Cristina gave him a cryptic look.

He shrugged. "I like smart women—like you, like Brianna. The dumb ones bore me."

He turned back to the screen and watched as Brianna led Laura to the makeup room and introduced her to Sheri.

"Would you like some almond tea, Laura?" Brianna asked.

"Yes. Thank you."

"It can be a little bitter, so I added some sugar." Brianna poured the tea into a cup and handed it to Laura.

Laura took it then set it on the desk without taking a sip. She picked up a jar of makeup. "What's this for?" she asked Sheri.

Sheri pinned Laura's hair back. "Honey, that's the best stuff in the world. It catches the light and makes your skin look like you've been out in the sunshine."

Laura's dark eyes lit up. "I wondered how the movie stars always looked so dewy."

Sheri spritzed a large cotton pad with liquid. "Close your eyes. I'm going to remove your makeup."

Laura complied, and Brianna let her smile fall. "Laura, please try to drink at least a little of the almond tea. It'll help your voice when you're on camera."

Laura waited until Sheri had finished taking off her makeup then picked up the teacup and took several large sips. She looked at Brianna for approval.

"Good girl," Brianna said. "I'm going in the other room while Sheri does your makeup."

"Okay." Laura picked up a small spray bottle. "Sheri, what's this?"

Rolling her eyes, Brianna left the girl-in-a-woman's-body with Sheri and hurried back to the control room.

"Where's Cristina?" she asked Marcio.

"She's prepping in one of the bedrooms. I think she wanted to give us some privacy."

"That was nice of her." Brianna shut the door behind her then locked it. "Remind me why Laura is on our list of suspects. She has the personality of a ten-year-old."

"She's had a crush on Lorenzo for three years, since the day she was hired."

"Just Lorenzo?"

106

Marcio grimaced as he plopped down on the bed. "What does that mean?"

Brianna turned down the sound on the makeup room monitor. "If I worked for two gorgeous, identical-looking men, I'd have a crush on both of you. Flirt with both until one flirts back."

"Lorenzo had just gotten divorced when we hired her. He was wounded." He picked at the comforter on the bed, searching for the right word. "Laura sensed his vulnerability. They never had an affair, but he leaned on her like he would a little sister. I think she took it the wrong way."

Brianna looked at the screen where Laura was sipping her tea. "So she wanted more than a little-sister/big-brother relationship."

He nodded. "But he could not give more. Valentina hurt him badly. She taught us both a lesson. A beautiful face is a good distraction for an evening or two, but a real relationship requires a woman of substance. He and I created a list of attributes our perfect woman must have." He looked down at her. "She must be smart, witty, confident, and successful by herself." Marcio gazed into her moss-green eyes. "She must be someone like you."

Brianna looked up at him. He had her attention.

"Laura is a nice girl, but you are right. She is just a girl." He rubbed the back of his neck as if he had an itch. "When she is eighty, she will still be a girl. She is dependent. She needs the adoration of another to feel good about herself."

Brianna looked away, fidgeting with a knob on the control panel. "Did Laura get upset when Lorenzo didn't ask her out?"

He nodded. "She started stalking him. Recently she started showing up at our apartment late at night. And then she talked the concierge into letting her into our apartment. When Lorenzo came home, she was waiting for him. Naked. On the kitchen counter, covered in honey and Saran wrap."

Brianna's eyes widened, and she laughed out loud. "I thought that just happened in movies."

"Truth is crazier than fiction. When Lorenzo rejected her, Laura went crazy. My brother and I realized things were getting out of hand. Last week we decided to fire her. We had been working with our human resources manager to put together a package for her. We were going to offer her three months' salary and a good reference. We planned to fire her the same day my brother was killed."

Brianna whistled. "That's convenient. Do you think Laura found out you were going to let her go?"

Marcio shrugged. "I cannot prove that she knew, but there is a saying in Panama: it is only possible to keep a secret between three people if two of them are dead."

"Ouch."

"Yes, I know." Marcio crossed his arms. "It is possible that someone overheard us talking or that our HR manager Stella Rodriguez told someone." He looked away. "For Laura's sake, I hope she is not guilty. She never would survive prison."

Brianna snapped her fingers. "Oh, I have a piece of good news. We tracked down Ana Maria Lopes. She'll be here in an hour." Brianna looked at her watch. "We have just enough time to do this interview."

Marcio stared at her. "How did you find her?"

"Turns out we had the wrong phone number. Babs, my producer at ADN, found her and set it up."

Cristina knocked on the door and made a twirling motion with her forefinger, knowing they could see her on the monitors.

Show time, Brianna thought.

She turned and gave a long look at the door to the control room. "We have so much to talk about," she said. "But first I have to find what secrets our little Miss Laura is hiding."

He watched as she left, then followed her on the monitor as she took her spot in front of the cameras. When Laura came out of makeup, Brianna already had her work smile glued in place.

Brianna pointed to Carlos. "Laura, this is Carlos, our sound technician. He'll get you set up with a wireless microphone."

Laura nodded and lifted her arms to let Carlos attach the microphone.

"I'm done," Carlos announced. "You can go sit next to Brianna in front of the camera."

Laura walked to where he had indicated and perched on the edge of the chair. She blinked at the bright lights, terror morphing her features into that of a scared animal.

Brianna straightened her blouse and licked her teeth to make sure she removed any stray lipstick. "Start the countdown, Mike."

Mike held up his fingers. Three, two, one…

"Good evening. I'm Brianna Morgan. Welcome to The Morgan Report. I'm reporting from Panama, which is becoming known as one of the best places in the world to retire. The lower cost of living, year-round good weather, and dollarized economy are just some of the reasons Americans are flocking to Panama.

"With me today is Laura Mareno, from Grupo SilCasa, one of the hottest real estate development companies in Panama. Laura, welcome."

"Thank you," Laura said, smiling like a third-grader on picture day.

"Laura, what's it like working in Panama right now?"

She flipped her highlighted hair behind her shoulders. "It's fun. We have some really cool projects, and our sales have been—you know— really great."

Cristina turned to Marcio in the control room. "Eloquent, isn't she?"

Marcio snorted. "If she spent as much time polishing her public speaking skills as she spends filing her nails, our sales would break records."

Brianna continued. "What do you do for Grupo SilCasa?"

Laura crossed her legs and pulled her skirt up a few inches. "I am the administrative assistant for a developer who sells beachfront condos."

"You're so pretty. I bet you sell a lot of condos."

Laura's face lit up at the compliment. "Thank you. I just do admin work right now but I want to move into sales."

"You're so fit. Do you work out?"

"Almost every day," Laura said proudly.

"I can tell." Brianna's brow pulled together, as if she were confused about something. "Laura, who does your company sell beachfront condos to?"

Laura leaned forward, showing off her abundant cleavage. "Americans."

"Americans?" Brianna acted surprised. "Aren't you Colombian?"

"I was born in Colombia, but I love Americans."

Brianna leaned back slightly. "Yes, I can tell. Your fake blond hair gives you away."

Laura scrunched up her face. "What?"

"If you were proud to be Colombian, you'd be proud of having dark hair. But you're not, are you?"

Marcio turned to Cristina. "What is she doing?"

Cristina curved her mouth into a slow smile. "She's playing good cop and bad cop. It gets them off balance."

Laura crossed her arms, trying to protect herself from the verbal attack. "I am proud to be Colombian."

Brianna arched an eyebrow. "How long has it been since you've lived in Colombia?"

"Eleven years."

"Have you been in Panama all that time?"

Laura nodded.

Brianna smiled, once again hiding the wolf behind the sheep's facade. "Tell me what Americans like about your beachfront condos."

Laura let her arms fall to her side. "In the United States, beachfront condos are expensive. In places like Miami or Southern California, they can go for millions of dollars, and monthly homeowner fees and insurance can cost several thousand dollars per month. In Panama, you can buy a brand-new beachfront condo for just two hundred thousand dollars, and the monthly fees are only a few hundred dollars a month."

Brianna's smile stayed in place. "That's a great deal for Americans. No wonder Panama's real estate market is so hot right now."

Laura nodded, relaxing a bit as Brianna showered her with smiles.

"Tell me about your company. It's owned by a Spanish family, correct?"

"Yes, two brothers." Laura's face pinched. "But one of them just died."

Brianna feigned surprise. "Really? What happened?"

Laura's eyes gleamed; she was eager to be the bearer of juicy news. "They found him in a cave. The police haven't said for sure, but people are saying he committed suicide."

"You're talking about the former professional soccer player, Lorenzo Silva, correct?"

Laura nodded.

"Do you think he committed suicide?" Brianna leaned forward toward her prey. "He was smart, well educated, successful, and one of the most handsome men on the planet. Why would he commit suicide?"

Laura shrugged. "You never know what's going on with a person."

"But you worked with him every day, yes? If he had been depressed, wouldn't you have noticed?"

"No. Lorenzo didn't show his emotions at work, but I think he was lonely. He didn't let anyone inside, especially after his divorce. He probably never got over it."

"What makes you think he never got over it?"

Laura shrugged. The little girl was back.

"Was it because of something he told you?" Brianna asked. "Or because you wanted a relationship with him and he rejected you?"

Laura jutted her chin out in defiance. "Lorenzo didn't reject me."

"Really? According to my sources, you emailed and texted him constantly."

"I worked for him. It's normal to text and email your boss."

"Is it normal to show up at his residence late at night?"

Laura shrugged one shoulder.

"Is it normal to stalk your boss?

Laura curled into herself, not saying anything.

"Is it normal to wait at your boss's apartment naked?"

"Why are you attacking me?" Laura whined.

"I'm just trying to find out the truth."

Laura's entire body shook. "The truth is my boss just died and you're being mean to me."

Brianna pushed herself forward so her knees almost touched Laura's. "Isn't it true that Lorenzo Silva rejected you, and you retaliated by killing him?"

Laura's head snapped back as if she'd been slapped. "You're crazy. Why would I kill him?"

"The oldest reason on the planet. You loved him, but he didn't love you."

Laura shook her head violently. "No. That's not true. Lorenzo loved me."

"And when he rejected you yet again, you poisoned him. After all, if you couldn't have him, no one could."

"I would never hurt Lorenzo. I was going to marry him." Big tears slipped from Laura's eyes. "With Lorenzo's death, I feel like a widow. No one will ever know how much he loved me, how much he confided in me."

Brianna made a twirling motion with her hand and looked toward the control room. "Lorenzo, come out now. I can't take this farce anymore."

Marcio walked out of the control room. "Cut the crap, Laura. I never loved you."

Laura looked at him through her tears. "Marcio? I didn't know you were here."

He lifted an eyebrow. "You messed up, Laura. You killed the wrong brother."

Laura's tears dried as she studied him. "Lorenzo?"

He nodded. "I want you to hear me when I say this." He walked over to her chair, looking down at her as he towered over her. "I do not love you. I have never loved you. And I will never love you. Do you understand?"

She nodded like a child who'd just been scolded.

"I was going to fire you on Friday. I was tired of you stalking me, of your moodiness. But then you killed my brother." Marcio's jaw clenched so hard that a muscle twitched. "Now, not only am I going to fire you, but I am going to send you to jail."

"Lorenzo, I love you. How can you do this to me?" The tears started again.

"Why?" he asked. "Why did you kill my brother?"

"I didn't," she sobbed. "You have to believe me. I would never hurt you. Or him. I was angry, yes, but I always thought you would come to love me as I love you." Tears flowed down her face, streaking her mascara, as she stood up and threw her arms around him. "Lorenzo, I love you so much. Let me be the one who helps you through this."

Marcio pushed her away and jumped back. "By the way, you were right the first time. I am Marcio. But I know for sure that my brother never loved you. He used to laugh at you, at how pathetic you were."

Laura crumpled to the floor, her sobs breaking the quiet in the room.

Brianna stepped between Marcio and Laura, using her body as a barrier. "Marcio, stop. She's had enough."

He looked at Laura with disgust. "This girl did not kill my brother. She might be manipulative and delusional, but she is not strong enough to commit murder."

Chapter 19

Detective Bethancourt sat at his desk, reviewing the evidence photos. His phone rang, and he reached for it, distracted. "Bethancourt."

"John, it's Eric Pinto from BonitaMar. I have news, and it's not good."

"Talk to me."

"Pedro Gonzalez was on duty in the control room when the electricity went out the night of Lorenzo Silva's murder."

"I remember. I talked to him the next day." Detective Bethancourt shuffled through the evidence file until he found the page with the security guard's interview notes.

Pinto hesitated. "He hasn't shown up for work in two days, hasn't answered his phone. I sent someone over to his house this morning, and he's gone."

"What do you mean?"

"The house has been cleaned out. No clothes, no suitcases, no food in the fridge. He's gone, his wife is gone, his three kids are gone."

"Does he have family nearby?

"He has family in Arraijan. I sent my guy there too. No one's seen him. His mother's house is small. There would be no place for him to hide if he was there." Pinto paused. "I'm sorry about this, John. I didn't see it coming. I never thought he'd do something like this."

Detective Bethancourt scrubbed his hand through his hair, giving him middle-of-the-day bedhead.

"That's the problem when workers struggle to put food on the table. A crisp green Benjamin can get them to do just about anything." Detective Bethancourt rapped his knuckles on the desk. "Thanks for the call, Eric. Let me know if you hear anything else."

He put the phone down. He wasn't surprised, but he should have seen it coming. Someone had paid Pedro Gonzalez to turn off the security cameras the night of the murder. That same person was the one who had killed Lorenzo Silva. But with Gonzalez gone, one of the few witnesses was gone as well.

He picked up the phone again and dialed Moses. "Kid, stop what you're doing. I need you to check something for me in the customs database."

Moses clicked a few keys. "I'm ready."

"I need to find out when someone left the country." Detective Bethancourt looked at Pedro's interview notes. "A Panamanian named Pedro Juan Gonzalez Esteban."

"Checking now," Moses said, his fingers clicking the keyboard. "Found him. He left Panama yesterday, headed for Colombia, traveling with four family members."

"Damn."

"Isn't that the security guard from the BonitaMar?"

"Affirmative."

"He must have gotten scared when his little prank helped cover up a murder."

"That's the way I see it." Detective Bethancourt picked up a stack of notes. "Thanks, Moses. I'm on my way to BonitaMar, if you find anything else. I want to interview all the security guards again. Go at them harder until someone cracks."

Chapter 20

Marcio stormed out of the presidential suite.

Brianna followed him out but kept her distance as he waited for the elevator. "Are you okay?"

He met her gaze, his eyes burning with rage. "My brother has been murdered, and I do not have a clue who did it."

Brianna's face softened. "Where are you going?"

Marcio shrugged. "Nowhere. Anywhere." A muscle twitched in his jaw. "I need to go for a drive."

"Do you want company?"

"No. I will call you in a little while." He held up his phone as proof that he would keep his promise. The elevator door opened. "I just need to get away. I need to think."

"Okay," she said. "Be careful. It's never a good idea to drive when you're upset."

He nodded, watching her as the elevator doors closed.

When he reached the lobby, he pushed through the throng of vacationers, avoiding eye contact with everyone around him.

Marcio's hands shook as he slid behind the wheel of his Range Rover. He took a deep breath, flexing his fingers to get rid of the shakes for the second time that day. He had to hold himself together.

He started the SUV and turned out of the resort. The road toward the city passed through dense jungle on either side of him. His body relaxed as he focused on driving around the curves, keeping his speed under check as he drove past banana and papaya trees that grew within inches of the road.

As he rounded the last bend through the mountain area, a Mack truck was trying to pass another eighteen-wheeler on the short stretch of road that ran parallel to the ocean. Marcio realized the driver coming toward him in his lane couldn't go fast enough to finish passing without hitting him head on.

He slammed on the brakes. The Range Rover slowed but didn't stop. He stepped on the brakes harder until he was standing on the brake pedal.

"Not now, not now!" he screamed.

The driver of the Mack truck barreling toward him tried to stop, but it was going too fast. The tires spewed smoke, but the driver couldn't move over to his own lane yet. The eighteen-wheeler it was trying to pass had slowed as it started up a hill. The two big trucks were still next to each other.

Marcio wasn't going to stop in time.

He had to make a choice—hit the Mack truck head on or go into the ocean. The tide was on its way out, so the water wouldn't be deep. He pulled the emergency brake and turned his steering wheel hard to the right just a second before the Mack truck could hit him. The SUV flew over the embankment into the water.

Chapter 21

People tell lies every day. To understand someone, you must separate the important lies from the lies of convenience. — Brianna Morgan

Brianna studied her notes for the final interview. She read the same note card for the third time then gave up. She couldn't concentrate. She was worried about Marcio. He was putting on a strong front, but he'd just lost his twin. She shouldn't have let him go off alone.

She pulled out her phone and called him, but it went straight to voicemail.

That was odd. When he showed her his phone, it had been on. She dialed again. Voicemail again.

Perhaps he was on the phone. She went to the kitchen and made some tea. Five minutes later, she tried once more. Voicemail yet again.

She tapped her nails on the desk. Something was wrong.

"I need to go find Marcio," she announced to the room as she grabbed her purse. "If Ana Maria Lopes gets here before I get back, put her in makeup."

She dashed out of the hotel and went to the concierge desk at Casa Bonita. She should have thought to bring a translator.

"Marcio Silva?" she asked, an exaggerated question in her voice.

The concierge shook his head. "*Él no está aqui.*" He spoke in rapid-fire Spanish, using his arms to indicate that Marcio had left by car.

"Gracias." Brianna thought for a minute. She needed to go after him. "Taxi?"

The concierge nodded and picked up the phone, talking in short bursts to someone who was hopefully a taxi driver and not a mass murderer. "*Cinco minutos.*"

Brianna nodded and stood by the door, waiting for the taxi. She tried calling Marcio again. Voicemail.

When the yellow taxi pulled into the valet area, she jumped into the backseat. "Amador Marina, *muy rapido*" she said, hoping the driver understood her Spanglish.

The driver nodded and stepped on the gas. He had a friendly face, but she didn't have the mental energy to try to chitchat with him.

She clicked her seat belt into place as the force of the acceleration pulled her back into her seat. Thank God Panamanians like to drive fast, she thought.

The driver followed the mountain road. On the way, people kept flashing their headlights. Either the police had a roadblock up ahead or there had been an accident. Brianna's pulse quickened. Please God, not an accident.

Traffic slowed then stopped. The drivers ahead of them had turned off their engines, and many were standing on the road, chatting in small groups. No cars passed from the other direction.

Brianna wrapped her Prada bag around her torso messenger-style and burst out of the taxi. "What happened?" she asked the group of men closest to her. They just looked at her, and Brianna realized none of them spoke English.

She ran to the next group. "*Habla ingles?*"

"I speak English," one of the younger men said.

"What happened?"

"A bad accident. Two trucks collided. The road is closed."

"Trucks? Like SUVs?"

"Not SUVs," he said. "*Camiones*. Mack trucks."

Brianna sighed. "Thank you. Thank you so much."

At least Marcio was safe.

She turned and headed back to the taxi. A motorcyclist pulled up and spoke animatedly to the group of bystanders Brianna had just left. She looked over her shoulder and saw the motorcyclist make a flying motion with his hand. She didn't understand much, but she heard him say, "Range Rover." Her heart flipped. She ran back to the man who spoke English.

"What did he say?"

"He said a blue Range Rover went off the road into the ocean. The police are trying to rescue the driver now, but they can't get him out of the SUV."

119

Brianna didn't bother to say thank you. She took off, running as fast as her stilettos would let her. After a few strides, she gave up and pulled one heel off, and then the other, and continued running barefoot down the deserted side of the road, carrying one shoe in each hand.

Her taxi driver yelled at her, but she ignored him and kept running. She transferred her shoes to one hand and pulled her cell out of the side pocket of her bag. She punched Marcio's number on her phone as she sprinted down the road. Voicemail again. Damn! She ran faster.

Brianna was an athlete and ran several 5K races each year, but she had never run barefoot before. The road wasn't hot, but small pebbles covered the mountain road. It would have slowed her down too much to try to avoid them, so she ignored the pain and focused on speed. By the time she got to the spot where the accident had happened—which was at least a mile away—her feet were bruised.

A crowd had formed around the perimeter. Everyone was looking over the embankment toward the ocean. Brianna slipped her shoes back on and pushed her way to the front of the crowd.

Marcio's Range Rover was upside down in about eighteen inches of water. Thank goodness the tide had been going out, or his car could have been swept out to the ocean. As she watched, the rescue workers pried the door open. Brianna gasped as two of them pulled Marcio's limp body out of the SUV. They put him on a surfboard and pushed him through the shallow water toward shore.

Trying not to cry, Brianna covered her mouth with one hand.

"Miss Morgan, I'm not surprised to see you here," Detective Bethancourt said, coming up behind her. "Every time something happens to a Silva brother, you're in the middle of it."

Brianna ignored the accusation. "What happened?"

"You don't know?"

"No. I was in a taxi trying to find Marcio. When I heard an accident had happened here, I left the taxi and came to find out if it was him."

"Marcio Silva took a dive over the cliff to avoid an accident." Detective Bethancourt stared at Brianna. "Witnesses say he never slowed down."

Brianna snapped her head to look at him. "You think someone did this on purpose?"

Detective Bethancourt shrugged. "You would know better than me."

Brianna's eyes widened at the accusation. "You think I tampered with Marcio's brakes? Why in the world would I do that?"

Detective Bethancourt took a step toward her until she felt his hot breath on her face. "I don't know yet, but I promise you I'm going to find out."

Brianna broke off the staring contest to watch Marcio being carried up the embankment toward a waiting ambulance. "I'm going with him. If you need to accuse me some more, I'll be at the hospital with Marcio."

Detective Bethancourt called after her, "You can't go with him in the ambulance."

Brianna whipped her head around. "Just try and stop me."

Chapter 22

Detective Bethancourt watched Brianna elbow her way through the crowd. She made big gestures with her hands as she spoke to the paramedics. After a short one-sided conversation, one of the paramedics shrugged, and she climbed into the back of the ambulance.

He didn't understand what was going on. One brother was dead; the other brother was injured; and the common link was Brianna Morgan.

Normally he wouldn't have shown up at a traffic accident, but he was on his way to the BonitaMar Hotel when the accident happened. He'd used his flashers to get to the site, then took charge of the scene until Officer Raul Hernandez arrived.

He walked over to Hernandez. "I want that Range Rover out before the tide comes in."

Hernandez scratched his head. "We don't have the equipment to do that."

"Find it. Borrow it. Steal it. I don't care if you use a boat, a truck, or your bare hands. That Range Rover is part of a murder investigation, and I want it out today."

"Yes, sir," Hernandez said.

Detective Bethancourt stared at the Range Rover. The water had dropped to just a few inches. He wasn't an oceanographer but living in Panama with a twenty-foot tide made him aware of the impact of the tide differential on daily life here. At low tide, the area below him looked like a barren desert, with miles of mud-like sand stretching in both directions as the ocean floor became exposed. At high tide, the same spot would be covered in twenty feet of water. He looked at his watch: 3:15 p.m. They had two hours to get the Range Rover out before the tide started coming back in. In six hours, the vehicle would be completely underwater.

Detective Bethancourt was a realist. They would never get the Range Rover out in time. What he really wanted—and needed—was to have an expert inspect the brake lines while the tide was still out.

He pulled out his cell and called his mechanic. It would take him an hour to get here.

When he hung up, he called his Moses. "Hey, kid. I need information, and I need it by the end of today. I want you to find any connection you can between Brianna Morgan and the Silva brothers. I don't care how tenuous it is, I just need something, anything."

"I'm on it," Moses said, typing even before the call ended.

Detective Bethancourt closed his phone. There was nothing to do now but inspect the car and get photos. The tide was almost out, so he went to his car and swapped out his leather lace-ups for an old pair of tennis shoes. He couldn't wait for his mechanic. Time to go walking in the mud.

Chapter 23

Moses Souza was a geek, and he relished his geekiness. After all, the biggest geek in the world was also one of the richest men in the world. While other boys his age had chosen role models like Arnold Schwarzenegger or fútbol player Lionel Messi, from a young age Moses had considered himself a billionaire-in-training. He wanted to emulate Bill Gates in every way.

He entered every variation of Brianna's name with Lorenzo Silva and Marcio Silva into his proprietary search engine. He'd nicknamed his search engine "Miracle" because when he wanted something, his search engine always did the impossible—it sifted through tens of thousands of various inputs and spat out the exact thing he was looking for. He didn't need to turn water into wine or turn straw into gold—his Miracle was putting bad guys away. And soon it would be his ticket to endless wealth.

When he hit a wall with his search terms, he pulled up Brianna's passport information and checked entry and exit stamps. Then he did the same with the Silva brothers.

Moses couldn't find any overlap with their passport stamps. They'd never been in the same country at the same time, except when they were in college. Brianna had been a freshman at UCLA when the Silva brothers were seniors at UNC. They had been educated on opposite sides of the US, three thousand miles apart, but at least they were in the same country. Since that was the only thread he had, he picked at it.

He bypassed firewalls and accessed secure school records, starting with the University of North Carolina. The only thing interesting he found is that both brothers graduated cum laude. *Since when did jocks graduate with honors?* he wondered.

Abandoning their academic records, Moses focused on their extracurricular activities. In 2001, when the twins were seniors, UNC won the NCAA championship against the Indiana Hoosiers. Brianna would have been a college freshman that year.

Turning to a different computer screen, he searched Brianna's academic file at UCLA. She had majored in journalism and spent her extracurricular hours at the school paper and on the debate team. She wasn't involved in athletics.

He poked around the online yearbook until he found a photo of Brianna with her roommate and gal pal, Chrissy Kratz, a statuesque blonde with the longest legs he'd ever seen.

Moses scratched the peach fuzz on his post-pubescent face. He would like to get to know Chrissy. He did a search to find out where she was now.

"Yes!" he screamed, jumping out of his chair and pumping his arm in the air in jubilation. "I found the link!" He turned to the framed photo of Bill Gates that he kept on his desk and saluted him. "Bill, my friend, you might have put a computer in every house in America, but Moses parted the Red Sea."

Chapter 24

If you were desperate, what would you be willing to do to survive? I realized I would say anything, even if it were a lie. I would do anything, even if it were immoral. I would use anyone, even if I hurt their feelings. If you think you wouldn't do the same, then you've never been pushed to your limit. — Brianna Morgan

Brianna sat in the waiting room at Pacifica Salud Hospital—a Johns Hopkins–affiliated medical center in the wealthy area of Panama City—frantic for a man she barely knew.

Marcio hadn't gained consciousness in the ambulance, and she couldn't understand what the paramedics were saying about his injuries. When they'd arrived at the hospital, the nurse had brushed her aside when she realized Brianna wasn't a relative. Brianna knew nothing about Marcio and couldn't help with his medical history. His brother was dead, and his mother was on a plane.

She hoped the doctors knew what they were doing.

She dragged her fingers through her hair. Marcio's accident couldn't be a coincidence.

Someone wanted Marcio and Lorenzo dead…and wanted her to be the scapegoat.

She got up and paced. She was missing something.

She needed a friend, someone analytical who could look at the situation objectively. The problem was, Brianna had trust issues. Ever since her brother's death, she had kept people at a distance. There were only a few people she allowed inside her glass walls—her father, her brother, and her best friend.

Her ex-military dad would know what to do, but her parents had just left on a three-month cruise around the world. Hoping for a miracle, Brianna walked to an empty corner of the waiting room and tried his phone. It went straight to voicemail.

She choked back a sob. She had to keep it together.

Her only living brother, Jack, had followed in their dad's footsteps by joining the Navy after graduating from West Point. But unlike their father, he'd become disillusioned with the military when he lost half his SEAL team due to bad intel. When his term was up, he left the Navy and went to work for a defense contractor. She felt safe when he was around, but getting in touch with him when he was on assignment was complicated. Although he earned a big paycheck, he worked in countries that didn't have running water. They often went months between phone calls.

She tried his number. It went straight to voicemail. No surprise.

That left Katherine Kelly, her socialite best friend. Keeping track of Katherine's whereabouts was almost as difficult as catching fireflies. Katherine flitted from country to country, socializing with rich friends and attending exclusive events. She could be visiting an orphanage in Kenya in the morning, wearing khakis and a T-shirt, and playing craps in Monaco by nightfall, decked out in a designer gown and dripping with jewels. Right now she could be on a yacht in the middle of the ocean or eight miles high in a private jet. The only person who could keep up with her schedule was her social secretary, Georgina Smythe, a matronly Brit whose efficiency rivaled that of Brianna's father.

Even though Katherine was a wild card, she was the only one left. Brianna found Katherine's number in her contacts, pressed the "call" button, and held her breath.

Katherine answered on the third ring.

"Where are you?" Brianna asked after exchanging hellos.

"Dubai. Do you remember Sheikh Mohammed al Abbar?"

"I know who he is."

"Of course, you do, darling. His birthday is in two days, and he's throwing himself the most lavish birthday party ever. Every guest has been given a Rolls-Royce and a driver to use while in Dubai. Tomorrow we're leaving on a week-long cruise on his two-hundred-foot yacht."

They had been friends since their freshman year at UCLA, so Katherine's A-list friends no longer made Brianna's jaw drop.

"Sorry to interrupt, KK, but I need your help."

"Of course. What is it?"

A glass tinkled in the background, and Brianna heard muffled conversation. It sounded like a cocktail party.

"What time is it there?" Brianna asked, looking at her watch.

"Almost midnight. The party is just getting started. Let me move to a quieter location."

Brianna heard high heels clicking on a stone floor.

"Okay, it's quiet here." Katherine's perfect diction was relaxed, but her words weren't slurred. Socialites knew their limits—well, at least Katherine did. "Tell me what's going on."

Brianna gave her the bullet-point version of the past three days.

Katherine sighed. "And I thought my life was exciting. What are you going to do?"

"I don't know. I was calling to see if you had any ideas."

"Do you want me to fly there? If so, just say the word."

Brianna wanted to say yes, but Katherine seemed so excited about the sheikh's birthday party. It would be like someone trying to pull her away from a natural disaster when she was the only journalist covering it.

"No, I can handle it. I just wanted to pick that great brain of yours."

Katherine laughed. "I've been drinking, so my espionage skills aren't at their sharpest. Why don't I send a plane for you?"

"And take me where?"

"Anywhere you want to go. You could join us on the yacht for a week. Drown your sorrows in sunshine and champagne."

"Out of the frying pan and into the viper's nest of socialites and backstabbers. Katherine, I couldn't survive in your world. No, thanks. I'll take my chances here."

"Do you need cash?"

"No, I'm okay."

"I don't mean vacation money, darling. I mean money to disappear."

Brianna sighed. "I hope it won't come to that, but thanks for the offer."

Katherine hummed under her breath, an endearing tic that happened when she thought. Brianna squeezed her eyes shut to keep from crying. What she wouldn't give to be back in college, living a simple life of classes and exams, listening to Katherine hum as they studied for finals.

As Brianna thought about the past, her dam broke. She turned toward the wall and let the emotion come. Tears rolled down her face as she sobbed into the phone.

"Hush, darling. Everything will be okay."

"KK, I finally met a man who could have been it. You know, the one. And after one date, he gets murdered. What's wrong with me? Why can't I meet a normal guy and have a normal life?"

"You think 'normal' would make you happy? It won't. You're extraordinary, and you need a man who shines as brightly as you do. Don't worry, this will pass, and you'll find your other half. Until then, you'll have to settle for me."

"If only you were a man." Brianna made a choking sound as she laughed and stifled a sob at the same time. "Want to know something crazy? I think I met Lorenzo our freshman year in college."

"What do you mean?"

"Remember when Chrissy Kratz and I flew to Indiana to go to the playoff soccer game?"

"Yes, I remember," Katherine said. "Chrissy was dating the captain of the soccer team for Indiana. She wanted me to go too, but Mommy Dearest was coming into town, so I couldn't."

"Yes, that was the weekend. I met some UNC soccer players at a party, and it turns out Lorenzo was one of those guys. I think he put his arm around me for a photo."

"That's right. You had a crush on him for a year, but he never called you."

"He didn't even ask for my number. Remember how I moaned about it for months, thinking I should have given him my number?"

"Oh, yes, I remember," Katherine said with a chuckle.

Brianna sighed. "I always wondered what happened to him. He had such kind eyes."

"And quite the sexy body, if I remember correctly."

"Fate is playing with me. I finally find this guy I've been dreaming about for fifteen years, and then he's murdered." Brianna brushed the tears away just as new ones formed. "And then there's the bottle of Disaronno. Could someone be trying to frame me? I feel so out of my depths here.

It's like picking up a novel at the end and trying to figure out what's going on."

"Brianna, darling, breathe. Remember when you took that military science course at UCLA?"

"Yes, we had to compete with the other students in a war game."

"You thought of every single possible outcome and beat everyone in the class. The professor said he'd never seen anyone with your analytical ability—the ability to think twelve steps ahead."

Brianna sniffled. "That was Daddy's doing. Chess was never a game for him. It was always a lesson in strategy."

"Brianna, you're the smartest woman I know. Stop feeling sorry for yourself and outthink your enemy."

Brianna took a deep breath. Katherine was right. This was war. She had to think like a general, not like a private.

"What's the worst that could happen?"

Brianna snorted. "I could go to jail."

"Then I'll come break you out."

Brianna laughed, wiping her eyes with the back of her hand. "Why do I think you're only half kidding?"

"Brianna, I'm not kidding at all. If the worst happens, I'll hire an army of mercenaries to break you out of jail. Of course, we'd have to live in a country without an extradition treaty for the rest of our lives, but I hear Venezuela is beautiful if you stay on the dictator's good side."

Brianna giggled. "Thanks, KK. You've helped more than you know."

Katherine paused. "I won't have cell coverage for a week. The sheikh confiscates our cell phones before he lets us on the yacht. He's a bit paranoid. If you need anything, you'll have to contact me before seven tomorrow morning Dubai time."

"I'll be okay. I'll put my thinking cap on. By the time you're back on terra firma, I'll have caught the killer and trussed her up like a stag after the hunt."

Katherine's laughter echoed through the stone halls. "That's my girl. And after you sell your memoir, you'll have rich men from around the world vying to breathe your rarified air."

They exchanged air kisses and hung up.

Brianna called her producer, Babs Whitaker, in Dallas and updated her on Marcio's accident.

"Brianna don't worry," Babs said. "I spoke to Legal. If you get popped for this, ADN has an attorney on standby in Panama."

"An attorney? That's your plan?" Brianna couldn't keep the annoyance out of her voice. "I might rot in a third world jail while your attorney files motions?"

Babs paused. "I thought you'd be pleased."

"Babs, I work for one of the most powerful TV networks on the planet. You should have an army of people down here helping me."

"Brianna, if it were up to me I would." Her voice softened. "All I hear about are cutbacks. I went to Scott Baker directly, but he won't authorize anything more than a local attorney."

"Scott's the GM of a major market. Why can't he authorize it?"

"He's under pressure from corporate. We need to have a strong first quarter to keep the stock price up." Babs sighed. "Just keep doing what you do. If you end up in jail, I'll turn up the heat. I promise."

Brianna disconnected the call and looked at her watch. Four-fifteen. How long until she heard something about Marcio?

Just then, a lanky dark-skinned doctor came out in scrubs, his face mask pulled down around his neck. Since she was the only one in the waiting area, he walked up to her. "Are you waiting on information about Marcio Silva?" He had a soft voice and kind eyes. She trusted him immediately.

She nodded. "I'm Brianna Morgan. A friend."

"I'm Dr. Eduardo Hidalgo. Your friend has come through surgery like a champion. He has a fractured clavicle, a broken rib, and a damaged spleen. We hope he won't need a blood transfusion for the spleen injury, but it's too early to tell."

"When will he wake up?"

"We don't know yet," the doctor replied. "He will be in surgery for a few hours. I will come out again when we're finished."

Chapter 25

Detective Bethancourt pulled into the police station. During the drive there, Moses had been texting him nonstop with cryptic messages, but the kid refused to divulge his secret over the phone.

Detective Bethancourt didn't stop at his desk. He went straight to the IT department and found Moses. "What did you find?"

Moses grinned, his lopsided smile adding to his geeky charm. "Before Brianna Morgan arrived in Panama, she and the Silva brothers were in the same country at the same time only once. That was the four years Lorenzo and Marcio spent at the University of North Carolina. Brianna went to UCLA, which is three thousand miles away, so that had me stumped. Social media hadn't been invented yet back then. If it had, I would have found this information sooner."

Detective Bethancourt rolled his eyes at the reference to 2001 being in the technological stone ages. He would strangle the wunderkind later. "And? What did you find?"

Moses pointed at his third monitor, where a photo of a beautiful blond woman's face stared back at them. "This is Chrissy Kratz, Brianna's roommate her freshman year in college. She looks like a typical southern California girl, but guess where she's from?"

"I haven't a clue."

"Indiana." Moses's voice buzzed with excitement.

"So?" Detective Bethancourt moved his hand in a circular motion, trying to get the kid to hurry along. He wanted the punch line.

"In 2005, UNC beat the Indiana Hoosiers at a playoff game in Indiana. Our two young coeds from UCLA attended the game."

"How do you know?"

"I found a picture online." Moses clicked a few keys, and a picture of Chrissy Kratz and Brianna appeared on one of his screens, with the soccer game in the background. The girls glowed with youthful vitality.

Moses pointed at the picture. "Take it from me. They're not just pretty. They're hot."

Detective Bethancourt picked up a stress ball from Moses's desk and squeezed it rhythmically. "Okay, they went to the same game. So what?"

"Apparently our little hotties got invited to an after party with the players." On his big screen, Moses pulled up a grainy photo that showed five people at a party. "That's one of the Silva brothers." He pointed to a handsome young man who could only be one of the twins. "And the woman he has his arm draped around is none other than Brianna Morgan."

Detective Bethancourt stopped squeezing the ball. "Well, I'll be damned. They knew each other." He slapped Moses on the back. "Kid, I owe you dinner."

Chapter 26

A life-and-death situation tests what you're made of. It can spur an average Joe to risk his life to help a stranger, or it can make a mother abandon her child so she can save herself. — Brianna Morgan

At Tocumen International Airport, Brianna held a sign that read, *Isabella Silva*. She hoped Marcio's mother would be rational, but one son had been murdered and the other was in the hospital in critical condition. Brianna would have avoided her altogether, except she was desperate. She needed an ally, and Marcio's mother needed a ride. Marcio had mentioned the time her flight was arriving, so Brianna was taking a chance that nothing had changed. Hopefully they could start there and find common ground.

Her stomach gurgled. She hadn't been this nervous since she'd interviewed for her job at All Day News in Dallas. She took a sip of bottled water and ignored the nausea.

Brianna knew Marcio's mother as soon as she saw her. In a sea of bedraggled travelers, Isabella Silva stood out like a blood-red rose in a pile of gray ashes. She looked like Sophia Lauren, with the same high cheekbones and generous lips her sons possessed. Brianna guessed her age to be late fifties based on what Lorenzo had told her, but Isabella looked a decade younger. She wore a tailored black suit that showed off her hourglass figure, and a low-cut white blouse that emphasized her cleavage. A white silk scarf encircled her neck and floated after her as she sashayed out of customs, looking like a well-preserved movie star. Two porters trailed after her, carts piled high with matching Louis Vuitton luggage.

She might have been poor at one time, but wealth fit her like a custom glass slipper. Rather than marrying her prince, though, she had given birth to her two princes.

Brianna waved her sign, trying to get Isabella's attention, but the woman didn't glance her way. She was looking for Marcio.

Brianna ducked under a rope and intercepted her.

"Hello, Mrs. Silva. My name is Brianna Morgan. I'm here to pick you up."

Isabella managed to look down her nose at Brianna, even though she was two inches shorter. "Thank you, but I am waiting for my son."

"Marcio sent me. I will take you to him."

Isabella looked at her sharply. "Who are you?"

Brianna forced a smile. "My name is Brianna Morgan. I'm a journalist from the United States. I'm helping Marcio through this difficult time. He asked me to pick you up."

Isabella studied Brianna as if she were a science specimen. "My son never would send someone else to pick me up."

Brianna opened her mouth to speak, but no words came out. So she shut it, feeling like a mute guppy.

"Speak up, young woman. Just say what you have to say."

Brianna sighed. She had wanted to wait until they had some privacy, but she had no choice. "Marcio wanted to pick you up himself, but he was in a car accident. He's in the hospital."

Brianna saw the steel settling over Isabella's features. She was a single mother who'd had to be strong her whole life; she would handle the crisis in front of her now and grieve later.

"Let us go then," she said matter-of-factly. "Bring the car to the front. I will wait for you."

"The car's already here." Brianna indicated a black Lincoln Navigator idling directly outside the glass doors.

Isabella nodded. "I will oversee my luggage." She spoke to the porters then watched with hawk eyes as they loaded her luggage into the back of the Navigator.

When the rear hatch closed, Isabella stepped up into the backseat. Brianna sat next to her. As soon as the door shut, the Navigator pulled away from the curb and merged into the busy airport traffic.

Isabella turned to Brianna, looking her up and down. "Tell me what happened. Do not leave anything out."

She sounds just like Marcio, Brianna thought.

Brianna explained how the accident had happened and said Marcio had just gotten out of surgery when she'd left the hospital to go to the airport.

"My son is not awake yet?"

"No. I asked the hospital to contact me the moment he woke up." Brianna lifted her cell phone. "They haven't called yet."

Isabella sat still for a moment. Then she folded her hands in her lap before returning her gaze to Brianna. "Tell me about my other son."

Brianna already had decided to be honest. If she wanted Isabella on her side, she had to tell her everything, from the kiss in the sand with Lorenzo to the taped interviews with Marcio.

When she finished, Isabella grasped her hand, the first glimpse of grief on her face. "Thank you for being blunt with me. You could have left out the embarrassing details, but you did not. I appreciate that."

"Mrs. Silva, I believe someone murdered Lorenzo, and that same person tried to kill Marcio. I think you should hire security for the hospital. I'd hate for something to happen to him while he's incapacitated."

Isabella nodded, eyeing Brianna out of the corner of her eyes. "That is very shrewd of you."

Brianna shifted positions in her seat, tucking the chest portion of the seat belt under her arm so she could turn and look directly at Isabella. "My father and brother are both ex-military. I grew up being a little paranoid."

"Do you have anyone to recommend?"

Brianna barked a harsh laugh. "I wish I could, but my Spanish is nonexistent. My brother works for an international security firm, but I can't reach him. I'm sure he's in some fourth-world country and might not emerge for months. We need help now."

Isabella patted her hand. "Do not worry. I will handle it." She opened her phone and punched a contact number.

Brianna watched as Marcio's mother spoke in Spanish, first to one person and then to another. She might be brokenhearted, but she was tough as rebar when conducting business. Brianna already liked her.

"I have hired a security firm. They will have three men here within the hour. My son will be watched around the clock until he is well."

"Mrs. Silva," Brianna began, "I'm so sorry for your loss. I know my words aren't sufficient, but I'll do everything I can to help."

Isabella studied her for a long moment. "Thank you. And please do not call me Mrs. Silva again. It makes me feel like my mother. Call me Isabella."

Brianna smiled. "Okay, Isabella. I appreciate that."

Isabella picked up Brianna's right hand and studied the peachy-pink gemstone in her ring. "That is a beautiful stone. What is it?"

"It's a Morganite, named after J.P. Morgan, who financed its discovery in the early twentieth century in Madagascar. My last name is Morgan, so it's become my signature stone."

"Is it a diamond?"

"No, it's a beryl, a cousin to an emerald. It gets its color from manganese."

"It is as lovely as it is unique." Isabella squeezed Brianna's hand. "I want to be clear about one thing. I will trust you and work with you, but if I find out that you have lied to me about anything, I promise you will be sorry."

Brianna nodded and gently pulled her hand away. "Fair enough."

"I'm not finished." Isabella grabbed Brianna's face under the chin, forcing her thumb and middle finger above Brianna's jawbone to keep her face immobile. Brianna saw a ruthlessness in Isabella's oval eyes that she hadn't seen earlier. "If I find out you have hurt either of my sons, the wrath of the Old Testament God will rain down on you—an eye for an eye, a life for a life. Do I make myself clear?"

"Crystal," Brianna mumbled, barely able to speak.

Isabella let go and turned to face the front. "Okay. Let's find out who is doing this."

Chapter 27

Detective Bethancourt parked his car at Pacifica Salud Hospital, where Marcio had just come out of surgery. He was betting Brianna Morgan would be there.

He flashed his badge at the emergency room nurse. "I'm looking for Marcio Silva. He was brought in a few hours ago, a victim of a car accident."

The nurse tapped a few keys on her computer. "He just got out of surgery and isn't awake yet." She pointed to the far side of the waiting room. "The doctor is updating the family, if you would like to talk to him."

Detective Bethancourt saw Brianna Morgan—no surprise there—holding the hand of a chic older woman while listening to a tall doctor speak. A burly man stood a step behind the ladies, glaring at the detective with a look that telegraphed private security. He'd bet his pension this bear of a man had been special forces in some army or another.

Detective Bethancourt strode over to the group, returning the bodyguard's glare as he approached. Rather than wait for a break in the conversation, he took immediate control and flashed his badge at the doctor. "I'm Detective John Bethancourt. Are you the doctor treating Marcio Silva?"

"I am," Dr. Hidalgo said. "I was just updating his family."

Detective Bethancourt flicked his gaze to the woman with Brianna. She looked like an older, feminine version of the Silva brothers. She had to be their mother.

The doctor continued. "Marcio pulled through the surgery like a champ. We were worried about the injury to his spleen, but I repaired the damage without a blood transfusion. He has a contusion from the crash, and he hasn't woken up yet. We have the best neurosurgeon in Panama with him right now. At this point, we need to wait for the swelling in his brain to go down before we can give a prognosis."

"When can we see him?" the older woman asked.

"The best thing for all of you to do is go home, get some sleep, and check back with us in the morning." The doctor looked around the group.

"If you don't have any more questions, I will leave you for now. I will talk to you again tomorrow."

As soon as the doctor walked away, Detective Bethancourt turned toward the older woman. "I'm Detective John Bethancourt. Are you related to Marcio and Lorenzo Silva?"

She looked him up and down, appraising him. "I am their mother, Isabella Silva." She didn't offer her hand.

"I'm sorry for your loss. I'm investigating Lorenzo's death. I only met him a few times, but he made a big impression on me."

Her face softened. "Thank you, Detective."

Detective Bethancourt flicked his eyes toward the burly man, who hadn't stopped glaring at him. "Is he with you?"

"Yes, Detective. One of my sons has been murdered, and the other has had a brush with death. My son will have round-the-clock protection until you catch the person trying to destroy my family."

"Smart move." He gestured with his chin toward Brianna. "I see you've met Miss Morgan."

Isabella nodded.

"I can't prove it yet, but I think she's behind all your troubles." He looked at Brianna, giving her his stern-cop look. "If I were you Mrs. Silva, I wouldn't let this woman near Marcio."

"How dare you." Brianna took a step toward Detective Bethancourt, invading his personal space. "From the moment I discovered Lorenzo's body, I've done nothing but try to solve this case for you. And now, because you're too lazy to find the killer, you're using me as a scapegoat."

Detective Bethancourt kept his face blank at her outburst. "I know about your freshman year at college, about the trip to Indiana to watch the playoff game with UNC. You knew Lorenzo before you arrived in Panama. It won't take me long to figure out a motive."

Brianna blinked.

"I have no doubt the lab will come back with positive proof that you were at the crime scenes for both brothers," he continued. "Once that happens, I'll have you for murder and attempted murder."

Brianna pulled out her phone and pressed a button. "I'm calling the American embassy. These accusations are outrageous."

Detective Bethancourt looked unfazed. "I'm not arresting you. Yet. But I am going to confiscate your passport." He held out his hand.

Brianna hesitated a beat then reached into her bag for her passport. She turned to Isabella and the bodyguard. "I have two witnesses to the fact that I'm willingly surrendering my passport. If you lose it, or say you never received it, there will be hell to pay." She released the passport into Detective Bethancourt's palm.

"Make your call," he said. "And while you're at it, hire an attorney."

Chapter 28

The problem with telling lies is they catch up to you. — Brianna Morgan

Brianna watched Detective Bethancourt disappear into the elevator. She turned to Marcio's mother. "I didn't do this, Isabella. Someone's trying to frame me. I don't know who yet, but I'm going to find out."

Isabella looked at Brianna for a long moment, as if making an internal decision. Then she nodded once. "I believe you. For now. I have already told you what I will do if you are lying. But at this moment, I will allow you to go." She grabbed hold of Brianna's hand with a grip that belied her age. "Just remember, if you are guilty, there is no place on earth where I cannot find you."

"I understand." Brianna craned her neck in each direction, looking with wild eyes to see if anyone was following her. "I have to go, Isabella. I can't solve this case if I'm locked up." She focused her gaze on the older woman. "Take care of Marcio. I'll call you if I learn anything."

They exchanged phone numbers and said goodbye.

Rather than take the elevator, Brianna followed the signs to the stairs. She felt like a caged animal and didn't want to get caught alone in an enclosed box with nowhere to run.

She needed cash. She looked around the hospital lobby for an ATM and was surprised to find a row of them from different banks. Thank God Panama is a banking haven, she thought.

She pulled out one of her debit cards and withdrew five hundred dollars, the card's daily limit. She then used two other cards at different machines to withdraw the max amount of money for each credit card. Fifteen hundred bucks wasn't enough to run, but she hoped it would be enough to hide for a while. If she used her credit cards after this, the police could track her. She'd have to make the money last.

As she walked through the automatic doors, she saw Detective Bethancourt, leaning against a four-door sedan in a no-parking zone, arms crossed. Waiting for her.

He made eye contact. "I just got a call from my office. Guess whose fingerprints the lab found on the bottle of Disaronno?"

Brianna's breath quickened. She'd been fingerprinted when she entered the country. She didn't have to guess.

"Yours." He sucked his front teeth. "That makes you my prime suspect."

"There are many reasons why my fingerprints would be on that bottle. That doesn't mean I killed Lorenzo."

He pushed himself off the car. "That's why I'm taking you to the police station for a formal interview." He removed a pair of handcuffs from his belt. "You can come willingly, or I can throw you to the ground first. One way or another, you're coming with me."

Brianna held up her hands, palms toward him. "There's no need to get hostile. I'll go with you."

"Get in," he said, opening the back door and tucking the cuffs on his belt. "The back doors can't be opened from the inside, just in case you were wondering."

As they drove, she paid attention to the route, her inner navigator making a map of the area. Once they arrived at the headquarters of the Policia Nacional, Detective Bethancourt used a security card to get in the back entrance. This must be the way cops brought in the bad guys, Brianna thought, horrified to be lumped in with thieves, rapists and murderers.

The detective parked in a reserved spot and held her elbow as he walked Brianna into the building. Unlike police departments she'd been in before, this one seemed more like a rickety old house than a public building. The dark hallways had one single light bulb along each corridor, making the narrow hallways seem even narrower. Rather than institutional green, like US facilities usually used, this place was dingy and gray with pitted concrete floors.

Detective Bethancourt deposited Brianna into an interrogation room that stunk of fear, sweat and piss. He hadn't signed her in, hadn't taken her handbag. He shut the door.

She choked on the smell, trying to breathe through her mouth, but that was worse.

She looked around. One rectangular metal table, bolted to the floor. Two hard plastic chairs, one on each side of the table. Four walls, one with a mirror so the cops could watch her.

Brianna willed herself not to gag, not to sweat. She would not show fear.

Rummaging in her bag, she found a small bottle of hand sanitizer and a packet of tissues. She squirted gel on a tissue and wiped one of the chairs and then the top of the metal table.

She perched on the front of the barely clean chair.

She pulled out her phone. She knew the police were watching her, wanting to see how she'd act, whom she'd call, what she'd say.

She dialed her father's phone number. "Daddy, please answer," she whispered. It went to voicemail. She blinked rapidly. Soldiers don't cry, she told herself.

She called Katherine. Voicemail.

Next, she tried Babs Whitaker. Voicemail once again. Doesn't anyone answer their phone anymore? she wondered.

She left her producer a message. "Babs, I'm being questioned by the police. I don't know when I'll be able to call you again. Get your lawyer down to police headquarters." She paused. "And if you have a plan B, now is the time to use it."

Brianna hung up and tapped her phone on the table. She wasn't ready to call Scott Baker, the network GM yet. She didn't want to push him into a corner and risk her career if she didn't have to. She put her phone back in her bag and sat with it on her lap, her hands folded on top. She used every interview trick she knew to keep her body still. She wouldn't give the police the satisfaction of seeing her squirm.

Minutes ticked by. She heard pieces of conversations through the thin walls. Then she heard a conversation in stereo. They must be in the next room, she thought.

"Hi. We're here to get fingerprinted for our residency application," a woman said. "They said you could help." She sounded Canadian, probably from the Toronto area.

"Yes, ladies, I can assist you. Let me get the fingerprint cards." The helpful-sounding male cop was Panamanian, but his English was good.

"We live down in the Coronado area," a second woman said. She had a strong Southern US accent but not a Texas accent. Maybe Tennessee. "Bless her heart, my friend Janie drove us here today. We're not used to all this traffic. She's waiting for us in the car out front. Will she be okay out there?"

"She is very safe. She's surrounded by cops."

"Some of the people we saw on the way in here looked a bit sketchy." It was the Canadian woman again.

"This is a police station," the officer said. "We bring the bad guys here, and their friends want to come visit. You ladies will be fine, though. I guarantee you will be safe." Brianna heard a smile in his voice. They must be attractive.

"Thank you, Officer. We appreciate finding someone as helpful as you." The Canadian woman was flirting back.

Without warning, the lights went off. Brianna looked around but saw nothing in the inky blackness.

"Oh, my word, what happened?" the Southern woman asked.

"The power went out, ma'am. It happens sometimes. Don't be afraid."

A man in some other part of the police station yelled in Spanish. Others soon joined him. Then came the sound of men singing. Apparently, the darkness brought out the crazies.

"I think we should go," the Southern woman said. "We can come back another day."

"Maybe the lights will come right back on," her friend offered.

"There must be a problem with the generator. Usually when the lights go off, the generator comes on. I hate to admit it, but the power could be off for quite a while. Perhaps you should come back another time."

"How do we find our way out of here?" It was the Southern woman again, fear in her voice.

"Just follow the hallway. When it ends, turn left. It will take you back to the entrance. The hall will be dark, but just use your hands along the wall to guide you, and you'll be fine."

Without thinking of the consequences, Brianna got up and went to the door. She had expected it to be locked, but to her surprise, the handle turned. She went into the hallway and waited. Two seconds later, a female hand knocked against her shoulder.

"I'm sorry," Toronto said. "I didn't see you." She laughed—a nervous laugh—trying to make small talk with a stranger in total darkness.

"That's okay," Brianna said. "I was coming to get fingerprinted for immigration but changed my mind when the power went out. I think the exit is this way. Here, take my hand."

"You're American?" Toronto asked, making small talk as they linked their hands and felt their way down the hall.

"Yes. I'm from Dallas. And you?"

"Toronto. My friend is from Nashville."

"Nashville, we're practically related," Brianna said. "We Southern gals have to stick together."

When the first corridor ended, Brianna turned left and kept going. A sliver of light appeared as they got closer to the front door. They held hands until they reached it, and then all three giggled with pent-up emotion as they burst out into the warm night air.

"This is going in my blog," the Canadian woman said, a six-foot tall woman with dark hair and tanned skin. "I'm Denise."

"Hi, Denise. I'm Jennifer." Brianna held out her hand as she lied about her name.

"And I'm Lynda." The other woman, a tiny blonde in her early fifties, looked relieved to be out of the dark hallway. "That was scary."

"Now I just hope I can get a taxi." Brianna looked at the mid-day traffic on the street, busy but not bumper-to-bumper yet. "Can I drop you ladies somewhere?"

"Thanks, but we have a friend waiting for us." Lynda waved frantically at a silver SUV parked a block away. The vehicle pulled out of its parking spot and crawled toward them.

"Where are you going?" Denise asked. "Maybe we can save you the trouble of getting a cab."

Brianna treated them to her biggest smile. "I'd appreciate that so much. I just need to get to a pharmacy. It doesn't matter which one."

"There's a big one at Albrook Mall. That's on our way." Lynda walked toward the SUV. "Get in. We survived a total blackout in a Panamanian police station. We're going to be friends for life."

Chapter 29

I've never been one to ask permission—I'd rather beg for forgiveness—but I've never thought about the consequences of not being forgiven. —Brianna Morgan

Brianna waved goodbye to her new friends and ducked into a large drugstore, keeping her head down to avoid the cameras. She grabbed the first box of dark-brown hair color she saw, along with other items she would need to alter her appearance. The first thing she had to do was cover her red hair. In a country of brown, her auburn locks stood out like a neon flame.

After paying with cash for her purchases, she locked herself in the drugstore bathroom, where she swapped her stilettos for nondescript flats and pulled a long, dark flowing dress over her clothes. She took some wipes out of her bag and scrubbed the makeup off her face. Then she untied the scarf from her handbag and wrapped it around her head.

She inspected herself in the mirror. Not satisfied, she opened the dark bronzer she had purchased and dusted it liberally on her face, neck, arms, and hands. She checked her reflection again. Not a great disguise, she thought, but it'll have to do.

She left the drugstore bathroom, keeping her head down and her shoulders rounded. She shortened her gait and slowed her pace to fit in with the relaxed tempo of the locals. She sauntered through the mall, looking for things she needed.

First, she needed to bulk up. She stopped at a casual clothing store and paid cash for oversize clothing she could wear in layers to make herself look heavier. Next, she went to a cell phone store and bought three prepaid cell phones and a handful of recharge cards.

With her purchases in hand, Brianna headed toward a mall kiosk. She found an optometrist on the directory, hoping the business would still be open. As she walked toward her destination, she sent a prayer of thanksgiving to the gods of capitalism that the eye doctor's office was still open late in the evening.

Ten minutes later, Brianna exited the optometrist's office with a small sack. She sauntered toward the nearest restroom, where she pulled a pair of dark-brown contact lenses from the bag. She popped them in her eyes then looked at the tortoiseshell librarian's glasses that also were in the bag, along with a pair of blue contacts, just in case.

She kept her head down as she walked out of the mall. She had the tools she needed; now she just needed to become someone else.

Chapter 30

My brother Jack always told me everyone should have an escape plan, a stack of cash, and a ticket out of Dodge. I wish I had taken him seriously.
— Brianna Morgan

Brianna stepped out of the shower an hour later, toweling off her now-dark locks. It took her an hour to blow-dry and flat-iron her curly hair then darken her skin with bronzer. She pulled on her the new dark slacks and blue button-down she had purchased, hoping to look like a bank teller who'd just gotten off work. She put the dark contacts back in her eyes and touched her lips with a dusky brown lipstick that never would have worked with her auburn hair and light skin.

She studied her reflection. She barely recognized herself. Hopefully no one else would either. And more importantly, she hoped no one would ask her to speak. Her gringa Spanish would shatter the illusion of a Latin office worker.

She used one of the new phones to call her father. It went to voicemail, though, and she didn't leave a message. Then she tried her brother. Still disconnected. Then Katherine. Voicemail.

When this was over, she was getting new friends.

She kept her head down as she left the lobby of the mid-priced hotel in El Cangrejo, a busy urban neighborhood in the heart of Panama City. She walked a few blocks to an Internet café and paid cash for an hour of computer time.

She'd left her flamboyant Prada bag in the hotel room and switched to a nondescript purse in a basic brown. After going to so much trouble to hide her features, she wasn't going to let her handbag be the one thing that made her stand out.

Once she got on the computer, she created a generic Gmail account and sent an email to Katherine. The subject line was the only thing real about the email:

KK use this email.

She wrote a puff paragraph about how they hadn't seen each other since college, and she'd love to get together for lunch the next time they were both in New York.

Brianna was the only person who called Katherine by the nickname KK, so she knew her friend would figure it out.

She drummed her fingers on the desk, playing a mental game of chess. She knew the person who had killed Lorenzo had to be the same person who had tried to kill Marcio. The same person who was trying to frame her. It just didn't make sense that she'd end up as the prime suspect without some manufactured evidence. But what she didn't understand was why.

She made a mental list of what she knew.

One, she didn't kill Lorenzo or attempt to kill Marcio.

Two, a bottle of Disaronno had been in the cave with Lorenzo. She had to assume it was the one she'd purchased, and it had her fingerprints were on it.

Three, Detective Bethancourt had found out that she'd met Lorenzo fifteen years ago. Why did he think it was important?

Four, she was being framed.

Five, the killer—and the person framing her—had to be a woman. Men kill with guns or knives or fists. Women kill with poison.

Brianna pulled up an incognito browser window on the computer. The woman framing her had to have left bread crumbs somewhere because she couldn't have shut off the power, turned off the backup generator at the BonitaMar, then lured Lorenzo to the cave if she was working alone. She had to have had help, probably someone she paid.

That person would now be terrified to come forward.

She needed to find someone who could speak Spanish and navigate the inner workings of the BonitaMar security team, without alerting Detective Bethancourt or the good old boys network in Panama that she was snooping.

Brianna searched online until she found what she was looking for. After making a few notes, she left the Internet café and disappeared into the busy streets of Panama City.

Chapter 31

Marcio swam toward the surface of the water. He kicked, his lungs burning. He saw the sun, but he couldn't reach it. He kicked harder, scratching at the water, willing himself to reach the top.

His mother's face loomed above him. If only he could reach her. He kicked even harder, his lungs feeling like balloons that were about to explode.

He couldn't give up. He wouldn't. Just as he reached a point of pain he thought was unbearable, he heard his mother's voice. He calmed as he listened to her singing *Duérmete Mi Niño*, a traditional Spanish lullaby from his childhood.

Sleep my child, sleep my love,
Sleep piece of my heart.
This boy of mine who was born at night
He wants me to take him for a drive.
This boy of mine who was born by day
He wants me to take him to the candy store.
Sleep my child, sleep my love,
Sleep piece of my heart.

Marcio heard the familiar voice singing the words he knew so well. He relaxed into the water and allowed himself to drift upward. He had almost reached the surface when he lost consciousness.

Chapter 32

Isabella stood over her son, watching him thrash in his sleep. He mumbled something incoherent. She leaned her head closer. He was trying to tell her something. His hands flopped on the bed while his legs kicked under the covers.

"What is it, my son?" she whispered.

He mumbled louder.

"Mamá is here. Tell me what is wrong, my child."

The heart rate monitor beeped louder.

She sang to him, a song from his childhood.

The heart rate monitor screamed with urgency as his heartbeat spiked to a dangerous level.

Instead of panicking, Isabella sang louder, caressing his hand in a rhythmic pattern. When he was a child, this was how she had calmed his active brain and coerced him into sleep.

She breathed a sigh of relief as he went still, relaxing with the sound of her voice. She continued to sing, this time more softly. She would keep him calm until he was ready to wake up. He needed his strength, and she needed her son.

Chapter 33

The good news is you can buy anything with a Wi-Fi connection and a bag full of cash. The bad news is you can buy anything with a Wi-Fi connection and a bag full of cash. — Brianna Morgan

Brianna sat at a back table in Starbucks, wearing her office-worker disguise. A piece of chocolate mousse cake sat untouched in front of her.

She'd placed an online ad for a mercenary the night before and had gotten only one response during her hour at the Internet Café. She didn't have time to collect resumes, so she set a meeting at Starbucks during peak coffee time. Although she pretended to read something on her iPad, she glanced up each time someone entered the busy coffee shop. She was as nervous as if she were waiting for a guy she'd met at an online dating site.

The Starbucks in Panama looked the same as the Starbucks in Dallas and had a mixed bag of patrons. The only thing these people had in common was that they were caffeine junkies looking for their midmorning fix—young moms pushing strollers, old men gossiping like schoolgirls, suit-clad businessmen conducting deals on their smartphones, European backpackers enjoying the free Wi-Fi.

A rough-looking man who'd been sitting nearby approached her table. He was shorter than average, with sun-darkened skin and a jagged scar that ran from his temple to his jaw. He looked like a laborer, with cheap jeans and a faded black T-shirt. If Brianna had met him in a dark alley, she would have run the other direction.

"Is the chocolate cake good?" he asked, his accent sounding more like a cholo from Los Angeles than a Panamanian.

She looked him up and down. "It normally is, but I've lost my appetite." She pushed the piece of cake toward him. "Help yourself."

"Gracias." The man pulled out the chair across from her and sat down.

They eyed one each other for a minute. Rather than glossy muscles from daily workouts at the gym, he had the sinewy strength of someone who worked with his back.

He picked up the fork and held it midair over the dessert. "Lady, you don't look like your picture. You did a good job." He put a big bite of cake in his mouth then pointed at her with the chocolatey fork. "You still look like a gringa, though. You're too tall to be Latin, and your cheekbones are too sharp."

She shrugged. "Should I chop off my legs to make myself shorter?"

He chuckled, a rusty sound.

He must not laugh much, Brianna thought.

"Feisty, aren't you? Don't worry. Maybe you could pass for Venezuelan." He studied her, his heavy eyebrows moving with his eyes. "How's your Spanish?"

"Bad."

"Then don't talk." He shoveled another big bite into his mouth. "Tell me what happened."

She gave him the short version of Lorenzo's death, the attempt on Marcio's life, and her attempts to find the killer. Then she explained her theory about the killer being a woman and how this woman had to have help from at least one other person at the BonitaMar Hotel.

He gazed at her with dead black eyes. "If someone helped her, I'll find him. Money talks in Panama. These security guys make six hundred bucks a month. Normally I could get the information for fifty bucks, but because someone was murdered, it'll cost more."

Brianna folded her hands on the table. "I understand."

He forked the last bite of cake into his mouth and pushed the plate away. "Let me ask you something, lady. Why don't you just go home? Go back to the States and get yourself a good lawyer."

"I can't." She leaned forward on her elbows to close the gap between them, then lowered her voice. "Detective Bethancourt took my passport. He's the one in charge of the case." She picked up her coffee, swirled it, then put it down again. "But I don't want to run back to the US. I didn't do this. I need to find out who did and clear my name. Can you help me?"

"Yeah. I can help." The man folded his small scarred hands on top of the table. "The most important thing is to keep you out of sight while I find out what went down at BonitaMar. I need to find the guy who cut the power and stopped the security tapes at the hotel. Then we have to hunt the hunter."

"That's what I thought." She studied his face. He had small crinkles at the corners of his eyes, so he must laugh often enough to have made grooves in his face. "How much?"

He wordlessly moved his mouth as he counted on his fingers. "It'll cost you two mil, plus expenses."

She leaned into him, screaming in a whisper, "Two million dollars! Are you out of your mind?"

He chuckled. "Sorry. Mil means a thousand in Spanish. It'll cost you two thousand dollars, up front, plus expenses."

Brianna leaned back in her chair. "By expenses, you mean bribes."

He shrugged. "That's how things are done here."

She stared at him, trying to make him uncomfortable so she could gain the upper hand. "How did you get that scar on your face?"

"I had a disagreement with a drug dealer. He wanted to sell drugs to kids. I objected."

"Who won?"

A dangerous smile snaked onto his face. "I'm scarred, but at least I'm alive."

She was probably getting into bed with the devil, she thought, but she had limited options.

"Okay. Two thousand, but you only get half now. You get the rest when we catch the killer and I get my life back."

The man stared at her for a moment, unblinking. She stared back.

He looked away first, nodding toward a small Starbucks shopping bag that sat on the chair next to hers. "Is that the cash?"

"Yes. The cash is under the coffee. One thousand, all in twenties."

"How'd you know how much to bring?"

"I'm a reporter. It's my job to know what things cost."

He opened the shopping bag and pulled out the bag of coffee, eyeing the cash underneath. He held up the bag of beans. "Thanks for the coffee. Nice bonus." He then slid the bag under the table and put it between his feet. "Now where are we going to hide you?" He scrunched up his face as he thought. "We have two choices. We can hide you in the Garibaldi."

Brianna's mouth fell open. "Isn't that the famous hooker hotel?"

"Yeah, but it's full of good-looking women, and you could blend in. The only problem is someone might want to…" He paused, lifting one eyebrow lasciviously.

She glared at him. "Might want to what?"

A corner of his mouth flicked up in the hint of a smile. "Might want to pay you for the pleasure of your company. Even without enhancements, you are prime goods, lady."

"Is that supposed to be a compliment?"

"I suppose. You look exotic." His eyes gleamed as his mouth stretched into a smile. "And expensive. You could earn enough to pay my fee in just one or two nights."

"What's my second option?"

"You can go into the interior and go native. You'll stand out, but if we get you in the right spot, no one will know you're the gringa the police are after."

Brianna tapped her fingernails on the table. "So my choices are a hooker hotel or a coconut hut in the middle of nowhere?"

The man shrugged. "It's not so bad. You could spend your days at the Garibaldi, getting massages and mud baths. Or spend them in the interior, rocking in a hammock. At least in the interior, the mud would be free."

She rolled her eyes. "Okay. The Garibaldi it is. Only because I want to be close to the city. If I go gallivanting into the interior, you might forget me and spend my money before I hack my way out of the jungle."

He nodded once, the corners of his mouth quivering as he tried not to laugh. "If you're going to blend in with hookers, you have to look the part. Do you have any other clothes?"

She looked down at her frumpy dress. "Why? Are you going to take me shopping?"

He shook his head. "No. You need to disappear, so shopping is out. But I have a friend who could loan you some clothes."

"Am I going to like my new look?"

"Probably not. But at least you won't end up behind bars. If they can't find you, they can't lock you up."

Brianna sighed. "Okay. Whatever it takes, I'm in." She looked around to see if anyone was listening, but all the other patrons were absorbed in their laptops and iPhones. "By the way, what do I call you?"

"El Pie." He pronounced it the Spanish way, "El Pee."

"What does 'L.P.' stand for? Luis Pedro? Leonardo Pablo?"

"No, lady. Not the initials L.P. The words 'El Pie.' It means 'The Foot.'" He used his fingers to make air quotes.

Brianna glanced under the table. "Your feet look normal. Why do you go by 'The Foot'?"

He laughed, a soulless sound. "They call me El Pie because I know how to put my foot up someone's ass and have him say thank you."

Brianna cocked her head to one side, like a dog trying to learn a new command.

El Pie handed her a slip of paper and a hotel key card. "This is my cell number. Call me only if it's an emergency. If I don't answer, don't leave a message. I'll call you back when I can. Got it?"

"Got it." She picked up the key card stamped with the Garibaldi Hotel emblem. Her brow knitted as she studied it. "Is this your room key?"

"No. It's for you."

"But we just decided that's where I'll stay. Why did you have it with you?"

He stared at her, his stern face emphasizing the violence behind the scar. "I knew you'd want to be close by."

She looked up at him, her brow still knitted. "How could you possibly know that?"

El Pie sighed, a hint of impatience in his expression. "Lady, you're a journalist. You're used to having the whole world revolve around you. There was no way you were going to melt into the jungle and hide under a rock."

She bit back a smile. She'd finally met a guy who understood her, and he was a knife-wielding maniac who associated with drug dealers. It was her lucky week.

"You have the room for one night. If you need to stay longer, you'll have to get a different room because this one is off the books."

"One night. Got it."

"You need more nights, I need more cash."

"More nights, more cash. Understood."

"I have a guy at the hotel who can watch out for you," El Pie said. "His name is Rodrigo, and he works the concierge desk. He'll give you a call if there's trouble." He grabbed her hand with one of his, his grip as strong as an eagle's talons. "If he calls, stop what you're doing and get out of the hotel right away. You understand?"

Brianna nodded. "Message received, loud and clear."

"The Garibaldi is not just a hotel but it's a casino too. It's got almost as many cameras as Vegas, watching you everywhere you go. If the cops have half a brain, they'll link into all the CCTV cameras in the city."

"But I'm not a redhead anymore."

He flicked his gaze up and down her face. "You're still hard to miss."

She closed her eyes and rubbed her temples. "Okay, watch out for cameras."

"Pay attention." He tapped her arm until she opened her eyes. "I'll leave a CCTV jammer for you in the stairwell on the second parking level. Use it only in case of emergency. It'll be hidden in a brown paper bag in the cabinet where they keep the fire hose and extinguisher. Rodrigo will make sure the cabinet is kept unlocked. If you need it, just pull it out and turn it on. Then keep it with you until you're someplace safe."

She nodded again.

El Pie eyed her. "You sure? Because when the crap hits the fan, everything gets messy. I don't want you to panic."

"I have a good memory." Brianna's tone was sharp.

He put his hands out, as if warding off an attack. "Just making sure. I might come by from time to time, but if you see me, pretend you don't know me. Okay?"

"Okay."

"And if I save your ass, you'll owe me another thousand."

Brianna forced a smile and nodded. She'd just given him the last of her money, but he didn't need to know that. She could take more out today, but she'd run the risk of the cops being on her trail. She'd just have to find another way to get the cash.

Chapter 34

Detective Bethancourt answered his desk phone, cradling it in his shoulder. "Bethancourt."

His junior detective, Diego Vialmo, was on the line. "Boss, I have bad news." He paused.

Detective Bethancourt continued to hunt and peck on his keyboard. "Don't just breathe in my ear. Spit it out."

"We can't find her. Brianna Morgan. She's gone."

Detective Bethancourt stopped typing. "What do you mean, you can't find her? She's probably the only tall skinny redhead in the entire country. She can't be that hard to find."

"She didn't go back to the BonitaMar last night."

"Did you check the security tapes?"

"Affirmative."

Detective Bethancourt ran his hand through his hair. No wonder middle-aged men went bald. "I don't care what it takes. Find her. And once you do, put her in cuffs."

"Yes, boss."

Detective Bethancourt slammed the phone down. He breathed in and out, trying to control his anger. He was going to catch hell for this from the chief of police. Why hadn't he put her in cuffs? He knew the answer. He hadn't treated her like a criminal because she didn't look like a criminal.

He drummed his fingers on his desk. If his junior detective wasn't up to the task, he'd bring in a professional.

He picked up the phone again and dialed an internal number. "Moses, get your skinny ass in here."

Detective Bethancourt leaned back in his chair and interlaced his fingers behind his head. This was his thinking position. He knew the IT kid was smarter than most of the cops on the force. He also knew they wouldn't be able to keep the whiz kid for long before an Internet giant like Google or Apple snatched him up. He crossed himself, sending a silent prayer of thanksgiving to Saint Michael, the patron saint of cops, that Moses could help him.

The door to the detectives' pit opened, the open area where a dozen detectives shared a common work space. Moses appeared, a lopsided smile on his face. "Yes, boss."

"Briana Morgan is gone."

Moses scratched the peach fuzz on his chin. "I thought you took her passport?"

"I did. But she slipped out of the station last night when the power went out. She hasn't gone back to the BonitaMar, and no one can find her. Any ideas?"

"What about using the media? Offer a reward and get all the locals looking for her."

Detective Bethancourt shook his head. "I want to keep it quiet. She's an American with resources. I'm not ready to tip my hand yet."

Moses picked up a stapler, clicking it open it and closed with OCD obsessiveness as he thought through the options. "The easiest way would be to hack into the CCTV cameras in the city. Panama City has more blind spots than Manhattan, but if she's here, we should be able to find her. After all, how many tall redheads are there in Panama?"

"That's what I said." Detective Bethancourt snatched the stapler out of Moses's hands and dropped it back on the desk. "Stop fidgeting."

Moses picked at his cuticles. "I can't help it, boss. It helps me think."

"How long will it take to find her?"

Moses scrunched up his face, looking at the ceiling, using his fingers to tick off time increments as he worked it out in his head. "Getting into the CCTV network is easy because I already have them linked. But our facial-recognition software isn't that great. I could hack into the FBI's computer, though, and borrow their system."

"*Dios mio!*" Detective Bethancourt dragged his hand down his face, biting the words off so he wouldn't explode. "That. Is. Not. An. Option."

Moses shrugged his skinny shoulders. "Okay. I had to ask."

"Give me legal options."

Moses clicked his teeth together as he thought. "I might be able to ask a friend for facial-recognition software that's faster than ours. I'll get started using our system then piggyback in another system. Maybe using two slower systems will double the speed."

"Do it," Detective Bethancourt ordered.

"Okay, I'm on it." Moses slunk out of the room.

Detective Bethancourt resumed his thinking position. His team had finished at the crime scene, and the autopsy was done. Now he needed to search Lorenzo Silva's personal property—his houses, cars, and boat. Who knew what gold he'd dig up, but now that he had a solid suspect, he knew where to focus.

Chapter 35

I used to love Halloween, the one day of the year when you can dress like a slut and get away with it. But when your costume makes men look at you like you're something that can be purchased, it's no longer fun. — Brianna Morgan

At nine that evening, Brianna strutted out of the elevator of the Garibaldi Hotel casino, clad in skintight leggings with a built-in butt enhancer, spiky stilettos, and a formfitting gold lamé top. The backless blouse had a plunging neckline and was held in place by two thin ties, one around her neck and the other around her waist.

She carried her cheap oversize handbag rather than slinging it over her shoulder. She didn't want it to alter the lines of her outfit—or inadvertently untie a precious strap. Unlike Vegas casinos, this one wasn't smoky, but that's where the positive comparison ended. The slot machine stools had cracks and tears in the vinyl, some of the slots had "out of order" signs posted on them, and the entrance chandelier had burnt lightbulbs. The whole place looked grimy and frayed.

Brianna scanned the room, looking for the perfect mark. It didn't take her long to find him.

She smiled as she made her way toward a loud, big-bellied American sitting at a pub table near the bar. He looked like a rumpled Paul Bunyan, his gaudy Hawaiian shirt untucked over baggy Dockers. Brianna felt oddly confident as she swung her hips from side to side, the gold dust on her darkened skin shimmering under the lights. She gave the man a come-hither smile and batted her false eyelashes.

He smiled lecherously as she approached, running his hands through his dark curly hair, leaving it a haphazard mess. "Well, hello there, beautiful," he boomed, his words blurry but not yet slurred. "This must be my lucky day. Would you like a drink?"

She nodded, looking down in a flirtatious attempt to be coy.

He stood up and called a waitress over, waving and using his outdoor voice. "Senorita, my friend would like a drink." He turned to Brianna as the waitress approached. "What'll you have, honey?"

"Vino blanco," she said, blurring the "v" into a "b" like the locals did, making it sound more like, "beano blanco."

"White wine for the lady and another Jack and Coke for me." The man opened his wallet, fat with cash, and tossed a folded twenty-dollar bill on the waitress's drink tray. "That's for you. I'll double it if our drinks are here un-de-lay pronto." He butchered the Spanish words, his diction as sloppy as his clothes.

The waitress snatched the tip off her tray with the practiced speed of a frog catching a fly. She hurried straight toward the bartender, shooting off commands to him in Spanish before she'd come within five feet of the bar.

The American turned toward Brianna, his double chin wobbling as he looked down at her. "What's your name, honey? You sure are pretty."

She set her handbag on the table and slipped onto the barstool next to him. "My name is Meli. It means 'honey.'" She used what she hoped was a Spanish accent.

"Meli, I knew you were as sweet as honey the minute I saw you." He traced a finger down her long neck, then let his hand rest on her hip.

She let him touch her, throwing her hair back and leaning into him for the benefit of the casino cameras.

When the waitress brought their drinks, he pulled another two twenties out of his wallet. "Keep the change, sweetheart." Then he turned to Brianna, lifting his drink in salute. "Cheers to you, honey."

Brianna brought the glass to her mouth, wanting to guzzle the wine but barely wetting her lips.

The man leaned into her, so close she could smell the whiskey on his breath. "Meli, honey," he said, louder than necessary, nodding toward her handbag. "What have you got in that big bag of yours?"

Brianna leaned into him and blew into his ear. "Implements of pleasure. Do you want to feel good?"

He looked at her with glossy eyes. "Oh, yeah, honey."

She used her fingers to play with the ends of his hair, taming the waves as she stroked. "I can make you good. Real good."

She tugged on his earlobe with her teeth and wrapped an arm around his neck, trying hard not to gag. No wonder hookers and dancers used drugs—she longed for a shot of oblivion right about now but her life was on the line and she needed to be sharper than ever.

The man groaned in pleasure.

She took his drink out of his hand, opening her palm over the glass as she set it on the table to release the crushed powder she'd hidden in her hand. She covertly stirred it into his drink with her finger then put her wet finger in his mouth.

The feel of his tongue on her finger made her skin feel like it had a thousand fire ants eating her from the inside. She shuddered involuntarily.

"Do you want to go somewhere more private?" she whispered, hoping he hadn't noticed.

He nodded, unable to speak with her finger in his mouth.

She pulled her finger out of his mouth and handed him his drink. "Finish your drink, mi amor, and let's find somewhere more private."

He knocked his drink back in one gulp and slammed his glass on the table. "Let's go, honey."

Brianna set her wineglass on the table and allowed him to nuzzle her for a moment. Then he swung into motion, putting his arm around her waist and pulling her along with him, away from the casino.

In the elevator, he punched his floor number then looked back at her, moving his hand from her waist and tracing his fingers up and down her bare arm. "Honey, you sure are gorgeous. This really is my lucky day."

She giggled, leaning into him while keeping her head down to avoid the cameras. "We are both lucky."

"I hate to be indelicate," he said, fumbling for words, "but how much is this going to cost?"

Brianna fluttered her eyelashes and pressed her breasts into his chest. "Don't worry, big guy. You can afford it."

He bent down and kissed her, crushing her lips with his wet mouth. He tasted like whiskey and salsa, a lethal combination.

Brianna resisted the urge to pull away and wipe her mouth.

When the elevator door opened, he pulled her behind him as he stumbled down the hall. When they reached his room, he pushed her against the outside of his door and kept one arm on either side of her, trapping her in his embrace. He kissed her neck as he fumbled with the key card.

The door clicked open and they fell inside.

He kicked the door shut, coming at her like a starving man who was about to capture his prey.

Brianna danced away from him, giving him a smile full of promises. "I need to use the bathroom, mi amor. Why don't you get comfortable? I'll be right out."

He smiled, humoring her. "Should I fix you a drink?"

"Sure, mi amor. I'll have whatever you're having."

Brianna went into the bathroom and locked the door. She turned the faucet on and rinsed her mouth out. She plucked several tissues from the box and wiped her mouth, careful to dispose of them in the toilet before flushing. Leaning her head against the wall, she studied her reflection. She looked like a Latina. If she hadn't done her own makeup, she never would have believed she could look so different, so sexy.

She started to shake. What was she doing? She'd bought benzodiazepine—a muscle relaxer that induced sleep—at a local pharmacy, but she'd never tried to knock a guy out before. He'd had a lot to drink, so she hoped her guesstimate was right when she'd crushed a few pills into powder. She didn't want to hurt him, but she needed him to be unconscious for the rest of the night. She was hiding in plain sight, and she couldn't afford to have any witnesses.

"Meli, Meli, where are you?" he crooned from the bedroom.

She looked at her watch. She hoped it wouldn't take more than fifteen minutes for the sleeping powder to work. Ten minutes had passed so far.

"Uno momento, mi amor," she called, turning the shower on. "I just need a quick shower."

"Hurry up, honey. I miss you." His voice sounded smaller.

Brianna opened her handbag and took inventory of the items she'd gotten from El Pie. He outfitted her from a friend's closet, and then borrowed a few other items she might need. Brianna didn't want to ask what type of friends they were. The less she knew the better.

Seven minutes later, she turned off the shower. "Mi amor, are you ready for me?" She cracked the door open. "Mi amor?"

She pushed the door open and crept into the bedroom. Her mark was sprawled on the bed, naked, snoring like a kitten.

"Your snores are music to my ears, big guy," she said, pulling a pair handcuffs out of her bag and securing his wrists to a bedpost in the center of the bed. "Sorry about this, but I can't have you waking up and catching me at a disadvantage. Especially since you weigh a good hundred pounds more than I do." She eyed his belly, a Mount Vesuvius of jiggling flesh. "Make that a hundred and fifty pounds."

She pulled a roll of duct tape out of her bag and taped his mouth shut. "I wish I didn't have to do this, but I can't have you disturbing the neighbors tonight if those pills wear off too soon." She draped a towel around his eyes then circled it with duct tape. "See no evil, hear no evil, speak no evil. Sleep tight."

Brianna pulled the covers over his body. "Let's find out who you are, big guy. Where's your wallet?" She picked up his discarded pants and went through the pockets. Nothing. Then she opened the top nightstand drawer. "Bingo!" She pulled out his wallet and wedding ring. "I had a feeling you were married. And I knew you'd be alone. Men like you don't come here for the gambling. That's why I chose you."

She flipped open his wallet and looked at his driver's license. "Tucker Carter from Toledo, Ohio. Well, Big Tuck, I need to borrow some cash." She plucked out all the cash, counting it on the bed. "A grand and change. Not bad, Tuck. I can tell you were planning to get lucky."

She rummaged in his wallet for a business card. "I'll send you the money as soon as I can. There will be no note, of course, but you'll know it's from me. I might even spritz the envelope with perfume to get you in a bit of trouble at work."

She put a twenty back in his wallet and stuffed the rest into her handbag, along with his business card.

Brianna surveyed the room as she looked for his laptop. It was a typical convention hotel, albeit frayed around the edges. The room held a king bed, a cheap desk with a straight-back chair, a stained lounge chair, and TV bolted to the wall. Like the casino, it needed more than a little freshening.

She spotted his laptop on the desk. "You don't look like a guy who messes around with passwords." When she walked over and turned it on, it booted and went to the home screen. No password required.

"I love being right. Thank you for being careless, Tuck. I needed a break." Brianna opened a browser and went to HideMyBadBehavior.com. She used his's platinum credit card to pay for a week's pass on the site, which would give her a fake IP address. She needed to send emails without sounding any alarm bells on her account. "Sorry if this gets you in trouble with the missus, Tucker, but she's going to find out about your philandering ways sooner or later."

She activated the VPN and created a new email address on Yahoo using a fake name, then typed in her cameraman's personal email from memory into a new email.

Hello, Mike,
Thanks for taking the time to do the private shoot with VA and MM. Please upload the raw footage from both interviews to a YouTube account I created: YouTube.com/MrEdTalkingHorse. Use this email as the access email. Remember what that person in the bar called me? That's the password.
I'm sorry I was unable to reconnect with you in person.
Cheers, mate.
—Ed

She pressed "send" and waited. Mike was addicted to his iPhone, and unless he was in the middle of a shoot, he would read the email right away. Brianna held her breath, hoping he would understand her cryptic message.

She didn't have to wait long. Her "new email" pinged, and her first message appeared.

Ed, buddy, good to hear from you. I was worried!
I remember what that schmuck called you. Will upload footage now. I've watched it already, and it's a bit ho-hum. Suggest we do it again with new subject. BTW, you owe me a beer. When can I collect?

Brianna didn't want him to worry, so she sent one last message.

Soon, my friend, soon. I'll buy you a beer and a steak to go with it. I'm buried in the sand now. Later, gator.

She knew he'd understand she had to hide out for a bit. She didn't want to involve him in her troubles unless she had to. He lived paycheck to paycheck and had two young kids at home. Any help he gave had to be peripheral.

While she was waiting for the raw footage of the interviews with Valentina Arias and Laura Mareno to be uploaded to YouTube, she got up and stretched. She was hungry. Living a secret life on the run used up a lot of energy.

She flipped through the room service menu. "What do you want, Tucker?" She looked at his prone body as if expecting an answer. "You're definitely not a vegetarian, but maybe you should be." She called room service. "I'd like two club sandwiches and a bottle of Duckhorn Cabernet."

She had time to kill before the food arrived, and the videos hadn't been uploaded yet. Her eyes scanned the room until she spotted what she was looking for. She crossed the room to the desk and picked up an inexpensive glass vase filled with sand and seashells, then carried it to the bathroom. She tossed the sand and the seashells into the trash. After wrapping the vase in a towel, she tapped it on the counter until she heard the grass crack.

She wrapped a small piece of glass in a hand towel and brought it to the bed. After pulling back the sheets, she gazed at Tucker's ample chest. She held the piece of glass with the towel, exposing a sharp edge. She then traced the edge of the glass along his chest just hard enough to make a mark without breaking the skin. She repeated the scratch three more times in a line, about an inch apart.

"There you go, Big Tuck. You had rough sex, and I scratched you in ecstasy. You'll have to get dressed in the closet for a few weeks so your wifey pooh won't see what a naughty boy you've been, but maybe you'll learn a lesson and stay away from prostitutes."

Brianna took the glass shard back to the bathroom, then flushed the piece of glass down the toilet and dumped the towel and the broken vase in the trash.

Returning to the laptop, she pulled up a local news feed on the incognito browser. She wanted to see if there were any new stories about Lorenzo's murder.

An ad for Zappos online shoe store preceded the video she wanted to watch. Brianna yearned for the days when her most important decision was whether to drop a few hundred bucks on a pair of designer stilettos or stuff the money into her 401K. She hoped she'd be in the mood to buy shoes again someday. This nightmare had to end soon. And hopefully it would end without bulky silver bracelets as her new must-have accessory.

The doorbell rang. "*Servicio,*" a male voice called.

Room service. That was fast.

Brianna pulled the covers over Tucker and tossed a towel over his handcuffed wrists. To the casual observer, he'd look like he was sleeping off a hangover.

Brianna looked through the peephole. A uniformed waiter stood in front of a room service cart. She pulled on a bathrobe over her clothes, kicked off her stilettos, and opened the door. The waiter started to wheel the cart in, but she used her body to stop him. "My husband is sleeping," she whispered. "Just give me the check."

The waiter handed her the bill, and she scribbled, "Mrs. Tucker Carter" on it, adding a generous tip.

She wheeled the cart in and shut the door, flipping the deadbolt before maneuvering the cart next to the desk. She then picked up the bottle of wine and studied the label. "Thank goodness you're not a cheapskate, Tucker. I needed a delicious wine after the day I've had." She pulled the cork out of the wine and poured herself a glass, sipping it with reverence.

Lifting the lid off her meal, she sniffed the air. Her club sandwich burst with fresh avocado and thick bacon. She popped a French fry into her mouth. "Wow, they're still hot. Who knew room service would be so good in a tired old hotel like this?"

Brianna turned on the TV and found the local news. She ate slowly, focusing on the fresh taste of the various ingredients. She was full after eating half the sandwich, but she decided to finish every bite. Like a soldier during combat, she needed the calories just in case she couldn't eat again for a while.

She finished the wine and poured a second glass, willing the email to come. Five minutes later, her email pinged, and she jumped to attention. Mike had uploaded the video footage of Valentina Arias to YouTube.

Brianna brought the video to full screen and watched the interview. Although Valentina came off as selfish and self-absorbed, nothing she said made her seem like a killer. She watched it again, pausing and going back to listen to every word. Everything about Valentina's microexpressions indicated that she'd been telling the truth.

Her email pinged again. Laura Mareno's video was on YouTube. She closed Valentina's video and watched Laura's video three times from start to finish. Laura was childish and petulant, but she was no murderer. Marcio had that right.

Either these women are great actresses or they're innocent, Brianna thought.

It was time to focus on the third suspect, Ana Maria Lopes, the latest in a string of Lorenzo's non-serious romantic interests. She Googled Ana Maria, but there were too many women by that name to get a good match. She tried Facebook but got the same result.

Brianna needed a break. She wrapped up the second sandwich in napkins and put it in the minibar fridge. It might come in handy later. She locked herself in the bathroom and washed the caked-on bronzer off her skin. She'd have to reapply it, but she wanted her pores to have a few hours of freedom.

She emerged from the shower dressed in the hotel bathrobe and used Tucker's credit card again to gain access to a "get all the dirt on someone" website. She began putting together a dossier on Ana Maria Lopes, a thirty-nine-year-old real estate broker who'd been divorced twice and, according to a tip from El Pie, was on the hunt for husband number three.

Brianna stared at the photo, looking at the woman's hook nose, long dark hair and overly full mouth until something in her brain clicked. Ana Maria was the woman she'd spotted in the BonitaMar bar with Lorenzo wearing the flamboyant yellow dress with matching stilettos. She was the woman who'd given Brianna a look of intense jealousy. Lorenzo must have given her the kiss-off before approaching Brianna.

She scanned the file. Ana Maria had grown up in a poor family. Her father was a laborer, and her mother was a maid. She had dark skin, which usually meant a lifetime of poverty in Panama's racist, classist society, but Ana Maria had been hungry and had clawed her way up the social ladder. From the photos, it looked like she hadn't been blessed with natural beauty, but she'd worked at it over the years with a personal trainers and regular blowouts to give her hair a silky sheen.

Ana Maria had gone into real estate after obtaining a degree in marketing from a middling university in Panama, and she hadn't stopped kicking and scratching until she was one of the highest paid workers in the country. But still she wasn't a business owner. She drove a Porsche Cayenne—like all successful people did in Panama—but unlike Lorenzo's brand new luxury SUV, hers was a ten-year-old year old base model.

As she thought, Brianna tapped her pen against the hotel notepad. She'd met a lot of social climbers who would do anything to have their names in the media. Unlike socialites who were born into prominence, social climbers had to smile and connive their way to social acceptance. But the name of the game was getting your name and your photo in the social columns as often as humanly possible. The super-serious social climbers even hired publicists.

She opened a new browser and searched for Ana Maria's name in the social pages of prominent Panamanian magazines. After combing through three years of back issues in four different publications, Brianna had found only three mentions of Ana Maria Lopes, and one of those didn't have an accompanying photo. She'd garnered nowhere near the amount of publicity a wannabe socialite needed to overcome her shabby beginnings.

Brianna studied one of the photos of Ana Maria. She wore a designer dress—probably a Versace. She was leaning away from the other woman in the photo, someone Brianna had seen dozens of times in the social pages after an hour of looking. Even though Ana Maria was smiling, she looked angry. Brianna made a note. "That's jealousy, Tucker. This woman has self-esteem issues and a lot of unresolved anger."

Could a moment of anger—or a lifetime of rage at having been looked over or subverted because of her humble beginnings—have

170

pushed her to commit murder? And would that same personality dysfunction make her devious enough to frame Brianna, a woman she'd never met but whom she felt threatened by when Lorenzo had ditched her?

Brianna needed more data—and she needed to have a face-to-face conversation with the enigmatic Ana Maria Lopes.

Chapter 36

Marcio's eyelids flickered open. He heard a machine beeping next to him. Turning his head toward the sound, he tried to focus his eyes, wanting to know what was making his bones ache. He grunted, pain shooting through his body as he attempted to move.

He felt a hand on his forehead and turned to look at the face attached to it. His mother's face. "You were in a car accident, mi amor," she said softly. "You have a broken clavicle, which is why your left arm is in a sling. You also have a broken rib. You need to stay still so your rib does not puncture your lung." She gently ran a hand over his cheek. "You had surgery to repair your spleen. The operation went well. Now you need rest. Let me get the doctor."

Marcio reached up to touch her with his good hand, but the pain made him stop. "Thank you for being here," he said hoarsely.

She found his hand and gave it a quick squeeze. "Where else would I be?"

She left the room and brought back Dr. Hidalgo. He checked Marcio's vital signs and made a few notes.

The doctor peered down at him. "We were worried about the bump on your head. Do you remember what happened?"

"I was in a car accident."

The doctor nodded. "That is correct. You might have some short-term memory loss, though. That is normal. Just rest and allow yourself time to heal. I will check on you later."

Isabella returned to her son's side. "I agree with the doctor. You should rest."

He let his head loll. "My brother is gone."

She grabbed his face between her hands, bringing hers within inches of his. "You are in pain. So am I. You must go on. It is hard, I know, but you are a Silva. We do not give up, and we do not give in. Not now, not ever." She kissed his forehead. "There will be time to grieve later. But now we must find out who is trying to hurt you. Tell me everything you remember."

He licked his lips, his tongue thick. "I was driving toward the city. A truck was in my lane. I tried to stop, but my brakes did not work. The last thing I remember was going over the side of the road into the ocean."

Isabella nodded. "That is what the police think happened as well."

"How long have I been here?"

"A day and a half, since Sunday. It is Tuesday morning, just after seven." She gave him a small smile. "You always were a morning person."

"How did you get here?"

She brushed his hair away from his face. "I flew in on Sunday. Remember?"

He dipped his chin in a modified nod. "I was supposed to pick you up."

"The reporter picked me up. Brianna Morgan."

He tilted his head to the side, his eyes darting around the room. "Where is she?"

"You mean Brianna?" She stared at him with mom eyes, waiting for his reaction.

He grunted. "Yes. Is Brianna here?"

Isabella moved away and busied herself at the tray next to his bed. "Would you like some water?" She poured water into the plastic hospital cup with a built-in straw. She put the straw up to his lips. "Drink a little. Your mouth is dry."

He took a sip to appease her. "Mamá, where is Brianna?"

Isabella put the cup down and turned back toward her son. "I do not know where she is, but she is not here. The police think she did it."

"The police think she did what?"

"Killed your brother…and tried to hurt you."

His chest rose and fell with rapid breaths "Is she one of the suspects?"

"I think she is the only suspect. Detective Bethancourt took her in for questioning, but she escaped."

"Escaped?" Marcio's eyes widened. "How do you know?"

"I have my sources." Isabella adjusted the monitor cords attached to her son. "I do not think she is running. I think she is trying to figure out who did this."

Marcio closed his eyes and exhaled. "Before Brianna became a suspect, we were working together, trying to figure it out."

Isabella stroked her son's head. "I know. She told me." She paused then added, "You like her. I can tell."

He looked at his mother. "Yes, I like her. She is like no one I have ever met." His eyes fluttered closed.

She took his hand in both of hers. "I trust your instincts. If you think she is innocent, then we should help her."

Marcio wrenched his eyes open. "Is she in trouble? Real trouble?"

"She could be. Detective Bethancourt is convinced she did it. She is in a country not her own, and she does not speak the language." She paused again. "What do you think? Is there a chance she did this?"

"No. Not the slightest chance." He looked at the IV in his arm. "How long until I can leave?"

She squeezed his arm. "My darling, you have broken bones and are recovering from surgery. You are not leaving anytime soon. But I can help you."

He raised an eyebrow.

"I might not be young anymore, but this old fox is still the cleverest in the henhouse."

Marcio snorted. "I never doubted that."

Isabella straightened her spine. "I have seen to your security. I lost one son this week, and I came close to losing you. I will not make the mistake of underestimating our enemy. I have a guard posted outside your door. He is on a twelve-hour shift and rotates out with another guard. They are mercenaries, not rent-a-cops, so you will be safe in their care."

A muscle twitched on Marcio's face, the first hint of a smile since he had woken up. "I would expect nothing less from you, Mamá."

She fiddled with one of the brass buttons on the fitted navy blazer she wore over wide-legged matching slacks. Her eyes gleamed as she squared her shoulders and adjusted t the short double-breasted blazer, looking like Napoleon planning a coup. "Any ideas who did this?"

"Brianna and I came up with a list. She is convinced it is a woman."

"I am inclined to agree." Isabella arched a perfectly plucked eyebrow. "Is Valentina on that list?"

"Yes. Brianna interviewed her, but I think Valentina is too self-absorbed to commit murder."

Isabella nodded. "I trust your instincts."

"Mamá, I need to speak with Brianna. Can you arrange it?"

"I will try, but I honestly do not know where she is."

Marcio grasped her hand. "Find her."

Chapter 37

"I'm innocent. I swear." Like they'd never heard that before. — Brianna
Morgan

Brianna unlocked Tucker's handcuffs at nine-thirty the next morning.
According to her calculations, he'd sleep until mid-day, but she didn't
want to take the chance of getting caught in his room.

"Take care of yourself, big guy," she said as she removed the duct
tape from his mouth and took off the blindfold. "Stay out of trouble. No
more prostitutes, okay?"

Drool dripped from his mouth.

She used a towel to wipe away any fingerprints she might have left
and slipped out the door. She kept her head down so the cameras couldn't
get a good shot of her face.

Instead of getting a taxi at the hotel lobby, Brianna walked a block
then flagged a cab. "Can you drive me to the mall?" she asked the driver
in English.

The driver gave her a blank look.

"Habla ingles?"

The driver shook his head.

"Good." Brianna settled into the back seat. "MultiPlaza Mall, por
favor."

The driver nodded and eased into traffic.

She sank into her seat and let out a long sigh. She looked at the driver,
but he had one eye on traffic and the other on his phone as he texted with
the urgency of a jilted lover.

Brianna pulled a maxi dress out of her bag and slipped it on over her
hooker clothes. After finger-combing her hair into a low ponytail, she
exchanged her dangly earrings for small studs and wiped the dark lipstick
off her lips.

She inhaled and exhaled with yoga breaths, trying to calm her nerves. When they arrived at the mall, she paid the driver and stepped into the humid air.

She walked ramrod straight, channeling her inner socialite, and avoided looking right or left. She walked to the food court, which was surprisingly busy for ten-fifteen in the morning. Surrounded by dozens of people on their phones, she pulled one of the disposable phones from her bag and punched in a number.

After a short conversation, she made a second call.

Isabella answered after two rings.

"Isabella, do you know who this is?"

"Yes."

"I need to talk to you in person. Can you meet me?"

"Of course."

"A taxi will pick you up in front of the hospital in thirty minutes," Brianna said. "Wear the same scarf you were wearing when I first met you. Can you do that?"

"I can."

"The driver will give you something of mine. The thing you commented on when we first met. If he doesn't have it, don't get in the taxi."

"I understand."

"See you soon." Brianna broke the connection.

Chapter 38

Moses clicked through images of women as his computer spit them out. He'd been looking at possible facial recognition matches for the past hour, and he was bored. He leaned back in his chair and put his feet on the desk as he continued to click through the potential matches.

His stomach rumbled, and he thought about lunch. He wanted a big bowl of pasta from the new Italian restaurant that just opened in the nearby Albrook Mall, but he couldn't be away that long. He'd have to settle for the food truck permanently parked outside the police station. The food was hot and filling, but they only served one thing each day. He hoped they had chicken today.

He was so focused on the idea of lunch that he missed her the first time. Two seconds after clicking past her photo, he scrambled forward in his chair, bumping his desk and knocking over his empty coffee mug. Ignoring a pen as it clattered to the floor, he clicked the "back" button. He stared at the photo. She had dark hair, dark skin, and dark eyes, but the cheekbones belonged to Brianna Morgan.

He looked at the data from the photo. This image had been taken from a security camera at an Internet café in El Cangrejo two days ago.

He might not know where she was at this exact minute, but he now knew what she looked like.

Moses's fingers danced over the keyboard as he programmed the system to search for the new image of Brianna in the CCTV camera network he'd set up. Even if she had her face turned to the side, he would find her.

It was only a matter of time.

Chapter 39

Isabella Silva waited in front of the Pacifica Salud Hospital, looking like a forties-era movie star. She wore a white fitted suit with a white scarf tied around her hair and a pair of oversize sunglasses hiding her eyes.

A taxi approached and stopped in front of her. The window lowered, and a Latin man with a scar on his face looked her up and down. "Isabella Silva?"

She stood tall, her spine as erect as a ballerina's. "Yes."

"I have something for you." He held up Brianna's Morganite ring. "Do you recognize this?"

She nodded.

He got out and opened the door to the backseat, holding the ring out for her to take.

She took the ring from his outstretched hand, and then got in the taxi, waiting to speak until the man was behind the wheel. "Who are you?"

"That's not important."

"Where am I going?"

"To see a movie." He handed her a ticket. "The theater is on the third floor of MultiPlaza Mall. When I drop you off, take the escalator to the top floor. Go into the theater. She will be waiting for you toward the back. Do not sit next to her. Sit in the row in front of her. Do you understand?"

Isabella studied the man behind the wheel, wondering how he got the scar and how he was connected to Brianna. "I understand."

"I'm going to drive in circles for ten minutes to make sure we're not being followed. It's important that no one knows about this meeting."

She nodded. "I understand. Thank you for being careful."

Neither one spoke until the taxi stopped in front of the mall ten minutes later. "This is where you get out. Do not look at her when you speak to her. There are video cameras in the theater, and you cannot be seen talking to her. When you're speaking, hold your phone up to your ear to make it look like you're on a phone call."

Isabella got out of the taxi and walked toward her destination with the carriage of a queen. Once she was in the mall, she improvised, taking the long way through the less-populated couture section. She glanced at her reflection in store windows to check for a tail. Although she didn't have a college degree, she had street-dog instincts. When she was sure she wasn't being followed, she made her way to the movie theater and gave her ticket to the attendant.

Looking around the theater, Isabella spotted a Latin woman sitting alone toward the back of the nearly empty theater. She checked her ticket stub to make sure she was in the right theater. She looked again and saw the telltale Caucasian cheekbones of the television journalist. A smile tugged at the corners of her mouth. She wasn't the only one with survival instincts.

Isabella sat in the row in front of Brianna and pulled her cell phone out of her handbag. She put it up to her ear as if she were making a call. "You are very clever," she said softly, without turning her head. "I did not recognize you at first."

"That was the plan." Brianna put her own cell phone to her ear.

Isabella held up Brianna's ring to her shoulder. "Here. This belongs to you."

Brianna leaned forward and pretended to get something from the floor before palming the ring. "How is Marcio?" she said, just as quietly as Isabella.

"He woke up, thank God."

"I'm so relieved."

"He remembers the accident, so I am hoping there is no permanent memory loss. He said his brakes did not work."

"I don't think it was an accident. Whoever killed Lorenzo is going after Marcio."

"I agree with you," Isabella said.

"Did he tell you what we found?"

"He told me about the voodoo charm under Lorenzo's mattress and the feathers in Lorenzo's wheel well. He also told me you think a woman is responsible."

"I do." Brianna sat in silence while a couple entered the theater. Once they were seated near the front, she continued. "We narrowed the list down to three women. I interviewed two of them before Marcio's accident: Lorenzo's ex-wife—."

Isabella cut her off. "Valentina has the emotional maturity of a hummingbird. I don't think she has the inner fortitude to kill someone."

Brianna nodded. "I agree. I've watched the raw footage over and over, and I don't see anything but narcissism." She paused as someone new entered the theater. "I don't think his assistant did it either; she's nothing but a child. That leaves the third suspect."

"And you need my help."

"Yes. I wouldn't ask if it weren't important."

"What do you need?"

Brianna leaned forward and whispered her plan in Isabella's ear.

Chapter 40

Moses grabbed the photo from the printer and raced toward Detective Bethancourt's desk. As he rounded the corner, he slipped on some spilled water and crashed into another detective. Moses's slight frame absorbed the impact, and he fell onto his backside, thin arms and legs splaying like matchsticks dropped from a box.

Detective Bethancourt looked up from his desk as the photo fluttered to the floor, his mouth twitching as he tried not to laugh. "What's up, kid?"

Moses pushed himself to his feet. He scooped up the photo and presented it to Detective Bethancourt. "I found her!"

Detective Bethancourt rubbed his forehead. "Found who?"

"Brianna Morgan. I found her. She's changed her look, but I found her through facial recognition, and I followed her on the CCTV footage to the Garibaldi Hotel. She's posing as a prostitute."

Detective Bethancourt's face lit up as he studied the photograph, the first genuine smile Moses had seen from him since Lorenzo Silva had been murdered. "I'll be damned. That's her all right. Great job, Moses." He turned to the squad room. "Saddle up, boys. We're going to catch a killer."

Chapter 41

Many of Oprah's guests were shocked when they met her. Instead of a warm and fuzzy new BFF they encountered a sharp-edged businesswoman. When a female has succeeded against all odds, you shouldn't be surprised to discover she has a titanium core. — Brianna Morgan

Brianna took a taxi back to the Garibaldi Hotel. The naughty Big-Tucker-from-Toledo, might see her but it was a risk she had to take, as her hooker look wouldn't work at any of the other hotels. In the back of the cab, she morphed back into the professional lady of the night who had left the hotel several hours earlier, stowing her socialite clothes in her bag.

The taxi dropped her off at the Garibaldi's valet entrance. Brianna turned on a sensual half smile and strutted across the lobby, turning away from the cameras she had spotted earlier.

She headed to the concierge desk. "Rodrigo?"

He looked up at her. "Si."

"You have a key for me?"

"You have money for me?"

She shook his hand, slipping him a hundred-dollar bill.

Rodrigo tucked it in his pants pocket and gave her an envelope. "Your room number is inside. Be out of the room by eleven."

Brianna nodded and left without saying goodbye.

As soon as she was in her room, she slouched against the door. It was exhausting to be a hooker. She looked around the quiet room. She needed a nap.

She flopped onto the bed, not bothering to kick off her shoes. Her mind raced for a few minutes before she fell into a hard sleep, her body twitching as her synapses fired.

In her dreams, she heard a phone ring. It stopped then rang again. The insistent ringing pulled her from her slumber, and she grabbed at the handset, only wanting to slip back into her delicious sleep. "Hello?" she managed to say, her voice hoarse with sleep.

"It's Rodrigo. The police are here. Get out. Get out now."

Adrenaline surged through Brianna's system as the phone went dead. She bounced up, shaking her head hard to clear the fog of sleep from her brain. Thankfully she'd been fully dressed when she had fallen asleep. She grabbed her shoulder bag and a bottle of water and quickly left the room.

Brianna twisted the cap off the bottle and chugged the water as she hurried down the hall toward the stairs. She needed the hydration to clear the sleep from her system. After guzzling down the whole thing, she dropped the empty bottle into her bag. She didn't want to leave a trail of her DNA for the cops to find.

She approached the stairwell and cracked the door open. She listened but didn't hear anyone coming up the stairs. Not wanting to give away her position in case the cops came up the stairs, she slipped off her stilettos and tiptoed barefoot down the stairs.

How had the police found her? She'd changed her appearance, but maybe it wasn't enough. She had to assume they knew what she looked like now. If so, they'd be waiting for her in the lobby.

Her years of playing chess with her dad kicked in. She pulled the frumpy, conservative dress out of her bag and pulled it over her head as she raced down the stairs, floor after floor. She wiped the lipstick off her mouth with the back of her hand, took the earrings out of her ears, and dropped them into her purse.

Brianna pulled a scarf from her bag and once again wrapped it around her head. As she ran, she excavated the ballet flats from the bottom of her bag, pulling them on as she descended.

She stopped on the floor marked E-2, the second floor of the parking garage. She quickly opened the fire hose cabinet and found a paper bag tucked behind the hose. She pulled it out and peered inside. The bag contained a handheld electronic device. She picked it up and turned it over, looking for the "on" button. She found it and flipped it to the "on" position.

The CCTV jammer had two thick antennas. She stuffed the device into her bag and pushed herself out the stairwell door.

Keeping her pace slow, she slouched her shoulders and kept her head down. To the casual observer, she might look like a tourist, embarrassed at being seen at Panama City's famous den of iniquity.

Brianna removed a set of keys from her bag and pretended to look for her car as she walked down two floors of parking to the street level. At the exit, she tossed the keys back into her bag and donned her oversize sunglasses. Instead of going to the street to find a taxi, she strolled toward the El Colombo Hotel, which shared a parking lot with the Garibaldi.

Unlike the Garibaldi, the El Colombo catered to wealthy Latins and was one of the finest hotels in Panama City. Brianna entered, bypassing the front desk, and walked directly through the lobby, knowing that every great hotel had at least a few restaurants, and one of them had to be on the lobby level. She ducked into the first restaurant she saw—a sushi place with intimate booths and low lighting—and asked the bartender for a cup of coffee.

The restaurant had a few lingering diners, but the frenetic lunch crowd had disappeared. She headed to an empty booth in the farthest corner of the restaurant and pulled one of her burner phones out of her bag. Her hands trembling, she punched in her dad's number but accidentally dropped the phone before she could press "send."

She took a deep breath to stop her body from shaking. With exaggerated slowness, she picked the phone up, held it steady, and pressed the "send" button.

Nothing happened. She looked at the phone and tried again. Still nothing. The jammer must have been blocking her cell signal. She reached into her bag again and turned off the device, careful to keep her head turned away from the restaurant's security camera. She tried again, but the call went to voicemail.

Then she tried El Pie's number, that she'd had enough foresight to program into each of the burner phones. Voicemail. She didn't leave a message.

Did El Pie know the police had found her? Had Rodrigo called him too? Did he know she needed help?

Panic rose in her chest. El Pie wasn't available. She needed her dad. She tried his number, but again it went to voicemail. Why did her parents have to be on a round-the-world cruise? Tears welled up in her eyes as the enormity of the situation crushed her.

Then she heard her dad's voice in her head, with his typical military-officer brusqueness: When you're cornered, don't panic. Panic can kill you faster than an enemy's bullet.

Brianna wiped her eyes, breathing deeply and willing her heartbeat to slow. She could find a solution. Although she'd never been a military officer, she was her father's daughter.

Chapter 42

Detective Bethancourt stood outside Brianna's room with six cops behind him, guns drawn, waiting for his signal. He doubted Brianna was armed and dangerous, but he wanted a show of force so she wouldn't slip away again.

He motioned for his team to be ready, and then used the master key he'd gotten from the hotel manager. When the electronic lock blinked green, he pushed the door back so forcefully that it slammed against the wall. "Go, go, go!" he shouted at his troops. At his command, they invaded the room like hungry ants that had just found food.

Within seconds Detective Bethancourt knew the room was empty. He saw the indentation of a head on the bed pillow and took off one of his gloves to touch it. "Still warm," he said. "We just missed her."

He pointed to his troops. "Team A, go door to door on this floor and check every room. Team B, take the stairs and go up to the roof; then take them back downstairs. Team C, search the lobby—the restaurants, the casinos, even the women's restrooms. Go now. Use your radios to report in."

As the cops scattered, Detective Bethancourt called the hotel manager. "I need to see the security tapes."

Chapter 43

The reason the show Survivor *is so successful is that we all want to know what we'd be willing to do to survive.* — *Brianna Morgan*

Brianna paid for her coffee and walked deeper into the elegant hotel, keeping her head down and her pace slow. Finding a row of gift shops, she pretended to look in a boutique window before entering. Without slowing her pace, she grabbed a little black dress off the rack and took it to the dressing room.

After checking for security cameras, she changed into the dress and looked in the mirror. It fit like it was made for her. She turned from side to side. If she had tried on a dozen dresses, this is the one she would have chosen. She felt like Dolly Parton, because the geometric neckline made her breasts seem larger and the sheath hugging her torso made her already lean waist appear even smaller.

She pulled the tags off and blinked in surprise. The little scrap of fabric cost almost five hundred dollars. That would eat into her cash, but she didn't have time to look for a cheaper clothing store. She changed back into her slutty stilettos—there was no more money for a new pair of shoes—then twisted her hair into a high chignon. She added a touch of nude lip gloss, stuffed her clothes into her purse, and went to the cash register to pay for her overpriced dress.

On impulse, she pulled a pale peach silk scarf from a nearby sales rack and wrapped it around her head, Audrey Hepburn style. "I'll take the scarf too," she said, pulling Big Tucker-from-Toledo's cash from her handbag.

After paying for her current disguise, she'd have about three hundred dollars left. She had to take it easy or she'd be out of cash again by tomorrow, but she couldn't dwell on that. Once she found the killer, she'd get her life back—her passport, her bank accounts, and most importantly, her freedom.

Brianna rummaged in her bag until she found the big sunglasses. She pushed them up her nose and gazed at herself in the counter mirror while the attendant counted back her change. She inclined her head at the image looking back at her. She didn't look like the pale-skinned, red-haired, green-eyed Brianna Morgan whose reflection she'd seen in mirrors her entire life. With her darkened hair, skin, and eyes—and the sunglasses, which hid her telltale Slavic cheekbones—she could be Italian, Greek, or Latin.

She was still too tall, especially in her hooker heels, but there was nothing she could do about that. Dropping her purse into a shopping bag, she exited the boutique with a confident gait. Hopefully the security guards would be so busy looking at her caboose that they wouldn't bother with her face.

Brianna strode toward the back of the hotel, got into an elevator, and pressed the floor for the conference center. She heard the thrum of people before she saw them. When the elevator doors opened, she exhaled with relief. The tides had turned: a big conference was a lucky break.

Slithering into the sea of convention goers—all chatting in English— she saw a sign that read, Welcome to Panama Shopping Center Real Estate Investors. Brianna smiled for the first time that day. All the women glimmered with style, their scarves and jewels accentuating little black dresses like hers.

She'd been to dozens of conventions just like this. She knew there would be a closing talk, followed by a cocktail hour, where she could mingle without being recognized. She found the main ballroom and picked up a stray convention binder. She lowered her scarf so it wrapped loosely around her neck; the she removed her sunglasses, pretending to search for someone as she did.

People were sprinkled around the ballroom, making phone calls or chatting in small groups. She spotted a fiftyish man in a designer suit working his smartphone in his chair, probably waiting for the final speech of the day. He wasn't wearing a wedding ring. She entered his row and sat down, keeping an empty chair between them.

Men liked to think they were the ones making the first move.

He glanced at her—a quick primordial check to see if she was friend or foe—then did a double take. His gaze started at her bare, toned legs then worked its way up to her oval face. Brianna felt him trying to come up with a pithy opening line.

He turned to her. "I'm Jake Tanner with Simpson Property Group. I haven't had the pleasure of meeting you."

The direct approach, Brianna thought.

"Hi, Jake. I'm Jennifer Thomas," she said, using an alias from her childhood. From personal experience, she knew there were too many women with that name to cull any meaningful information online.

He smiled, a bit too big and bright for a man having a polite conversation with a stranger. "What do you do?"

She gave him a flirtatious wink. "As little as possible."

Jake leaned toward her. "Where are you from?"

"All over." She softened her smile. "But now I live in Manhattan."

"Who do you work for?"

This guy doesn't give up, she thought. Brianna had read that the best lies were close to the truth. "I'm a freelance journalist," she said. "This week shopping centers in Panama, next week hotels in Dubai."

He fiddled with the knot in his tie, a preening gesture. "Are you staying here at the hotel?"

She lifted her brow. He was direct.

"I'm staying close by. I don't like people putting their noses in my personal business, so I avoid staying at the same hotel as the convention."

Jake smiled, a genuine smile that comes from meeting one of your own. "Jennifer, how is it that we've never met before?"

She leaned toward him and dropped her voice to just above a whisper. "I have a secret to confess."

He leaned his head in, a coconspirator. "I'm all ears."

"I'm bored out of my mind." She looked around to see if anyone else was listening. "But don't tell anyone."

"Your secret's safe with me."

She held out her pinky in a crooked hook. "Pinky-swear promise?"

Jake wrapped her pinky with his. "I pinky-swear promise."

"Jake, can I tell you another secret?"

He grinned. "You can tell me all your secrets."

"I think you're kind of cute. Much too cute to be in this crowd of old geezers."

"I'm glad you think I'm cute, because I think you're gorgeous." He untwined his left pinky from hers and held up his hand, back side toward her. "I know an empty ring finger means nothing these days, but I really am single. My divorce is signed, sealed, and collecting dust in my desk drawer."

Brianna touched his arm, turning his wrist to look at his watch, a solid-gold Rolex. "I think this is a record, Jake."

He frowned, not understanding.

"We went from hello to marital status in under three minutes. At this rate, we'll be in a committed relationship before the plane touches down on American soil."

"Does that mean you're single too?" he asked.

"I bet if you were a dog, you'd be a pit bull. You never let go of a bone, do you?"

He chuckled. "Quite the comedian. But are you a single comedian?"

"Would it make a difference?"

Jake leveled his gaze at her, heat radiating toward her in intense waves. "At this moment, maybe not."

"Don't worry, Mr. Pit Bull. I'm single. There will be no adultery committed tonight."

Jake smiled with the confidence of a man who realized he was about to get lucky.

Brianna just hoped her own luck would hold.

Chapter 44

Moses Souza downloaded the Garibaldi Hotel's surveillance videos from the cloud, compliments of the hotel's security chief. He clicked to the footage time stamped 3:02 p.m., when Brianna had exited her room and entered the stairwell. There were video cameras in all the guest-room corridors but none in the stairwells. He saw her enter the door to the stairs, but there was no record of her leaving the stairwell. According to Detective Bethancourt, his team had searched the stairwell multiple times, starting at 3:10 p.m., and they were positive she wasn't still there.

Moses should be able to find her on the surveillance videos, entering one of the floors from the stairwell door. He was methodical, so he started at the bottom floor and worked his way up. He queued the tapes to start at the time Brianna had entered the stairwell and watched each one for twenty minutes.

On several floors, there were random glitches where the video skipped and stuttered. "Crappy equipment," Moses muttered. "You'd think that a hotel like the Garibaldi would have better video equipment. I bet they've got dirt on everyone in town."

After watching footage for from all the floors within a twenty-minute span, he extended the search to forty minutes. Still nothing. At this rate, he'd be here all night.

Moses stopped watching the tapes, leaned back in his chair, and thought about what he would have done to avoid the cameras. "Dios mio." He sat up so fast that his chair tipped over, knocking him to the floor. Without getting off the floor, he reached up to his keyboard and found one of the places where the video had skipped. He watched the time stamp. It went from 3:04 p.m. until 3:07 p.m. on the second parking level. It wasn't a glitch; it was a three-minute blackout.

He pulled himself back into his chair and found the next glitch on the first parking level at 3:07 p.m. until 3:09 p.m. The final two-minute glitch occurred on the entry level to the parking garage from 3:09 p.m. until 3:11 p.m.

Brianna had to have used a low-frequency CCTV camera jammer. That's exactly what he would have done. But why hadn't she turned the jammer on before she'd left her room? Why did she wait until she'd left the stairwell?

Moses queued up the tapes. He wanted to watch them again. The answer was here. He just had to find it.

Chapter 45

A wolf will chew its own leg off to get out of a steel trap. If an animal will maim itself to get free, imagine what a human is capable of. — *Brianna Morgan*

Brianna studied Jake Tanner with her peripheral vision as the keynote speaker droned on about how technology was changing the future of shopping malls. With a full head of salt-and-pepper hair and smile lines around his hazel eyes, Jake had the well-groomed good looks that telegraphed money and power. He also had the physique of someone who had been—and still was—an athlete.

If Brianna hadn't been running for her life, she would have enjoyed their witty repartee. She felt a twinge of guilt at using him, but right now she'd do anything to stay out of jail and catch Lorenzo's killer. Even if that meant crossing a few lines. After all, pretending to flirt was small potatoes compared to drugging a man and stealing his money. A few short days ago, she would have been horrified by her actions. But just like her dad, she was a survivor, and she would do whatever she had to do.

She leaned toward Jake. "Want to find something more interesting to do?"

"What do you have in mind?"

"Are you up for an adventure?"

A smile broke across his face. "With you? I'm up for anything."

"Why don't you get up and pretend you're going to the bathroom? I'll leave in a few minutes and join you."

"Where are we going?" he asked, his eyes bright at the prospect of a mischievous adventure.

"You'll find out. Just go to the main entrance and wait for me in a taxi."

He frowned. "You're not going to ditch me, are you? Let me wait alone in the cab for an hour while you find another man to flirt with?"

"Been stood up before, have you?" Brianna pulled off her Morganite ring. "My father gave me this when I graduated from college." She handed it to him. "You can give it back to me when I get in the taxi."

Jake brought her finger to his lips and kissed the spot where she'd taken off the ring. "I can't wait to give you your ring back. See you in a bit."

She watched him leave, a handsome man in a bespoke suit. How far was she willing to go? She knew the answer: as far as she had to.

Chapter 46

Detective Bethancourt was leaving the confines of the Garibaldi security office to answer his phone when Moses called. "Talk to me, kid."

"I know two things. She's already left the hotel, and she had help."

The detective raked his fingers through his hair. "Start at the beginning. Tell me everything."

Moses took a deep breath. "There are gaps in the footage. Each time there's a time jump in the video, Brianna Morgan is nowhere to be seen. It took me a while to figure it out, but I'm ninety-nine percent sure she used a CCTV jammer."

"Which is why there's no video of her."

"Yeah, but there are a few weird things, so I've built a plausible scenario."

Detective Bethancourt paced the empty hallway. "Like I said, start at the beginning."

"The cameras saw her leave her room just before you got there, and then there's no trace of her. If she'd had the jammer with her in her room, why didn't turn it on before she left her room?"

"Because she didn't have it yet."

"That's exactly what I was thinking. If that's true, it must have been waiting for her in the stairs. I checked out the video, going back a full day, to see if there were other gaps." Moses scraped back in his chair. "I found another set of time jumps yesterday."

Detective Bethancourt stopped pacing. "This is what you meant when you said she had help."

"Yep."

The detective resumed his pacing. "Any idea where she went?"

Moses clicked his teeth. "I don't know. All I can tell you for sure if that she left the Garibaldi through the back entrance to the parking garage. She could have gotten a taxi or left in a car. She could have walked to the El Colombo Hotel, to its attached casino, or maybe she just walked away. The problem is the footage from other businesses won't help me unless I get the original video so I can find the time gaps."

"How long ago did she leave?"

"Forty-five minutes ago."

"I'll get you the original footage." Detective Bethancourt hung up without saying goodbye, then pulled the walkie-talkie off his belt. "All teams, stop what you're doing right now. The suspect has left the building. Team A, search the streets. Team B, get the original security tapes from every business within a two-block radius and send it to Moses. Team C, go to the El Colombo Hotel and the attached casino." He clicked his walkie-talkie off and then on again. "Team C, meet me at the entrance to the parking garage. I'm going with you."

He hustled to the entrance and met up with Team C on the street. "Alvarez, go to the El Colombo casino and get the security footage. Any problems, call me." He strode toward the El Colombo Hotel. "Guzman, do the same for the El Colombo Hotel. Delgado and Cruz, come with me. We're going to search every nook and cranny of this hotel."

Chapter 47

When you're on the run, you can't just think about where you're going next. You have to think about the next five places you're going, how you'll get there, what you'll eat, where you'll sleep, and then how you'll get away. — Brianna Morgan

Brianna closed the taxi door. "Bio Museum, Amador Causeway," she told the driver.

Jake grinned. "Let the adventures begin."

As she turned to respond, Brianna spotted Detective Bethancourt striding toward them. She pretended to drop something on the floor and ducked as the taxi pulled out of the valet area.

"What are you doing down there?" Jake asked.

"I dropped an earring." Brianna slipped an earring out of her right ear and covertly dropped it to the floor as the taxi merged into traffic. "Here it is." She sat up and showed off the earring like a lost treasure.

"Speaking of jewelry, I have something that belongs to you." Jake held up her Morganite ring. "Please, allow me."

She held up her right hand, and he slid the ring onto her fourth finger. Their gaze held as the taxi wove in and out of traffic.

He let his hand linger on hers. "Are you going to tell me why we're going to a museum?"

She gently pulled her hand away and winked at him. "Roads were made for journeys. Not destinations."

"Okay, Confucius. You win. I'll find out when we get there. But my guess is we're going to an opening party."

"Oh, you clever, clever man."

"I read about it in the Panama tourist info they gave us. I just hope they have a cash bar instead of an open bar. Cash bars stock better booze."

She turned slightly to look him up and down. "Heaven forbid you have to drink Jack Daniels instead of single malt."

Jake arched an eyebrow. "Jennifer, you understand me so well." He fingered a stray curl that had fallen from her chignon. "Let them eat cake while you and I feast on champagne and caviar."

Brianna tried not to flinch. In her desperation to make Jake like her, she was feeding his inner narcissist and lying about everything that mattered. She felt a twinge of guilt but let it pass. Her life was on the line, and if she broke a rule—or a heart—along the way, she would apologize later. In the meantime, she needed to take this man's amorous advances down a notch.

"Jake, what do you do for Simpson Property Group?"

He turned toward her, resting his left hand on the back of the driver's seat, settling in. "I'm the senior vice president of luxury leasing."

She gave him a cockeyed look. "What exactly does that mean."

He chuckled and gave her a practiced aw-shucks look. "I'm responsible for negotiating leased space in our high-end malls to retailers. We start with the anchors—stores like Macy's and Nordstrom—and work our way to the smallest space in the food court."

She kept her gaze focused on him while her thoughts scrambled ahead. She had to stay out of sight and hope Marcio's mother still believed in her innocence.

Brianna kept him talking with leading questions until they reached the Bio Museum, a huge open structure with a roof made up of geometric blocks in bright primary colors.

Jake paid the taxi driver and they got out. "Wow, what is this place?"

She walked toward the museum, turning to make sure the taxi drove back toward the city. "It's a museum dedicated to the diversity of life originating in Panama and how it impacts the planet. It was designed by Frank Gehry, the famous Canadian architect."

She slung her bag over her right shoulder and slipped her left arm through Jake's. "You have three guesses about our agenda for this evening."

"We're going to a museum."

"No." She led him past the museum to a waterfront path behind the museum. "Two more guesses."

Jake looked around the path, which was lush with flowering bushes and mature trees. "We're going to a secret society meeting where you have to know the special knock and secret handshake."

"Great guess." Brianna gave him a sidelong glance as they walked. "But wrong."

As they rounded a curve, he saw dozens of boats parked in the bay. "We're going on a boat."

She pointed to a sparkling white hundred-foot catamaran. "We're going on that one."

Jake smiled. "Just a joy ride or do we have a destination?"

"We have a destination, to be sure. We're going to a secret society dinner on a private, uncharted island. Once we get on the boat, I'll teach you the secret handshake."

He cocked a brow, trying to figure out if she was serious. "Really?"

Brianna chuckled. "Well, we're having dinner on an island, but when we tell our friends, we should add the part about the secret society and say it was an uncharted island. Sounds more mysterious."

He squeezed her hand. "Jennifer, I will never get bored of you."

Brianna led him down the dock to the catamaran.

A middle-age man with tanned skin and beige Dockers held a clipboard. "Welcome aboard," he said in a Canadian accent. "Do you have reservations?"

"No," Brianna said. "Is that a problem?"

"No at all." His eyes twinkled as he talked. "Dinner is one hundred and fifty a person. That includes dinner, an open bar, and transportation to the island. You pay at the restaurant after dinner."

"That's fine," Jake said, putting his hand possessively on Brianna's arm. "Please add our names to your list—Jake Tanner and Jennifer Thomas."

The man wrote their names down and then gave them a bright smile. "I am Captain Thaddeus. Welcome aboard." He offered his hand to help them on the boat. "Would you like a glass of champagne?"

"We'd love champagne," Jake said.

"My steward, Reynaldo, will help you. Enjoy your evening."

Jake led Brianna to the waiting steward and plucked two glasses of champagne from Reynaldo's tray. He handed a glass to Brianna. "Jennifer, cheers to you, the most fascinating woman in Panama."

She looked him in the eye. "To a grand adventure."

They clinked glasses, and she took a sip. She wanted to gulp it, but she needed her wits about her. She would need to ration her sips.

She set her glass down and took Jake's hand, leading him through other guests to the front of the catamaran, where cushioned deck chairs were set up. They sat next to each other, watching the sun dip below the horizon.

"This is amazing," Jake said. "I thought I was going to a boring convention, full of the same group of people I've been around for decades. Who knew it would turn into such an adventure?"

Brianna let out a barely audible sigh. "Yes, who knew?"

"What's on the agenda for tonight?"

She pulled out her journalist's voice. "We're taking a champagne cruise to the island of Taboga, where we will be picked up by private transportation and whisked to an elegant restaurant called La Vista, high on the cliffs. There, we'll listen to live music and eat a six-course dinner, overlooking the water and the Panama City skyline. Afterward, we'll take the boat back to shore."

"And if we want to stay the night?"

She looked at him through her lashes. "We'll see how the evening goes."

Chapter 48

Moses let out a whoop of satisfaction. He'd found the gaps in the security tapes. His boss would be thrilled. He imagined Detective Bethancourt' face—the piercing stare and blank expression. Well, he'd be ecstatic on the inside, even if it didn't show on the outside.

Moses punched a cell number into his desk phone.

His boss answered after one ring. "Bethancourt."

"Boss, she was at the El Colombo Hotel. She left as you were walking over there. You just missed her."

Detective Bethancourt muttered a multilingual curse. "If she walked away, I would have seen her."

"That's what I thought," Moses said. "She probably took a taxi. Many of them have darkened windows, so she could have been right next to you and you might not have seen her."

"Can you find out where she went?"

"Doubtful. The jammer was on, so we can't get a taxi number."

"I'll ask the guys at valet. Maybe they'll remember." Detective Bethancourt paused. "Can you find her again?"

"I don't know. If she keeps using the jammer, then facial-recognition software won't work." Moses leaned back, using the long squeak of the chair to give himself time to think. "Maybe it's time we put her face on TV."

"I was hoping it wouldn't come to this, but I think you're right. Get it done."

Chapter 49

Marcio opened his eyes as his mother walked into his hospital room. "What did you find out?" His voice sounded rusty.

"The police have not found her yet, but they are not far behind." She pulled a CCTV photo out of her handbag and held it up for Marcio to see. "The security team I hired gave me this. She has changed her appearance, but they know what she looks like now."

Marcio studied the photo. "Her skin is darker, but the shape of her eyes and cheekbones make her easy to spot. I would have recognized her immediately."

Isabella gave her son a sharp look. "She is cunning. She dressed like a prostitute, went to a hooker hotel, and even changed the color of her eyes. Are you still sure she is innocent?"

Marcio grasped her hands. "Mamá, on the life of my brother, I know she did not do this. We must help her."

Isabella smoothed his brow. "I was just asking. If you are sure she is innocent, then of course we will help her. As you can see, I am already doing what I can."

Marcio's eyes flicked to the wall. "Dios mio. There she is." He pointed to the television, where Brianna's face filled the screen. "Turn it up."

Isabella grabbed the remote and unmuted the TV.

"An American journalist, Brianna Morgan, is wanted for questioning in the murder of prominent Panamanian businessman Lorenzo Silva. She has auburn hair and green eyes, but she might have changed her appearance." A new photo appeared, the same one Marcio had just seen from a CCTV camera, showing the Latina version of Brianna. "She's been seen recently with dark hair and dark eyes. The screen changed again, and both pictures appeared next to each other. "If you have seen this woman, please call the Policia Nacional tip line."

"Mamá, you must do more." Marcio tried to sit up, but it took too much energy. He sank back into his pillow. "You must help her. I owe her that."

Isabella leaned down and kissed his forehead. "I promise you I will help her." She stroked his hair. "Not because I am convinced she is innocent, but because I know it is only then that you will relax."

He grasped her hand and squeezed it. "Thank you, Mamá."

She brushed his hair back. "Rest now, my son. I will take care of everything."

Chapter 50

Have you ever been at the right place with the wrong person? It sucks. —
Brianna Morgan

La Vista was the type of restaurant where men proposed marriage and women announced pregnancies. It had every element conducive to romance: soft music, attentive wait staff, a salty breeze, and incredible views.

Built high on the cliff, La Vista was part of Villa Caprichosa, a boutique hotel made to look like an Italian estate. The open-air restaurant had a panoramic view of water and the Panama City skyline. The restaurant was decorated in neutral shades of beige, cream and tan, allowing the brilliant blue of the ocean to be part of the color palette. Brianna felt like she was a guest in someone's villa rather than a customer at a restaurant.

Brianna had an attractive man across from her, but her stomach was tied in knots. She picked at a tiny bite of lobster and brought it to her lips, forcing herself to put it in her mouth. If this were any other time, she'd be thrilled to be experiencing this restaurant with an attractive man. But it was wasted on her now.

She feigned interest in Jake's nonstop conversation as her mind calculated escape routes. Although her eyes were pointed at him, her peripheral vision focused on everything around her; she wondered when the police would find her and how she could get away if they did.

After the fifth course of the tasting menu, she excused herself to go to the bathroom. Instead of going to the toilet, she walked along the path on the cliff, fighting the urge to just keep walking. She didn't want to draw any undue attention to herself by disappearing, even though her flight instinct was kicking her like a mad kangaroo.

Brianna took a deep breath, stopping to look out over the bluff. She had to concentrate on her next move. She'd probably be safe on Taboga Island for the night. No one knew she was here, except for Jake and

Captain Thaddeus—who both thought she was Jennifer Thomas—and she hadn't spotted a CCTV camera anywhere on the island. Heck, they probably didn't even have cable TV out here. Even if she saw a camera, she could turn on the jammer, but she would rather not alert the iPhone-addicted patrons that anything was amiss by stopping their cell phone connections.

The problem was Jake. If she'd met him under different circumstances, she might even like him. But there wasn't room for him in her life right now. She had to survive, and he was a means to an end.

The thought of having to spend the night in his arms turned her stomach contents to bitter bile, not because he was repulsive, but because she wasn't that woman—the one who casually slept with a man to get what she wanted. She sighed. She would do what she had to do, but there had to be another way to stay safe.

Brianna looked out over the harbor, yearning for freedom. She could steal a boat and hide in the darkness of the ocean, but what would happen in the morning? Where would she go?

She stifled a sob. Her problems felt heavy, a lead apron she couldn't escape.

Her father used to say that the only way through was through. She hadn't understood it at the time, but now she did. Running wasn't an option. She had to face this ordeal head on, fight her way through the eye of the storm, and find out who had murdered Lorenzo. Because Lorenzo's murderer was also responsible for the attempt on Marcio's life and for putting Brianna in the crosshairs with the cops. She would bet her freedom on it.

She had to get in front of this. To do that, she had to trust Isabella. Again.

Brianna hugged herself in the cool evening air. Trust didn't come easily for her, which was why she'd only had three people to call when her life had fallen apart.

She pulled one of the burner phones out of her handbag and turned it on. As soon as she did, she saw the text from Isabella.

You made the news. They even showed you in disguise. Keep out of sight.

Brianna's stomach flipped. This was the moment she'd been dreading. She, of all people, knew the power of the media. She took a deep breath to steady her nerves, and then she punched in Isabella's phone number. Isabella answered after one ring.

"You are not safe."

"I know."

"My son wants me to help you."

Brianna paused. She hadn't expected that. "Thank you."

"You can thank him when this is over. For now, tell me where you are, and I will send someone to get you."

Brianna paused. The moment of truth. Did she trust Isabella? I guess I'll have to, she thought. "I'm on Taboga Island at a restaurant called La Vista."

"You're with a man," Isabella said. It wasn't a question.

Brianna hesitated for a moment. "Yes."

"That is what I would have done."

Brianna closed her eyes in relief. The simple act of having someone understand her lifted a little bit of the weight off her chest.

"Do not leave the island. I will send someone for you. Check your phone again in one hour for the details."

"Isabella…"

"No, my dear. Do not say anything now. There will be time when this is over." Isabella hung up.

Brianna turned off the phone. Now that help was on the way, she could relax a little. If Isabella turned her over to the police, though, this could be her last evening of freedom. She might as well enjoy it.

She walked to the restroom, wanting to splash water on her face. She looked in the mirror and realized she couldn't wash her face without smudging her bronzer. She settled for washing her hands and touching up her lipstick. Although Jake didn't know it yet, his time with her was almost over.

She swung her hips as she walked back to the table, enjoying the feel of his eyes on her. She didn't want him in a carnal way, but that didn't mean she didn't like the attention.

"I missed you," he said, drinking her in with his eyes. "I asked them to wait until you got back to serve dessert."

"Dessert can wait." Brianna stopped short of her chair and held her hand out to him instead. "I'd rather dance with you."

A smile blossomed on his face. "It would be my pleasure." He stood up, whisking her into his arms. "I'll take you over dessert any day."

They joined other couples on the dance floor, moving in rhythm to the sultry jazz the band was playing. Jake twirled her, and Brianna smiled her first real smile in days, intoxicated with the feel of freedom.

They danced for nearly an hour, stopping only to refill their champagne flutes. She looked at her watch as the restaurant manager made the announcement that the restaurant van would soon be departing for the boat that would take them back to Panama City. She and Jake were asked to settle their bill.

"I need to use the restroom before we leave." Brianna slipped away before Jake could suggest they stay the night. She wanted privacy when she checked her messages. As she headed down the path, away from the restaurant, she turned on her disposable phone. A new text had arrived from Isabella.

A man named Jorge will pick you up at 10:00 p.m. on the dock. He will be wearing my white scarf.

Brianna looked at her watch. It was almost ten now. She used the restroom and returned to the table. Jake already had paid the bill. He was the type of man used to picking up expensive checks.

He stood up.

"Thank you for a lovely evening," she said.

He started to speak, but she stopped him with a soft kiss on the lips. "Shall we go to the van? I'd rather sit in front, where there's more leg room."

He held out his arm. "Let's go get a good seat."

They walked arm in arm to the van and sat in the front bench seat.

Jake stretched out his long legs. "This is the one disadvantage of being tall in a country of short people. Nothing is made for people our size."

Brianna giggled. "The toilets are so low that my knees touch my chin every time I have to use a public restroom."

He traced a finger along the bare skin of her upper thigh. "A small price to pay for such beautiful long legs."

"Says the man who gets to stand up when he pees."

Jake laughed. "Touché."

They rode in silence with other dinner guests until they reached the dock. Brianna glanced at her watch. It was five minutes after ten. She hoped Jorge would be there. If not, she'd have to invent an excuse to miss the boat back to the city.

They got out of the van and walked toward the dock. She spotted a solid man wearing tight black jeans, a formfitting black T-shirt, and a flowing white scarf standing halfway down the dock. Only in Latin America could a man make a silk scarf look masculine and hot.

Brianna squeezed Jake's arm. "Uh-oh."

"What?"

"That's my husband."

"You're married? I thought you said you were single."

"I never said I wasn't married. I said there would be no adultery tonight." She pulled her hand from the crook of his arm. "Jorge!" she called, giving a little wave. "What are you doing here?"

The swarthy man looked at her, frowning.

"I told you I wanted a divorce," she said, loud enough for those around her to hear. "Didn't you get the divorce papers?" She hoped he spoke English...and that he would play along.

Understanding flashed in Jorge's eyes. "There will be no divorce." Although he had a strong Spanish accent, his words were clear.

She stopped short of where he stood, leaving a few yards between them. Jake stood motionless beside her.

Jorge closed the distance between them in a few powerful strides, standing as close as a lover would. She felt his warm breath on her face.

He ran his hands down her arms. "You and I made a vow before God, mi amor." He spoke in a low voice only she and Jake could hear as he pulled the white scarf from around his neck. It made a scratching sound as it caught on his three-day stubble. He wrapped the scarf around her neck, taking his time as he tied it in a loose knot. "You will be my wife until death separates us. But until God takes you, you are mine."

Brianna swallowed hard. Although she'd just met this man, the deliberateness of movements made her knees weak. She knew it was a carnal reaction to the intimacy of his touch, but it caught her by surprise.

He finished tying the scarf and tucked a loose lock of hair behind Brianna's ear. Only then did he acknowledge Jake with a glare. "You can go now."

Jorge pulled Brianna to him and draped his arm around her shoulders. He kissed her temple, gave Jake a hard glare, and led her toward the end of the dock, keeping his arm around her shoulders as they walked.

Brianna glanced over her shoulder at Jake, his face frozen in a tableau of shock. "Sorry," she mouthed. She turned back around, walking in sync with Jorge until they reached a sleek white speedboat. "Thank you," she said, just loud enough for him to hear.

"My pleasure, mi amor." He looked down at her and winked. "It's a good thing we are not really married, for I would never let you out of my sight."

She pulled away. She had to put some physical distance between them. His peanut-butter skin, iridescent hazel brown eyes, and square jaw made him look like an underwear model. Her hormones had been on overdrive since the moment she'd landed in Panama.

"Where are you from?" The journalist in her couldn't help asking questions.

"Venezuela."

She thought he might say more, but he didn't. With his country in crisis, his personal story must be worthy of a Lifetime movie, she thought.

She pointed to the speedboat. "Is this our ride?"

"Yes. Take off your shoes." Jorge's demeanor quickly changed from flirtatious to authoritarian. "I can't return this beauty with a hole in the seat."

She leaned down and slipped off her stilettos, slinging both straps in one hand. She gave her other hand to Jorge and allowed him to help her into the boat. When she was seated in the front, she looked over her shoulder and saw Jake still watching her. She kissed her forefingers and held them up in his direction in a sad farewell.

The devastation on Jake's face gave her a moment's guilt, but she let it pass. He'd move on to the next woman as soon as he saw Brianna's face on the morning news. He would know she had lied about everything, and then anger would fuel his rebound.

She turned to her new companion. "Thanks for playing along."

Jorge winked at her. "Any time. I'd offer my other husbandly skills, but something tells me Senora Isabella would not approve."

The more Brianna knew about Isabella, the more she liked her. No wonder her sons had turned out so well. The sudden thought of Lorenzo made her gasp as if a knife had sliced her heart.

How could the death of a man she barely knew cause her such physical pain?

Jorge started the engine and pulled away from the dock. As soon as they were clear of the bay, he shifted into high gear and headed back to the city.

Brianna wrapped the scarf around her head to protect her face from the sting of the salt as they skimmed the waves. She was grateful the powerful motor made conversation impossible. She rode in silence, wondering what Isabella had planned.

Instead of going back to the commercial dock where the catamaran had departed, Jorge skirted around the city and headed north. They slowed as he came within visual distance of a secluded beachfront house, the dock and backyard lit up with soft lights. Huge bay windows on the rear of the house offered unobstructed views of everything going on inside.

The two-story house had to be at least twenty thousand square feet of modern geometry. A wide set of concrete stairs led from the dock to the back door. The swimming pool cascaded down three tiers on either side of the stairs before ending just feet from the ocean. A helipad was attached to the dock.

"This doesn't seem very private," she said when Jorge put the boat in low gear.

He waved his hand along the empty shore. "No one comes by here except local fishermen. No one will spot you from the sea, and the front of the house is a fortress worthy of Senor Noriega himself."

He slid the speedboat next to the dock and cut the motor. He secured the moorings then hopped off with an agility that belied his size. He held out a hand to help Brianna out of the boat. She scooped up her bag and her stilettos and took his hand, hoping she wouldn't fall as she got out.

He held her hand for a moment too long, a residue of their feigned intimacy. She took the time to regain her land legs then pulled her hand away. Even though he was mind-blowingly sexy, she didn't want him getting any ideas.

Although the dock lights were on, Brianna didn't want to take the chance of stepping on something that slithered, bit, or stung, so she slid her heels back on.

"This way." Jorge motioned for her to follow. She worked to keep up with his long strides as they headed up the path toward the house.

Isabella appeared at the back door, dressed in a white one-shoulder crepe pantsuit with white strappy sandals. She looked as if she were going to afternoon tea at Bloomingdales rather than running a covert op late at night. She watched them approach.

"Hello, Isabella," Brianna called. "This is quite a place."

"It belongs to a friend of my sons. They are traveling in Europe right now."

Brianna stopped short of the woman, not sure how to greet her.

"Your safety is important to Marcio. Therefore, it is important to me." Isabella pulled her into an embrace, kissing both of her cheeks. "I will do everything in my power to protect you."

She collapsed into Isabella's arms, giving in to the tears she'd kept at bay.

Isabella stroked her hair. "Hush now. You are safe here."

They stayed locked in an awkward embrace while Brianna cried. When her tears began to subside, she pulled away. "Thank you."

Isabella brushed the wetness from Brianna's cheeks. "You have had your cry. Now you need to be strong. We must figure out who is trying to harm my son."

Brianna pulled air into her lungs. Isabella was right. She had to keep going, keep pushing.

Isabella turned and led her into the house. "For now, you sleep. We will need our strength tomorrow to plot the demise of a treacherous snake."

Chapter 51

Detective Bethancourt leaned back in his chair as he tossed a small rubber ball in the air. It bounced off the ceiling, and he caught it before it hit the floor. He continued this in a rhythmic pattern: bounce, catch, pause…bounce, catch, pause. The ceiling bore dozens of marks from when he'd done this in the past.

When he was stuck on a case, the physical act of throwing, catching, and bouncing helped clear his head. He had spent the night at the station, taking calls on the tip line. Some people had seen Brianna at MultiPlaza Mall; some had seen her at the Garibaldi Hotel; others thought she had been sighted with Elvis. Tip lines always attracted the crazies, and the more media a case got, the wackier the calls.

Detective Bethancourt caught the ball once more and checked his watch. It was just before 7:00 a.m. Moses had fallen asleep at his desk several hours ago. He should have sent the kid home, but he desperately needed the scrawny genius. He'd wake him up in a bit, as soon as the morning shift arrived.

Four days had passed since Lorenzo Silva's murder. Although Brianna Morgan was his best suspect, something didn't add up. Instead of leaving Panama after Lorenzo's death, she'd stuck around and befriended Marcio Silva. Then, when Marcio was hurt and she had another chance to leave, she had hooked up with Marcio's mother.

When he took her in for questioning, she could have lawyered up or gone running to the consulate. Instead she changed her appearance and stayed in town. Why wasn't she running?

Detective Bethancourt threw the ball at the ceiling again. She was a cool one. In fact, he'd never met anyone so self-possessed. She didn't seem frightened of him either. Most people were terrified when he came calling as a homicide detective.

He yawned, missing the ball as it came down from the ceiling. He needed sleep, but he didn't want to take the time to go home. Instead of going to his house, which would take fifty minutes in rush-hour traffic, he would go to his cousin Guillermo's casita in Veracruz, a little fishing

213

village on the ocean, only ten minutes away. Detective Bethancourt often went there during the day if he needed a shower or a nap. Guillermo would be at work, so he could catch a few hours of uninterrupted sleep.

Veracruz was right down the beach from where Lorenzo Silva had been murdered. Perhaps being in the vicinity would help him achieve the breakthrough he needed.

He grabbed his keys and headed to the parking lot.

Chapter 52

Until you've walked a mile in my stilettos, you have no right to judge me.
— Brianna Morgan

Brianna wandered into the kitchen, looking for coffee. The house was worthy of Architectural Digest's cover. The ceilings had to be thirty-five feet high, and the entire back side of the house was made of glass. The house seemed to be part of both sky and ocean as white light infused the home in sunshine and warmth. The huge walls held massive paintings in bright colors.

Brianna's dark hair was pulled into a high ponytail. Fresh faced and green eyed without the dark bronzer and brown contact lenses, she wore a pair of shorts and a tank top Isabella had provided, making her look more like a coed than a woman on the lam.

She spotted Isabella in the backyard, doing tai chi. One of the hired security men stood guard on the shoreline, a large handgun strapped to his chest. Brianna wasn't sure if the obvious weapon made her feel more secure or more at risk. As her father had been in the military, weapons weren't foreign to her, but men with guns always made her tense.

She deposited her handbag on a barstool. Although she probably was safe here, she wanted her belongings close by, just in case. Looking around, she saw a Nespresso machine on the counter and put a coffee pod in. Rummaging in the cupboards, she found a mug. She missed the aroma of brewing coffee, but she couldn't argue with the convenience of pods for on-demand coffee and espresso.

The machine whirred and hissed while she watched Isabella's fluid workout. Dressed in workout attire, Isabella looked like a model for AARP's wellness catalog.

Brianna found some milk in the fridge and poured a generous amount into her coffee mug. She preferred cream—a daily indulgence—but milk would have to do. At least it was real milk and not that dreadful soymilk many people preferred these days.

She was about to go outside and sit in the sun when she heard a car pull up out front. Her pulse increased as she scanned her surroundings, looking for a place to hide. The speedboat was still behind the house at the dock. Did Jorge take the keys with him or had he left them in the boat? Why hadn't she paid attention?

Isabella came into the house. She must have seen the panic on Brianna's face.

"Do not worry, Brianna. It is Jorge. I sent him out for breakfast."

Brianna let out her breath, unaware that she'd been holding it. She tried to pick up her coffee mug, but her hands were shaking too badly. To hide their trembling, she walked to the sink and washed her hands. "Breakfast sounds good. I was too nervous to eat much at dinner last night."

"I thought so." Isabella touched Brianna's cheek. "You need to eat to keep up your strength."

A key turned in the front door, and Jorge came in with two big bags of groceries.

"Guess who I just saw?" He looked from face to face as he set the bags on the counter. "Detective Bethancourt."

Isabella tapped a pen on the counter. "Where did you see him?"

"I was pulling out of the Veracruz Market, and I saw him drive past. I thought he was coming here, but he turned a few streets before. I drove around for a bit to make sure he wasn't following me or waiting to see where I went. When I was sure I hadn't been followed, I went back to where he turned. His car was parked in front of a little casita."

"What do you think he was doing there?" Isabella opened a bag and pulled out bananas, mangos, and pineapples before putting them in a hand-carved wooden bowl on the counter.

"Maybe he was talking to an informant," Jorge replied. "Maybe it was unrelated."

"We cannot take the chance that his presence here is unrelated." Isabella put a container of blueberry yogurt in front of Brianna and handed her a spoon. "Eat," she ordered.

Brianna pulled out a barstool and sank into it, grateful for its support.

Jorge put a six-pack of bottled water in the fridge. "The detective saw me at the hospital, but I don't think he saw Diego." He motioned to his colleague, who stood outside on the rocks, scanning the horizon. "We could send him to the casita to do recon."

"Do it," Isabella said.

Jorge strode outside to talk to Diego, all flirtatiousness from the night before gone.

Isabella handed Brianna a banana. "Eat this too."

She peeled the banana and ate it without speaking. When she was finished, she pulled the tab off her yogurt and ate it as well.

Isabella handed her a protein bar and watched as she ate it with focused precision.

Brianna got up from the barstool and deposited the trash in the garbage. "My dad was a military officer. I'm hardwired to follow orders."

Isabella laughed. "I will remember that."

Brianna settled back onto the barstool. "Where are we? I know we're north of the city. Are we near the BonitaMar Hotel?"

"You are very astute." Isabella pulled up a map on her iPhone and showed it to Brianna. "We are here, at the edge of Veracruz, the fishing village next to the BonitaMar." She traced her finger along the coastline from their location to the BonitaMar. "As you can see, we are just up the coast. By car, we are less than ten minutes from where my son was murdered."

The two security men entered the house through the sliding glass door to the backyard.

"You should change clothes before you go." Isabella tapped her chin as she inspected Diego's all-black ensemble. "You look like a mercenary."

"I am a mercenary."

"But you should not look like one."

"Yes ma'am." Diego double-timed it upstairs to change.

"See if there is a car in the garage that is less conspicuous than our black SUV. Maybe a maid's car. We must not forget this is a poor village and an expensive car will stick out."

"Yes ma'am." Jorge disappeared into the garage.

Isabella smiled. "I like dealing with people who have been trained in the military. It is so much more efficient than having to explain everything first."

Brianna chuckled. "I couldn't agree more. When I was growing up, orders were obeyed and never questioned. Now I have an assistant, Darcy Pendleton, who's an Ivy League grad, but she needs to understand every detail before she'll do her job. If she doesn't agree with me, she'll debate with me for an hour. Sometimes I think it would be easier to do her job myself."

"She must be a millennial," Isabella said. "She sounds just like my nieces."

Before they could debate the personality traits of each generation, Diego came downstairs, dressed in a blue polo shirt, old jeans, and well-worn tennis shoes.

Isabella inspected him. "Much better."

Jorge returned from the garage. "There's an old Hyundai Tucson SUV in the garage with a full tank of gas." He handed Diego the keys. "The windows are tinted, so you should blend in."

"Did you remove the front license plate?" Diego asked. This would make it more difficult to identify the vehicle from someone in front of the Tucson.

"Affirmative."

"I want to swap out the license plate on the back, just to be safe."

"The local market does not have cameras."

Diego shook his head. "Too many witnesses."

Jorge snapped his fingers. "I know! There's a tourist area as soon as you cross the Bridge of the Americas. Places like that always sell old license plates."

Diego nodded. "A bit out of the way but a great idea."

"Here are the coordinates for the casita." Jorge typed them into his iPhone. "I just sent them to you on WhatsApp."

Diego's phone dinged. "Got 'em."

Isabella looked at her watch. "Check in every thirty minutes."

"Will do." Diego stuffed three protein bars into his pockets and grabbed a bottle of water before disappearing into the garage.

They were all quiet until they heard the garage door shut.

"Jorge, eat breakfast then resume lookout duty. I do not want anyone to surprise us from the sea."

"Yes, ma'am."

Isabella turned to Brianna. "It is time to catch a rat."
Brianna nodded. "Time for the second part of our plan."

Chapter 53

Moses finished his café con leche. He needed more caffeine. He wanted a caramel macchiato, but he couldn't spare the time it would take to go to a coffee shop with a barista. Although they were becoming more popular in Panama, they weren't on every corner. Yet.

When he'd woken up, he'd had the F, G, and H keys tattooed on his forehead. He'd grown up the youngest of eight children and could sleep through a rocket launch. The problem was he needed nine hours of sleep, not five.

He wandered into the break room and refilled his coffee cup, then rummaged through the fridge, looking for food his colleagues wouldn't miss. He found a pudding cup and a mozzarella stick. He ate both in a few bites then washed it down with coffee. As he filled his cup again, he remembered a bag of microwave popcorn in the cupboard. Not breakfast food, but it would have to do.

He put it into the microwave and continued to search the nearly empty cupboards for other forgotten snacks while it popped. When the microwave dinged, he grabbed the popcorn, his coffee cup, and a pilfered bag of fried plantains and headed back to his desk.

An email from Detective Bethancourt was waiting for him.

We've missed something. Start at the beginning. Look with fresh eyes. I'm going to get a few hours of sleep. Call me the second you find something.

The best place to start, Moses thought, was with the original security footage from the BonitaMar. Instead of starting when the power went out, however, he went back to that morning. If something had happened earlier that day, he wanted to see it.

He put the split feed on his big screen, showing the most common areas: the lobby, the restaurants, the bar, and the pool entrance.

He turned on the surveillance tapes and leaned back in his chair, munching a handful of popcorn. He smiled to himself. This was better than going to the movies.

Chapter 54

To catch a rat, you need bait. — Brianna Morgan

Brianna scurried a half step behind Jorge, scribbling in a notebook as she ran behind him. Dressed in a conservative navy-blue suit two sizes too big, she had padded her lean frame with a bulky sweater to make herself look twenty pounds heavier. Her hair, now platinum blond thanks to Isabella's skill as a former beautician, had been trimmed shoulder length and flat-ironed straight. A fringe of bangs shortened her face, and the straight sides diminished her cheekbones. Navy ballerina flats minimized her height, making her legs look less inviting. Her skin was once again white and free of makeup, giving her a youthful look. Blue contact lenses and a pair of nonprescription eyeglasses completed the illusion of a chubby Norwegian executive assistant.

She had wrapped Isabella's white silk scarf around her collar to hide her lean neck. In this tropical heat, she longed to unwind the scarf, but her long neck was one of many things that could give her away.

Jorge had transformed himself into a banking executive, with slicked-back hair and a clean-shaven face. He sported a Brioni suit, borrowed from Marcio's closet. The hard lines of his face were softened with an owlish pair of eyeglasses.

Rather than use Brianna's press pass, they purchased full-fare tickets to the banking summit. Jorge used the name of Isabella's personal banker in Spain, Juan Antonio Ojeda, who had the right credentials to get in. Jorge had lived in Spain for a few years and could fake Juan Antonio's Castilian accent if necessary.

Once they were through the doors, it was just a matter of blending in with the Swiss bankers, Caymanian dignitaries, and European bureaucrats.

Brianna tapped Jorge's shoulder mid-stride. "That's him," she whispered.

He stopped and looked to where she was pointing. A tall, portly American man stood behind a high-end video camera, collecting footage of the attendees.

Jorge held his iPhone to his ear with his left hand, pretending to be absorbed in an important call. He held a carnival-style hot dog in his right hand. He surveyed his surroundings, as if searching for a place to take a break and eat a quick late afternoon snack. As he meandered toward the cameraman, he stopped several times to speak in Spanish to his nonexistent caller. Brianna stayed a half step behind him, her head down and her shoulders slumped, trying to look shorter.

When he was just one step away from the cameraman, Jorge ended his fake call and slipped his phone into his breast pocket. He retrieved a small piece of paper from his pocket. In a voice just above a whisper, he said, "Mike, I have something for you."

Mike looked up from his camera and squinted into the sunlight. He wasn't used to people speaking to him while he worked.

Jorge handed him a note Brianna had written earlier.

Mike,
Please do not react to this message…people are watching. I need you to help me find Ana Maria Lopes. We were supposed to interview her, but after Marcio's car accident, I lost track of her. I have good intel that she'll be here at the conference. The man who gave you this note is going to hand you a hot dog. Under the waxed paper is a disposable phone with my number programmed into it. Text me if you see her.
—Mister Ed

After reading the note, Mike looked up and locked eyes with Brianna. He'd seen her dozens of times without makeup on set, and he knew her in an instant.

His head tilted forward in an almost imperceptible nod. He crushed the note in his fist and stuffed it deep into his pants pocket.

"You like hot dogs, Mike?" Jorge handed him the hot dog in a red-and-white disposable tray. "Careful, it's messy."

Mike accepted it, cradling the tray in his beefy hand. "Thanks, man." He studied it for a moment, then picked up the hot dog, leaving the waxed paper on the tray to conceal the cell phone. "I was getting hungry." He took a big bite then put it back on the tray as he chewed for a few seconds. When he picked it up a second time, he palmed the phone in the waxed paper. "You're right. These are messy."

Finishing the hot dog in three more bites as only big men can do, Mike wiped his mouth with the waxed paper and stuffed the phone into his pocket. He tossed the tray and waxed paper into a nearby trash can.

Jorge pulled his iPhone out of his breast pocket and checked the screen. "Glad you liked it. See you around." He turned and walked away, Brianna hastening after him.

The keynote address was starting in twenty minutes in the grand ballroom. They wanted to arrive early so Brianna could get a seat in the middle of the melee without having to step over everyone. She needed to blend in with the other navy-blue suits.

Brianna held up her badge to the security guard. "Hilde Olson." She clipped her syllables to imitate a Norwegian accent.

The security guard waved her through.

The ballroom already was filling up, everyone anxious to hear the pearls of wisdom offered by Alan Greenspan, former chairman of the US Federal Reserve. Brianna found a seat in the middle of the ballroom, two-thirds of the way back.

She opened her iPad, which had a privacy filter so nosy neighbors couldn't see what she was seeing. On-screen, she watched Jorge's progress. His nerdy glasses disguised a spy camera, transmitting everything in his line of sight to her iPad in real time.

Jorge sauntered around the edge of the ballroom as if looking for a seat. With a practiced motion, he placed a spy camera the size of a nickel on the frond of a silk plant at the front edge of the ballroom, popping the lens through the leaf so the camera would be hidden by the leaf itself while the lens would provide an unobstructed view of the conference attendees. He waited a minute then found Brianna's gaze. She nodded once.

He moved to the back of the room, where he set a camera pen on the back of a table behind the water service. He drank a glass of water then texted Brianna. *Good?*

She messaged him back. *Yes. Good to go.*

Jorge walked to the other side of the ballroom, pretending to look for an outlet. He found one a moment later and plugged in his phone. He needed an excuse to stand up during the keynote so he could scan the faces. There were over a thousand attendees, but he and Brianna were only interested in one face.

The face of the killer.

Brianna studied face after face on her iPad as people walked in. She could discard many of them straight away because most of the attendees were men, and she was looking for a woman.

The buzz in the ballroom grew louder as more people entered, most of them working on cell phones or tablets while waiting for the keynote address to begin. Bent over her iPad, Brianna looked like the rest of the Type A workaholics.

Her phone vibrated. She read the text from Mike. *Ana Maria Lopes is with a group of Swiss bankers heading toward reserved VIP seats at the front.*

Of course, Ana Maria had attached herself to Swiss bankers, the rock stars of the summit. In a sea of bespoke suits and Rolex watches, they stood out with their elegant postures and self-assured smiles. After all, the wealthiest clients in the world would always choose a Swiss banker over a second-tier Caymanian or Panamanian option. They had every right to be smug.

Brianna texted the news to Jorge. His gaze darted to the back of the room, and Brianna watched the video feed as they sauntered in. Each man had a woman on his arm, the women dressed more appropriately for a nightclub than a power conference.

The fourth escort caught Brianna's attention. It was the same woman Brianna had seen her first afternoon at the BonitaMar, which meant it had to be Ana Maria Lopes. Her tight red dress stood out against the backdrop of dark suits, her breasts spilling out for everyone to see. Her weapon was raw sexuality combined with a cunning ruthlessness only found in those whom had clawed their way out of poverty.

The tip Brianna had gotten from El Pie was right—Ana Maria was shopping for a husband. But Brianna had spent time with the Swiss. Each banker would have a wife at home, and at least one mistress in a love nest.

This weekend tryst would be forgotten before the banker's jet touched down in Switzerland.

Ana Maria teetered on her stilettos as she strutted by. The man behind her steadied her with a hand on her hip, an intimate gesture. When they arrived at the front of the ballroom, he guided her to a seat with the gallantry of a medieval knight.

She checked her iPad screen. The spy cam in the silk-plant frond had a good angle on Ana Maria. She pulled out her cell and texted Jorge. *Camera 1 is on target. You can leave your post.*

Jorge read the text, then looked down at his hands and gave her a thumbs-up so she could see it on the video feed. He unplugged his phone from the outlet and wandered to the back of the ballroom, picking up the camera pen before sitting in the back row.

Brianna settled in to watch the show on her iPad. They had their prey. Now they just had to get her alone.

Chapter 55

Detective Bethancourt gave his car to the valet at the BonitaMar. He wasn't the type to spend money on valet parking, but he was in a hurry and didn't want to waste time trying to find a parking space.

Moses hadn't been able to locate Brianna Morgan on the CCTV cameras in the city, and the tip lines had gone quiet. With no other solid leads, he wanted to see if she showed up at the banking summit. Not only was the BonitaMar Resort ground zero for Lorenzo's murder and Marcio's attempted murder, but it also was where she was supposed to be before Lorenzo's murder had derailed her schedule. Perhaps curiosity would bring her here today. After all, criminals often returned to the scene of their crime, either to relive the thrill of what they'd done or to insert themselves into the investigation, wanting to be helpful so they could find out what the cops knew.

"Has the conference started yet?" he asked the valet.

"Si, senor. Everyone is in the ballroom. Alan Greenspan is speaking."

Everyone would be in one place for the keynote speech.

Detective Bethancourt walked the grounds, looking for loiterers. Aside from a few women lying by the pools, the outdoor area was deserted. He studied each woman he passed. They were probably wives of conference attendees, reveling in the tropical sunshine, trying to get a coveted January tan to show off to their friends at home.

He studied each one as he passed. None of them had the long limbs and athletic frame of Brianna Morgan.

After checking the beach area and all five pools, he slipped through the back door of the ballroom. Every seat was taken, and dozens of people stood around the edges of the room, hanging on every word Alan Greenspan uttered.

While Greenspan talked about reform that would prevent another mortgage crisis, Detective Bethancourt scanned the crowd. He looked at the back of every female head, searching for telltale auburn hair. He didn't think Brianna would have gone back to her natural color, but red was the easiest color to check. He let his gaze linger on a few redheads but dismissed them after more intense scrutiny.

Next, he looked at the dark-haired women, a much larger group. Coming up blank, he studied the neck of every woman in the room, looking for Brianna's swanlike neck. This was a more difficult task, as many of the women wore scarves or high-necked suit jackets. He found five possibilities and mapped in his mind where they sat. He would be able to see three of them from the left side of the room, and then he would have to change positions for the other two.

He moved closer to the front to get a better look at the faces and profiles of the three possibilities. He had to squeeze between two young men—most likely aides—who were standing against the wall. He nudged himself into the small space then studied the crowd, searching for his quarry.

Chapter 56

Detectives are just like journalists. They must know who, what, when, where, and how. But most of all, they need to understand why. — Brianna Morgan

Brianna caught sight of Detective Bethancourt as he made his way toward the front of the ballroom. Years of investigative reporting had taught her to be cunning, so she resisted the urge to stare. Rather than look at him directly, she studied her iPad as he moved into the spy cam's field of vision. No question, it was Detective Bethancourt.

She texted Jorge.

Detective Bethancourt is here. Left side of ballroom, midway to front. He is on Camera 1. Prepare diversion if he spots me.

Her mind raced. What was Detective Bethancourt doing here?

Her phone vibrated with a text from Jorge. *I see him. He's looking your way.*

She took a deep breath, willing herself not to panic. She couldn't get up and leave; she would stand out like a neon sign in an Amish community. She had to sit tight and blend in with the crowd. She rummaged in her handbag and pulled out a fresh pack of gum. She stuffed three pieces into her mouth, her jaw chewing in a sprint against time. Once she had gotten the gum to the desired consistency, she pushed it up inside her gums in the highest part of her left cheek toward her eye socket. Then she shoved three more pieces of gum in and did it again on the same side. She didn't care that she was lopsided; she only needed to fool Detective Bethancourt, not everyone at the conference.

She used her tongue to mold the wads of gum just under her left cheekbone. Then she tucked her chin into her chest and blew out the lower half of her face like a balloon. It was crude, but she hoped the detective's eyes would pass over a round-faced blonde without giving her a second look.

Chapter 57

Detective Bethancourt dismissed three of the potential women after seeing their faces and profiles from his new vantage point. He scanned the crowd again. When he let his eyes linger on a woman too long, he counted the seconds until she looked up and met his gaze. A sixth sense made people aware when they were being watched. They had to look—it was an innate survival instinct—to see if the person was friend or foe. The only people who didn't respond to his stare were those who were distracted by their electronics.

Once a woman met his gaze and he saw the shape of her face and the line of her jaw, he moved on to the next woman. Brianna Morgan might be able to change her hair color, eye color, and even the color of her skin, but she wouldn't be able to change the shape of her eyes or the sharp planes of her face.

He continued scanning the room. Most people in the audience seemed entranced with Greenspan's speech, watching him with the wide-eyed reverence people give to royalty and movie stars. Others were hunched over their smartphones, unwilling to stop working for even an hour.

He watched a blond woman. Unlike the others, she never looked up from her tablet to meet his gaze, and she never looked up at the speaker. Her neck was wrapped in a scarf, and she had a curtain of blond bangs. She was the right age, but the shape of her face was wrong.

He knew Brianna now; he had been in her file and in her head. She would be more aware of her surroundings. Having been trained by a military tactician from birth, she wouldn't be hunched over a tablet. She would be looking around, assessing the situation with those intelligent green eyes of hers.

He flicked his eyes away from the blond and moved on to the next woman.

Chapter 58

As a child, I used to cry whenever I watched Wild Kingdom. *It broke my heart when a lion attacked a sweet gazelle. But as I got older, I realized the lion must eat too. Sometimes, in the name of survival, someone else must get hurt.* — *Brianna Morgan*

When the detective's gaze moved away from her, Brianna closed her eyes and tried to slow her pulse. That was close, she thought. She wiped away a bead of sweat before it could trickle down her face. Her heartbeat reverberated through her body like a nightclub bass.

She had to keep thinking, and she couldn't do that while she was having a panic attack. The adrenaline overload was only good for a sprint out the door, but that would be suicide.

She took another deep breath, watching Detective Bethancourt on the camera feed.

When he walked out of range, she pulled out her phone and banged out a text to Jorge. *I need to see what he's looking at. Change positions!*

Jorge read the text and pushed himself off his position on the right-hand wall. After meandering back to the water station at the rear table, he poured water into a glass and drank it in one long gulp. When he was finished, he walked up the left aisle, looking at the people in the seated section as if he were searching for a seat. He kept walking toward the front, knowing no seats were available. When just four people separated him from Detective Bethancourt, he squeezed into a space against the wall with others who had come in late.

He pulled his camera pen and a small notebook out of his breast pocket. He looked straight ahead to keep Detective Bethancourt in the sights of his eyeglass cam and positioned the pen to see what the detective saw.

On her split screen, Brianna watched Detective Bethancourt scan the crowd until he found a tall brunette to focus on. He stared at her with unblinking intensity until the woman returned his gaze. Once she did, he averted his eyes and went back to scanning the crowd.

He repeated the stare three times, all with brunettes.

That was his game: intimidation. Brianna smiled. Now that she knew his strategy, she could beat him. At least long enough to get back in the game. Plus, she had the advantage of being a chubby blonde now. He already had scrutinized her and given her a pass. With any luck, Brianna could escape his eagle eyes long enough to accomplish her goal.

The crowd around her jumped to their feet, clapping like game-show contestants.

Brianna stood with the rest of the crowd, putting the iPad on her seat and then applauding while watching Detective Bethancourt out of the corner of her eye. She kept her shoulders hunched and her knees bent as she clapped, facing the podium, mirroring the look of adoration that was painted on every face around her, even though she hadn't heard a word of Greenspan's speech.

She clenched her teeth, trying to restrain her nerves. She hated not being in control, and for this to work, she had to trust other people. Her plan depended entirely on a stranger's charm, Ana Maria's narcissism, and a little bit of luck keeping Detective Bethancourt far away.

Chapter 59

Marcio pushed himself up in bed. Pain radiated from his neck and chest down his legs. During his years as an athlete, he had learned to compartmentalize his physical discomfort and separate it from what needed to be done. Rather than taking a pill, he drank some water. He needed to be sharper than he'd ever been in his life.

He picked up his iPhone and sent a text message. *Mamá, I am awake. What can I do to help?*

His phone beeped with her response. *Rest, my son. Brianna has a plan.*

He wanted to throw his phone at the wall. He was tired of being sidelined. He sent another message. *Where is Brianna now?*

Isabella texted back. *She is with one of the bodyguards I hired.*

Frustrated, Marcio punched his response into his phone. *Tell him if anything happens to her, I will hold him responsible.*

Isabella's final text caught him by surprise. *Jorge will protect her. He is halfway in love with her.*

Marcio started to throw his phone then thought better of it. He exchanged it for the television remote, hurling it against the opposite wall, feeling a sense of satisfaction as it smashed into tiny bits of plastic.

He needed to get out of the hospital. Right. Now.

Chapter 60

In order to get a journalism degree, students are required take at least one course in ethics. But idealism goes out the window in the real world. There is no black or white in journalism; there are only murky shades of gray. — Brianna Morgan

Brianna tucked her iPad into her bag and joined the crush of people rushing out of the ballroom. After just one hour of the conference, the lure of free drinks at five o'clock was like a siren's call, turning stuffy bankers and economists into free-spirited vacationers.

After exiting the sterile ballroom, she walked into the courtyard, which had been transformed into a tropical wonderland. A band played reggae music, the sound carrying in the humid air. Tiki torches flickered with ambient light as beautiful Latin women in form-fitting black dresses handed out welcome cocktails.

Brianna longed to be in front of the camera, catching the looks on the faces of these important men as they ogled the local girls, their indecent thoughts transparent for anyone to see.

She sighed. She had more important things to do tonight than philandering husbands looking to taste a slice of paradise.

She accepted a champagne cocktail offered from a young woman who'd been surgically enhanced from top to bottom.

Meandering from group to group, she listened to snippets of conversation.

"Greenspan hit the nail on the head."

"I used that economic principle last year and made a killing."

"I bet you a thousand bucks I can get that waitress to sleep with me."

Brianna smiled. Bingo! She'd found what she was looking for. She pretended to check her iPhone as she glanced at the guy in his early twenties who wanted to get laid. He was an inch or two over six feet, with the type of boy-next-door good looks that had catapulted Tom Cruise to superstardom.

He was surrounded by a pack of twenty-somethings—bright, young rising stars who worked hundred-hour weeks for their chance to someday earn multimillion-dollar paychecks. They were slamming free drinks, thrilled at a few hours of unsupervised party time.

Brianna approached the group and adopted her Norwegian accent. "Hello. I am Hilde Olson from Norway. I'm so relieved to find some people my age. Can I join you?"

The mini-me Tom Cruise put his arm around her shoulder, drawing her into their group. "Darling girl, of course you can join us." His British accent dripped of trust funds, prep schools, and a top-notch education. "I'm Colin Wentworth, and these are my pals. We're all overworked and underpaid, but damn if we don't have fun anyway."

Sucked into their group with the ease of a puppy rejoining its pack, she raised her glass to clink with his.

"Hi. I'm Julie." A petite brunette with a pixie haircut turned to her, waving at her even though she was less than a foot away. "What company are you with?"

"A private bank in Norway." Brianna gave them a convincing smile. "I'm so glad I found some friends. I have the juiciest piece of gossip that I've been dying to share."

"Do tell," Colin said. "Gossip is our currency."

Brianna looked around, as if to see who might be listening. "My boss is from Spain. He went to a high-end strip club last night and got robbed by a Latin dancer named Ana Maria."

"Did the little vixen take his wallet?" Colin lifted his glass in mock salute. "These Latin whores are sneaky bitches. One of them tried to snatch my wallet last night as well. But I caught her in the act and made her give me free lap dances for an hour so I wouldn't turn her in."

Julie rolled her large cornflower-blue eyes. "If you didn't hang out with the pigs, Colin, you wouldn't wake up in the mud."

"Darling girl, I didn't go to the club to meet the future Mrs. Wentworth. I just wanted a bit of fun. Don't get your knickers in a wad."

Julie turned back to Brianna. "Was your boss pissed?"

"Like you wouldn't believe. There was something in his wallet that his five-year-old daughter gave him, and he wants it back." She leaned in to share her next bit of gossip. "Here's the best part. This dancer, Ana

Maria, showed up today at the conference, walking in with a group of VIPs."

Colin shrugged. "Old news. Look around you. Half the women here are either prostitutes or gold diggers. Not that there's much of a difference."

A girl with long California-blond hair leaned forward to share in the gossip. "Was this Ana Maria one of the people who walked in late and got escorted to the front row?"

"Yes, that was her. She was the woman with the red dress and the large…" Brianna used her hands to indicate both breasts and butt.

"Oh, the J-Lo booty," Colin exclaimed. "Yes, I definitely saw her. A girl with that much junk in her trunk is bound to be nasty. Just my kind of girl. I might even be willing to lose my wallet to her."

Julie pouted. "The only one nasty is you, Colin. Why do you guys find it so sexy when girls stuff silicone in their chests and butts? If it's that entertaining, why don't you just get a silicone doll? Then you could squeeze it whenever you wanted to."

"Now there's a thought," said a guy joined who looked like a real-life Ken doll. "What do you think, Colin? Should we chuck our jobs and start selling Silicone Suzies?"

"Not a bad idea, Justin. Think of all of the wankers we'd be helping."

Brianna needed to rope them back in. "I really like my boss and was trying to think of a way to help him. I thought of something, but it's a little cruel."

"If she stole his wallet, she deserves a bit of payback." Colin leaned into her. "What cruelty do you have in mind for our naughty, nasty Ana Maria?"

"I think we should expose her to her new friends. Let them see who she really is."

"That's about as entertaining as reading to your grandmother." Colin leaned back, bored at the suggestion. "Twenty bucks says they met her at the same club your boss did, dirty rotten scoundrels that they are."

"I overheard her talking to them earlier," Brianna fibbed. "She told them she was in financial sales. She's here at the conference as a registered guest, posing as a banker."

"Nooooo," Julie said, her big eyes getting even bigger. "Isn't that identity theft or something?"

"I don't know if it's a crime," Brianna said, "but I think it's our job to make sure they know the truth about her."

Colin rubbed his hands together. "Lies and intrigue. That makes things a wee bit more interesting." He wrapped his forefinger and thumb around his chin, as if thinking. "Those VIPs might be dirty rotten scoundrels, but they're our dirty rotten scoundrels." He slammed the palm of his hand on the table. "Let's out the whore! At least this conference won't be as dull as the last one."

"How are you going to expose her?" Julie asked.

Brianna tapped her nails on her champagne flute, pretending to think. "I think we should let Colin do it." She smiled at him. "Are you up for it, Colin?"

Justin, the Ken doll, chanted, "Col-in. Col-in. Col-in."

"Of course I'm up for it." He tossed back the rest of his drink and smoothed his dark hair back. "Point me in the right direction."

Brianna looked around, pretending to look for Ana Maria. "There she is. My twelve o'clock."

Every head in their group swiveled toward their mark.

So much for being discreet, Brianna thought.

"A hundred bucks says I make her cry." Colin opened his wallet, pulled out a crisp hundred-dollar bill, and slapped it onto a table.

"I'll take that bet," Justin said, tossing his money on top of Colin's.

"I will too." Julie opened her purse and counted out five twenties. "I don't think you can make a stripper cry. Once you've made the decision to sell your body for money, there are no tears left."

Colin pushed a bit of blond bangs away from Brianna's face, a gesture much too intimate for a man she'd just met.

"You hold the pot, Hilde," he said, nodding toward the money, "since you don't have money on the wager."

Brianna scooped up the cash, fanning it out in front of her. "If I did, my money would be on you." She tapped him on the nose with the bills. "Good luck."

He leaned in for a kiss.

"Hold on. I see my boss. He doesn't know we're doing this. I want to make sure he doesn't stop us." Brianna ducked away from him. "Be right back."

Before anyone could stop her, she dashed over to where Jorge was sipping a club soda with lime as he kept an eye on Ana Maria.

"How is it going?" he asked.

"They say journalists have no heart." Brianna shook her head. "Those kids are vultures in Armani."

He chuckled. "Are they going to help us?"

She nodded. "Even better. They're taking bets right now to see if they can make her cry."

"It should be quite a show."

Brianna shook her head. "You have no idea. That kid Colin, the tall one with the dark hair, could star in his own version of Cruel Intentions."

Jorge cocked his head, a question in his eyes.

"It was a famous teen movie in America, but it's not important." She waved her hand as if shooing away a fly. "If Ana Maria is innocent, we'll apologize later." Brianna's eyes hardened. "If she's guilty, I want her to admit it to the world."

Chapter 61

Colin Wentworth had been raised in the system—not the government system of foster care and juvy—but the rich kids' system of boarding schools, nannies, and absentee parents. In some ways, the lack of parental attention was the great equalizer among the rich and poor. Kids who lacked attention acted out. Period.

His way of getting attention was to be the ringleader in every devilish plot a boy's brain could imagine, and he was nothing if not creative. At twelve, he'd "borrowed" his dad's jet so he and his mates could go skydiving, even though none of them had ever taken a skydiving safety course. One of his friends, Oliver Wood, broke both of his legs during a hard landing and spent a month in traction.

At fourteen, Colin paid an escort to pose as his mother and seduce Jean Botz, the headmaster of his prep school. Colin waited outside with a camera hoping to get blackmail photographs that would guarantee top marks. The plot backfired when Jean Botz rebuffed the woman's advances because he was gay, and then caught Colin lurking in the bushes. He'd managed to avoid expulsion but was kindly asked to pursue his education elsewhere.

His father's influence—and even more of his family's money—had ensured him a spot at Cambridge, although any other kid would have ended up behind bars with a permanent black mark on his record.

He had a natural cruel streak and had been in and out of therapy since he was twelve. In his final report, one psychologist had written, "Colin Wentworth is a classic narcissistic sociopath, destined for either prison or politics."

At twenty-four, armed with a business degree he detested, he had one more year before he could access his trust fund. He had no intention of working for even one minute longer than he had to, so staying out of trouble to keep his job never crossed his mind.

Colin loved to make wagers. It fed his addictive nature. Not only was he sure he could win this bet to make the whore cry, but as the victor, he might also have a shot with Hilde Olson.

His dad was a failure as a father. But having been married seven times to a string of beautiful wives, he was good at choosing genetically blessed women.

Colin had learned from his father how to spot good breeding from a woman's bone structure. Although Hilde Olson looked a bit thick in the waist, she might just have a bad wardrobe. She looked fantastic without makeup, a fresh-faced beauty with cheekbones that models dreamed about. When her scarf unwound a bit, shortly after she had joined their group, he caught a glimpse of her neck. The sight made him ache with desire. He wondered if under her bulky clothes she might be one of Victoria's secret angels. If he were successful in his quest, maybe he'd get lucky and find out for himself.

"Do you have a plan?" Brianna asked when she returned.

Colin smirked. "Darling girl, I always have a plan."

Julie shook her head. "He doesn't have a plan. He's just going to wing it. Like always."

"Jules, it may surprise you to learn I have a plan that would be approved by Sigmund Freud himself." He used a fork to clink his glass. "Ladies and gentleman, may I have your attention, please? I would like to present my glorious plan." He bowed low, twirling his hand like a Shakespearian actor.

His audience clapped and hooted, supporting their leader.

Colin put his foot up on the rung of a barstool, enjoying the limelight. "I will do a visual inspection of Ms. Ana Maria to find out what her insecurities are." He turned to Julie. "Jules, darling, if I told you that you were fat, would it make you cry?"

She chortled. "Of course not. I weigh ninety pounds. I'm always the skinniest girl in the room."

"Exactly!" he touched one forefinger to his nose, pointing the other one at her like a game-show host. "If I tell a skinny girl she's fat, she'll not only laugh at me, but she'll never think of my comment again." He turned to Brianna. "Likewise, if I tell a woman with flawless skin that she has a crater face, I'll be wasting my breath." He traced a finger along Brianna's cheekbone. "I might as well throw darts made of feathers."

Carly, the California blonde, raised her hand. "Colin, you're so right. I don't have a big ass, so if you tried to fat-shame me for my big booty, I'd think you were crazy."

"But if I said you were the dumbest girl in the room, I'd hit a nerve, wouldn't I?"

Her eyes expanded with a micro-expression of fear.

He walked toward her, smiling with the benevolence of an amused dictator. "Darling girl, I wouldn't do that to you." He kissed the top of her golden head. "Not unless you deserved it."

He turned back to his audience. "The key to making a woman cry is to uncover one of her deepest fears. I need to find out what this Ana Maria hates about herself so much that she's trying to camouflage it. In other words, what piece of history she's trying to rewrite."

A nerdy-looking guy in glasses looked at Colin with awe. "How do you know this?"

He winked. "I screwed one of my therapists, a hot little number who wore designer suits in the office and nothing but leather in bed. We had the most interesting pillow talk."

Brianna snapped her fingers in front of his face, bringing his attention back to the present challenge. "Colin, I have something you can use. My boss was online last night, trying to track her down. He found out that her mom is a maid and her dad is a laborer. That's not so important in Norway, where I'm from, but in Latin America, having poor parents is something she would want to hide."

A serpentine smile slithered onto Colin's boyish face. "Good, anything she's trying to hide can be used against her." He leaned in close. "A kiss for luck?"

Brianna leaned in close and whispered in his ear. "I'll do better than that." She put a pair of black lace panties in his hand. "Just in case you need proof of your conquest to her admirers."

Colin uncurled his hand and stared at the black lace, feeling like a fifth grader touching his first pair of panties.

She used her fingertips to tilt his head up to look at her face. "Be a good boy and you might even get a reward." She took the panties from his frozen hand and tucked them into his breast pocket. "There you go." She patted his chest. "Good luck."

Colin's cocky smile returned, and he saluted her. He pulled her into him for a hard kiss then turned toward his mission.

Colin picked up a flute of champagne from a passing tray. He preferred single malt scotch, but bubbly seemed appropriate since he was already planning his victory celebration.

Chapter 62

The ability to compartmentalize is what keeps soldiers alive on the battlefield. My father trained me to sequester my emotions from an early age because everyday life is full of skirmishes. It doesn't matter if I'm hot or hungry or frightened—I need to focus on what I need to do, rather than how I'm feeling. Unlocking my emotions during the height of conflict is never an option. — Brianna Morgan

Julie turned to Brianna as Colin walked away. "I'm sleeping with him."

"Darling girl," Brianna said, mimicking Colin, "I don't want him, and you deserve better." She looked down at sweet, wide-eyed Julie. "I'm sure he's a load of laughs, but he's not the guy who's going to be there for you when your mom gets cancer."

Julie sighed. "I know. But his personality is so big, and mine is so small."

Brianna gave her an impulsive hug. "Julie, you have a terrific personality. You're so bright and sweet. There are a lot of great guys out there who will adore you. You just need to break free from Colin's spell long enough for one of them to find you."

Julie gave her a smile of gratitude. "You're not really from Norway, are you?"

Brianna hesitated then shook her head.

"I saw your contacts move. Your eyes are green, not blue."

Brianna studied the young woman in front of her. It was always the quiet ones you had to worry about.

Julie looked up at her, eyes wide. "Are you with the CIA or something?"

"Something like that." Brianna grabbed Julie's hand. "Come on. We don't want to miss the show."

They followed Colin at a distance, the others trailing behind as they turned on their smartphone video cameras. No one wanted to miss a single moment of Colin's show. It would be recorded from every angle, for both posterity and social media.

The VIPs were all silver-haired men, past their physical prime but at the pinnacle of their power and wealth. Each one had a delectable piece of Latina arm candy nearby.

Colin approached the group. "Excuse me," he said, his upper-crust English charm oozing out of his million-dollar smile. "I'm sorry to disturb you, but I have something I'd like returned." He stood in Ana Maria's personal space.

At first she looked as though she wanted to snub him, but he was so much more handsome than the men she was with, and he reeked of money. "What can I do for you?" she asked, her voice sultry with promise.

"Darling girl, you can return my wallet."

She looked him up and down, sizing him up. "What are you talking about?"

Colin continued as if she hadn't spoken. "And in exchange, I'll give you these back." He pulled the black panties from his breast pocket.

One of the silver-haired foxes tried to protect his new companion. In a tone dripping with condescension, he asked, "Can I help you, Mr...."

"Mr. Wentworth. Mr. Colin Wentworth. Son of Lord Fenton Wentworth, grandson of Lord Ulysses Wentworth."

The silver-haired executive's demeanor changed as quickly as if he were a thumb puppet and someone had pressed his button. He held out his hand. "Mr. Wentworth, I'm Roger Baumann. I met your grandfather once. It's a pleasure to make your acquaintance."

Just like that, Colin's old-money family name had taken him from interloper to ultimate insider.

"I'm sorry to disturb you, gentlemen, but Ana Maria and I have unfinished business." He turned to her. "I'll give you an extra hundred if you return my wallet."

She shot him a mean look. She was street-wise enough to know he was up to something. "I have no idea who you are or what you want, but you are making a big mistake."

Colin chuckled. "You can't have forgotten me so soon. I paid you a thousand bucks last night, and you gave me an energetic night of...shall we say, naked gymnastics and oral negotiations."

Roger and the other Swiss bankers chuckled the way successful men do when they brag of their conquests. The hope of memorable sex was the reason they plied local girls with expensive meals and French champagne.

"I have never seen you before." Ana Maria spat out the words between clenched teeth. "Clothed or unclothed. And I certainly never slept with you or took your money."

"Darling girl, it doesn't matter that you're a working girl. We're all friends here." Colin leaned in for a kiss.

Ana Maria slapped him, leaving a red handprint on his face.

Colin made the sound of a tiger. "I'm glad you remembered that I like it rough. You gave me quite a working over last night. I was hoping for a repeat performance tonight."

A hint of fear flashed in Ana Maria's eyes. "I've never met you before. You have me mistaken for someone else."

Colin pulled a roll of bills out of his pocket. "Look, love, I'm willing to pay you, same as last night, but I really need my wallet back. You can keep the money, just give me the wallet and my cards."

The executive nudged her. "Go ahead, sweetheart. Give him his wallet back."

Ana Maria whipped her head around, glaring at Roger and his cronies. "I. Am. Not. A. Prostitute."

Colin smiled, reveling in his role. "Of course you're not a prostitute. That's such a low-class term anyway, and you're a classy girl. What do you call yourself? An escort? A companion? A temporary girlfriend?"

The VIPs chuckled, elbowing one another in the ribs. They clearly were enjoying this. One of them flagged a waitress and ordered a fresh round of drinks.

Ana Maria looked around and saw that her knights had shed their armor. She stabbed Colin's chest a manicured finger. "Look Richie Rich, I don't know who you are or what you want, but you'd better watch your back."

His mouth curved into a vicious smile. "Here she is, the real Ana Maria. You can take the girl out of the slum, but it's wicked hard to take the slum out of the girl."

Her eyes turned hard, mean, as she closed the space between them. "That's right. I come from nothing, which means I've got nothing to lose. You're in my country now."

Instead of backing up, Colin put his nose in her face. "You think that thing between your legs is going to bag you a rich husband?" He threw his head back and laughed, his eyes sparkling with amusement. "I have news for you. Rich men may crawl into your bed in the dead of night, but when they see you in the morning without makeup, they'll jump back out again. You can buy big boobs and a gigantic booty, but a clear complexion and the right bone structure only come from good breeding."

"You son of a bitch." Ana Maria attacked him, raking her fingernails down his face. "How dare you insult me?"

He pushed her arms away with the ease of a martial arts fighter defending himself from a nine-year-old.

"Tsk, tsk, Ana Maria. You're showing your ghetto roots." He held her arms back with one hand and waved his other hand up and down her body. "Of course, I'd expect nothing less from the spawn of a lowly maid and a laborer."

Ana Maria's body wilted as though Colin had landed a punch in her gut. She blinked a dozen times, trying to keep her emotions locked inside, her fight depleted.

Knowing he'd hit a nerve, he kept going. "Look at you. Your hands are thick, your skin is rough, and your face is pockmarked from acne. You'll never be anyone's wife. At least not anyone important."

She turned to her silver-haired companion, looking for support, but Roger turned his back in indifference. This wasn't his fight.

Her lip trembled as she turned back to Colin, imploring him with her eyes to show mercy.

He gloated, knowing victory was near.

Ana Maria opened her mouth, but no sound came out. Then the damn broke and tears spilled out of her eyes, tracking black muddy streaks down her face.

Chapter 63

Colin turned away from her with the exultant look of a prizefighter. He had won! He scanned the area, looking for his groupies.

He saw his buddies giving each other high fives. He caught up with them and gave Justin, a fist bump. "My good man, I hope you caught that."

Justin beamed, following his leader back to their table. "Yeah, Colin, I got it. You were a badass."

"Send me the video," Colin ordered. "We'll watch it later."

"Sure." Justin pressed a few buttons on his phone. "It's on its way."

Colin caught up with Julie and gave her rear-end a pat. "I do believe I just won a hundred bucks."

She pushed his hand away. "You won the money, Colin. Nothing more."

"Look who's become an ice princess," he retorted. "I'll look for a warmer reception elsewhere." He pulled away, searching for Brianna.

"Looking for Hilde?" Julie asked with the sweetness of a Southern belle.

He scrutinized Julie, his pixie-sized friend with benefits. Perhaps she wasn't as naïve as she seemed. "I wanted to thank her for the challenge. Plus, she's holding the pot."

Julie opened her purse and handed him a wad of cash. "She gave it to me. She knew I'd make sure you got it."

He looked around, ignoring the money. "Is she coming back?"

"I don't think so. She asked for your number, so I gave it to her. Said she was going to send you a WhatsApp."

Colin whipped out his phone from his suit pocket. A voice message from an unknown number was waiting. It had to be Hilde. He pressed "play." It was Hilde's voice but without the Norwegian accent.

Hi, Colin. There are two things you should know. First, Julie adores you. You don't deserve her, but if you work hard, one day you might see what an amazing woman she is.

247

Second, there's a chance that Ana Maria murdered a man five days ago and attempted to murder someone else to cover her tracks.

When I asked you to talk to Ana Maria, I didn't think I was going to put you in danger. But you were too good, and you pushed her too far. I don't know what she'll do to retaliate, but she could be dangerous. Stay away from her, and watch your back. Don't drink anything unless you buy it yourself. Don't get into a taxi unless you request it.

If it's possible to get an early flight home, do it. I saw her face as she ran out of the cocktail party. She's unhinged. I think you're a pompous ass, but I don't want you to get hurt.

Take care, Colin, and good luck.

Chapter 64

Detective Bethancourt heard a woman screaming across the courtyard. He pivoted and raced toward the melee. There were too many people for him to see what was happening, but he did spot the flail of arms and elbows above the crowd that always meant trouble.

He nudged and elbowed his way through the mob of bespoke suits, catching a glimpse of a woman walking away from the scuffle. Unlike most of the people in the crowd, who were looking toward the skirmish—rubber necking to see what was going on—this woman didn't glance back as she headed away from it. The mass of humanity closed in around him, and the woman disappeared.

Something about her reminded him of Brianna Morgan.

This woman was shorter and thicker than Brianna—not to mention blond—but there was something about the set of her shoulders. He bobbed left then right, trying to see her again, but she had vanished.

Chapter 65

I have many insecurities. Will I ever find lasting love? Will I still have a job once my face loses its youthfulness? Will I get over my trust issues? One thing I'm supremely confident about, however, is my ability to focus when I'm working. That's where I shine. — Brianna Morgan

Brianna strode away from the scuffle, calling Jorge on her cell before she was away from the crowd. "Ana Maria is leaving the reception."

Jorge pushed himself off his perch on a planter at the edge of the throng. "I've got her."

Sliding into a shaded chaise lounge that would hide her from the conference attendees—and from Detective Bethancourt if he happened to walk by—Brianna pulled out her iPad and watched Jorge's progress through his eyeglass camera. He followed Ana Maria at a discreet distance while she walked by the pools and then up the stairs toward the main level.

In the lobby, he pulled ahead, arriving at the bank of elevators a half minute before she did, time enough for him to send three elevators to various floors without passengers.

He called Brianna. "Play along," he whispered. And then louder for Ana Maria's benefit, he said, "Skip, I need you to commit to the purchase plan, or I'm going to find another buyer." He paused, watching Ana Maria in the stainless-steel surfaces of the closed elevator doors as she approached. "I know it's expensive, but no risk, no reward."

Ana Maria didn't look at him. She kept her head down while she pressed the elevator call button.

"We only have a minute before the elevators come back," Brianna said on the other end of the phone. "Get a close-up shot of her face."

"Look, Skip," Jorge continued, "I had three investors lined up when you came to me." He paced the elevator waiting area, his voice loud as he acted like a crazed businessman. "You convinced me to let the other investors go. I did what you asked. Now you need to do what I'm asking."

Jorge bumped into Ana Maria. "Sorry," he muttered, looking up from his phone to make eye contact.

Brianna had expected sadness in Ana Maria's face, but what she saw chilled her. Ana Maria didn't look sad or beaten. Her face was contorted comic-book style into a mask of rage.

"Did you see her face?" Brianna asked.

"Yes," he said.

"She's going to do something. I don't like that pompous ass Colin Wentworth one bit, but we need to protect him."

"Yes, I agree, Skip. How can we fix this?"

"Let her get off the elevator before you. Then get off on the next floor and take the stairs. Find out what room she's in."

"Okay, sounds good, Skip. I'm about to get in an elevator, so I'll talk to you in a bit."

Jorge ended the call as the elevator doors opened. He motioned for Ana Maria to get in first. She entered, pressing the seventh floor. He pressed floor fifteen and pretended to look at something on his phone.

When the elevator let her off on the seventh floor, he watched her walk down the hall to the right. Before the doors closed, he pressed the button floor number eight. On the eighth floor, he ran down the hall to the emergency stairs. Pushing the door open, he pounded down the stairs, opening the door a crack on the seventh floor to see where Ana Maria was.

She was standing in front of her room, trying to get her key card to work. He watched her try three times before the access lock blinked green. She kicked the door open and slammed it shut again after she was inside.

Jorge called Brianna. "Room seven seventeen."

"Leave a camera somewhere in the hallway. We need to know when she comes out."

Jorge pulled the pen out of his suit pocket then changed his mind. He put the pen back and pulled out the small camera that had been on the silk-plant frond during Alan Greenspan's speech. He had picked it up after everyone else had left the ballroom in search of cocktails.

He put the small camera in a flower arrangement near the elevator.

"Good decision," Brianna said in his ear. "I was worried someone might pick up the pen."

"I would like to leave another camera to show us the hallway leading to her room, but there is no place to put it."

"That's okay. If she leaves her room, she'll use the elevator."

"I don't like it. Two is one, and—"

"One is none," Brianna finished for him. "My father used to say that to me all the time. It must be a military thing."

Jorge looked down the hall again, searching for a place to put his pen cam. "Well, there's nothing to be done about it. One will have to do."

"It's not one," Brianna said. "Your eyes are one, and my eyes are two. I'll be watching the entire time. We have our redundancy."

"You're right." He pressed the elevator call button. "I'm coming back down."

"You need a new look," she said. "She's seen you as the suave businessman. It's time for you to become a tourist. The gift shop is still open. Find something gaudy to wear."

Back in the lobby, Jorge walked to the gift shop, trying on a few hats before settling on a large-brimmed Panama hat. Although Panama hats were made in Ecuador, they had become ubiquitous with tourists who wanted a Panamanian keepsake.

He also bought a white Panama shirt—made in Colombia—and went into the dressing room. Still wearing the spy glasses, he shrugged off his shirt jacket and unbuttoned his shirt, watching himself in the mirror.

His phone rang in the dressing room. "Nice abs."

Jorge chuckled. "I knew were watching." He tugged his dress shirt off and took a moment to pose from side to side.

"Magic Mike has nothing on you."

He was silent, his face a question mark.

She sighed. "You really need to watch more American movies."

He chuckled again as he slipped the Panama shirt on. "I can give you a private show later."

Brianna squeezed her eyes shut. "I'm kryptonite, Jorge. The last guy who wanted to give me a private show wound up dead." Her tone softened. "Hurry up. We don't want to miss whatever Ana Maria has planned."

Chapter 66

Detective Bethancourt flashed his badge to a silver-haired VIP at the location of the disturbance. "What happened?"

A muscle clenched in the man's jaw. "There was a misunderstanding, Officer. That's all. There's no need for the police to get involved."

Detective Bethancourt made a show of looking for the man's name tag. "And you are?"

"Roger Baumann from Zurich."

"Can you tell me exactly who was involved in this misunderstanding?"

Roger shook his head. "I'm afraid not. I really must go. Excuse me." The Swiss banker hurried away, brushing the detective off like he would a vacuum salesman.

Detective Bethancourt scanned the crowd. At least a hundred people had witnessed what happened. There had to be someone who was willing to talk. Trying to get a Swiss banker to divulge information was like asking a priest to break the seal of confession. He looked for someone less Swiss looking.

He spotted a group of kids barely old enough to drink giving high fives to a guy with movie-star good looks. Their frat-boy behavior stood out among the conservative bankers.

"Dude, I can't believe you made her cry," a blond guy told Movie Star.

Movie Star flashed some cash. "I always come through when there's scratch to be made."

Pushing his way into their ranks, Detective Bethancourt showed his badge again. "I'm Detective Bethancourt with the Policia Nacional. What just happened here?"

The gregarious banter stopped as quickly as if he'd pressed a "mute" button.

No one spoke, but every set of eyes in the group darted to Movie Star, who calmly put his cash back in his wallet. He clearly wasn't afraid of the police.

Detective Bethancourt fingered the conference ID hanging from a lanyard around Movie Star's neck. "Colin Wentworth from London," he read aloud. He dropped the name tag and stared at Colin, unblinking. "Mr. Wentworth, I just spoke to Roger Baumann from Geneva. He said you were involved in a misunderstanding."

Two guys in the group elbowed each other, trying to suppress their laughter.

Colin looked at Detective Bethancourt with the sincerity of a choirboy. "The misunderstanding wasn't mine. It was Roger's."

"Explain."

Colin sighed with impatience. "Roger thought the woman he was with was a businesswoman. Turns out she's a professional of a different sort." He winked.

The blond guy who'd been fighting to control himself burst into laughter. "When Collin called her out, the two-bit whore actually broke into tears." He mimicked a woman's high-pitched voice. "My name is Ana Maria, and I am not a prostitute."

"Ana Maria? Do you know her last name?"

"Beats me," Colin said.

Could they be referring to Ana Maria Lopes who appeared in the security tapes with Lorenzo Silva on the afternoon before his death? Detective Bethancourt wondered. He didn't believe in coincidences. "What did this Ana Maria look like?"

"See for yourself," the blond guy said. "I got it all on video." He pressed a few buttons on his phone and held it up so they could watch it together.

Detective Bethancourt watched Colin Wentworth humiliate Ana Maria Lopes in front of a group of silver-haired bankers.

"Are you sure she's the one who took your wallet?" he asked Colin when the video finished playing.

Colin smirked. "I've said enough. Why don't you go find the woman and ask her?"

The boy was lying. "She didn't take your wallet, did she?"

Something flashed in Colin's eyes. Detective Bethancourt was getting warmer.

"Did you even know her before you accused her of stealing your wallet?"

Colin's eyes met his.

"If she didn't steal your wallet, and you'd never met her before, why would you accuse her of being a prostitute? Just for fun?"

"He did it for Hilde," a girl said.

"Who's Hilde?"

A beautiful young woman with long flaxen hair pushed her drink around with a straw. "Hilde Olson, from Norway. Her boss was the one who lost his wallet to Ana Maria. It was Hilde's idea to humiliate her. She wanted to teach her a lesson."

"Where is this Hilde Olson now?"

The blond girl shrugged. "She took off."

Detective Bethancourt scanned the group. Everyone looked perplexed except a tiny woman with short brown hair. He walked closer to her. She looked like a deer about to bolt. "What's your name?"

"Julie." She didn't make eye contact.

"Julie, you know where Hilde went, don't you?"

"No." Her voice was small.

"Julie. This is important." Detective Bethancourt used his fingers to tilt her chin up, a gentle nudge so she'd look at him. "Where is Hilde?"

She shrugged. "I don't know where she went, but you won't find her."

He tried not to show his impatience. "Why?"

Her blue eyes looked up at him. "Because she's in the CIA."

Colin leaned forward, intrigued with the conversation. "Jules, why do you think Hilde is in the CIA?"

Julie shrugged again, a little-girl gesture, and looked down again. "I don't know."

Detective Bethancourt tried to keep his face a mask of patience. "Julie, tell me why you think Hilde is in the CIA."

Julie looked at Detective Bethancourt in earnest. "Because I saw one of her contacts slip. Why would anyone with such gorgeous moss-green eyes want to make them look blue? Blue eyes are so boring."

Detective Bethancourt stood straight up. There was only one woman he'd met recently who had moss-green eyes. "Do you have a picture of Hilde?"

Julie shook her head.

"Any of you?" Detective Bethancourt could no longer hide his impatience. "Did anyone get a picture of Hilde Olson?"

Colin moved closer. "My good man, why are you so interested in her? Did she rob a bank or something?"

Detective Bethancourt studied Colin Wentworth. The boy wasn't afraid. He'd probably been in and out of trouble his whole life. Threatening jail time wouldn't do anything but make him more uncooperative.

He pulled his phone out of his jacket pocket and scrolled through it until he found a file of pictures. He put his phone on the table.

"This is Brianna Morgan, a journalist from the US." He scrolled through the pictures from Brianna's news-show press kit. "She's the prime suspect in the murder of a prominent local businessman, Lorenzo Silva." He flipped to a new photo, showing Brianna on a CCTV camera as a Latina. "She's been able to change her look over the past few days and evade arrest." He flipped back to an auburn-haired version of Brianna with a long neck and high cheekbones. "Is this the woman you knew as Hilde Olson?"

Colin stared at him, a look of wonder on his face. "I knew she was a stunner under that hideous suit. Bone structure doesn't lie."

Detective Bethancourt glanced at his watch. "How long has it been since you saw her?"

Colin pulled out his phone. "Look, Detective, I don't think she did it. The last thing she told me was to be careful of Ana Maria. Listen to this."

Chapter 67

After my brother's death, my mother curled up in a ball and cried. Two decades years later, she's still in a fetal position, frozen in sadness. Whenever I want to throw myself a pity party, I think about her and wipe away my tears. I'd rather be cold and heartless than waste my life feeling sorry for myself. — Brianna Morgan

Brianna sat on a lounge chair by the pool, watching her iPad in split screen, seeing video from the spy cam on the hotel's seventh floor as well as the feed from Jorge's eyeglass camera. It was dark, and she had the entire pool area to herself. She was close enough to the convention to hear the gurgle of cocktail chatter, but she was far enough away to be out of sight. She positioned her lounge chair beside an L-shaped hedge of bougainvillea and turned it so the high back of the chair faced any stray convention goers. In the dimly lit area, someone would have to walk the narrow path between her and the pool to see her.

Onscreen, Jorge sat at a table at the back of the lobby bar where he could watch people from three different angles. He didn't have access to the video feed from the hidden camera on the seventh floor, but he'd spot Ana Maria if she exited the elevator.

Brianna settled in, not knowing how long they'd need to watch for her. A moment later, she froze as she heard Detective Bethancourt's voice.

"I just received confirmation that Brianna Morgan is here at the BonitaMar. Or at least she was less than twenty minutes ago. She was going by the name Hilde Olson, from Oslo, Norway."

Brianna clicked off her iPad screen so the glow wouldn't give her away.

"She now has blond hair and blue eyes," Detective Bethancourt said. "She was last seen wearing a navy-blue suit with a white scarf around her neck. I'm sending you the picture she took for her conference badge."

Damn those kids, she growled to herself. *They couldn't keep their mouths shut for one hour.*

"Shut the gates," Detective Bethancourt ordered. "No one gets in or out."

Brianna had hoped it wouldn't come to this, but she and Jorge were prepared with a contingency plan. She waited until the detective had passed, and then she texted Jorge. *Detective Bethancourt is in the conference courtyard. Moving to location B. Will be offline for fifteen minutes.*

Jorge texted back immediately. *Roger.*

Brianna slipped off her scarf and put it in her bag. Its brightness would attract attention like a beacon in the moonlight.

She unbuttoned her suit jacket and shrugged it off before unzipping her bulky sweater. Her head lolled back in ecstasy as she was released from the hot garment. She had worn only a navy one-piece bathing suit underneath the sweater, and the cool breeze felt delicious on her bare skin. Finally, she wiggled out of her suit pants. She longed to plunge into one of the hotel's pools, but she didn't have time to waste.

She bunched up her clothes and wrapped them in a pool towel. She then pulled a thin coverup out of her bag. She zipped it up and pulled the hood up over her hair before sauntering to the nearby towel hut. She stuffed her clothes and the pool towel in a basket underneath some dirty towels. Her bag slung over her shoulder, she strolled to the beach.

Brianna took her time walking down the beach, splashing her feet in the water like a carefree vacationer. A shallow river separated the BonitaMar from the Secrets Resort. During high tide, the river made it impossible to walk from one property to the next, but since it was low tide, she waded through.

Once she was on the neighboring property, she strolled to the edge of the resort, where an oversize hot tub gave its occupants an unimpeded view of the ocean as well as privacy from prying eyes.

An amorous couple soaked in the hot tub, oblivious to everything but each other. Brianna dragged two lounge chairs into the darkest corner of the hot tub area and turned them away from the couple. She sat in one and put her bag on the other. She then pulled out one of her burner phones and called Jorge. It went straight to voicemail.

"Hi, honey," she said at the beep, her voice full of romantic promise. "I'm all set up by the hot tub. Why don't you come join me? And bring a bottle of champagne. Call me back."

She put the phone on the chair between her legs and checked the time. She'd made it to the neighboring resort in less than twelve minutes. She turned on the iPad, opening the split-screen from the two cameras. The video feed on Ana Maria's floor showed an image of a gray-haired couple getting on the elevator, but Jorge's eyeglass camera had gone dark.

Brianna texted him. *No signal from your eyeglass cam. Where are you?*

No response. She sent another text. *Send status report ASAP.*

Nothing.

She tried calling again, but it went to voicemail once more. Something wasn't right.

She backtracked the eyeglass camera's footage, starting when Jorge had sat down in the lobby bar of the BonitaMar. Sensing time was of the essence, she watched in quadruple speed.

Chapter 68

Carrying two laptop cases, Moses trudged into the BonitaMar's security center. Detective Bethancourt had summoned him to find Brianna Morgan. Although a dozen cops were scouring the grounds, his boss had demanded him to join the search as well.

After unpacking his computer gear, he hooked his specialized electronics into the live CCTV video feed. There had to be a hundred videos running on different monitors, showing every inch of the property. He launched his facial-recognition software so it would monitor the images in real time.

Moses plugged in every image he had of Brianna—her natural look from her press-kit photos, the dark-skinned Latina look he had captured from the Garibaldi, and the new blond Scandinavian image he had gotten from Detective Bethancourt. Just for kicks, he uploaded a dozen other images he had of Brianna, including a few of her and Marcio taken by one of the detectives on the day of Lorenzo's murder.

He wanted to give the software an overload of images so he could catch her from any angle.

He set up the system for a manual facial check. If someone had biometric similarities to Brianna Morgan, her face would pop up on a special screen. If he didn't think it was a match, Moses would put the image into a digital file for later review. If he saw a woman who might be Brianna, he would call Detective Bethancourt, who would descend on the area with an army of cops.

Moses called his boss. "I'm set up at the BonitaMar security station. Want me to head over to Secrets Resort next door and do the same?"

"I can't spare you right now, Moses. I have men posted along the beach. She won't get there without a helicopter."

Moses clicked his teeth. "I can think of five ways to get to Secrets Resort undetected."

Detective Bethancourt barked out a laugh. "Thank goodness she's not you. Only a computer geek or a Navy SEAL could get there undetected."

Chapter 69

Think back to when you first watched Silence of the Lambs. Were you scared when Clarice was in danger? I wasn't frightened; I was exhilarated. That's when I knew I was an adrenaline junkie. — Brianna Morgan

Watching the eyeglass-cam video feed, Brianna saw Jorge sit down at a table in the lobby bar. A waitress approached, and they chatted for a minute. When she left, he kept his gaze focused on the corridor Ana Maria would need to take when she got off the elevator. When the waitress returned, she put a tall glass in front of him, most likely club soda with lime. She stayed at his table for forty seconds, standing between him and the corridor. Brianna's view of people getting off the elevator was blocked for the entire forty seconds as the waitress flirted with him.

She didn't look overly disappointed when she left his table. Brianna wondered how often this woman chatted up strangers, hoping for a connection.

When the waitress moved out of the frame, Jorge threw some bills on the table, bolted out of the bar, and raced down the winding lobby staircase.

Brianna watched the segment again. For the entire forty seconds, she could only see the waitress. Perhaps Jorge had spotted something in his peripheral vision.

She kept watching the footage, which showed him jogging toward the beach. When the palm trees became dense, he slowed down, flailing through the fronds. Suddenly the camera spun counterclockwise, as if Jorge were in a tide pool. Then the screen went black.

Brianna watched the last portion again. Something had happened to Jorge. The spinning camera could mean Jorge had gone down. But why? She watched it a third time, memorizing the path he had taken.

She tucked her iPad into her bag. She needed to find out what had happened to Jorge, but first she needed a weapon. Jorge had been special forces. For someone to take him out of commission without a fight meant his attacker was either armed or extremely clever. Or both.

Chapter 70

Moses expanded his facial-recognition parameters. He wanted to eyeball anyone and everyone who resembled Brianna Morgan. A few times each minute, his program pinged, putting the current CCTV image of a prospective match on his central screen.

He studied each image then clicked to the next when it wasn't her.

His computer pinged. He looked at the next image then did a double take.

He looked closer. "What the heck?"

He found the image on the raw video and watched it.

There was no mistaking who it was.

Moses picked up the phone and punched in a number. "Boss, we have a situation."

Chapter 71

Sometimes I wish I were normal. You know, the type of woman who could marry an accountant, have two kids, and go to barbecues on the weekends. The problem is I love the adrenaline I get from chasing a good story. — Brianna Morgan

Brianna approached the river that separated the two resorts. Only a quarter moon and a handful of stars illuminated the beach, but she had the hood over her head, just in case. Two uniformed cops stood watch at the edge of the river on the BonitaMar side of the beach about a quarter of a mile from where she was. She wouldn't be able to get to the BonitaMar without walking past them. She had to assume they had seen photos of her as a blond, so bluffing her way through wasn't an option.

She analyzed her options. She could walk out the front gates of Secrets Resort but getting back into the BonitaMar would be problematic if the resort was in lockdown. She could swim around the guards by going into the ocean and circling around to the other side of the bay, but she'd have to leave her iPad behind. Plus, swimming in stealth mode would take too long.

She needed a decoy.

Brianna went back to the pool area at Secrets Resort. Two boys, around ten years old, were splashing in the pool but other than that, the pool area was deserted. Perfect. Kids did what they were told and didn't ask questions, especially when their parents weren't around.

She crouched next to the pool. "You boys swim like fish."

"Like dolphins," a brown-haired boy said, wriggling his lean body to imitate a dolphin.

"No, like sharks," the other said, his bronze skin and white-blond hair proof of his time in the sun.

"How would you like to make twenty bucks?" she asked, pulling a bill out of her bag and holding it up for them to see.

The brown-haired boy's eyes lit up, but the other boy kept splashing, a bored look on his face. "Twenty bucks won't get us much more than an ice cream. Give us fifty, and we're in."

Brianna laughed, shaking her head. "Okay, you little extortionist, forty bucks. That's twenty each."

"Okay, deal." The blond boy popped out of the pool and sat on the ledge next to her. "You've got us for twenty minutes. Talk fast, lady."

He really was a shark. She had to get his name and hire him at the network when he was old enough to work.

"I'm in too," the brown-haired boy said, popping out of the water and sitting on the edge of the pool next to his buddy.

She smiled her best "trust me" smile. "I'm playing a game of hide-and-seek with my friends. Do you ever play hide-and-seek?"

They both nodded, their heads bobbing with the exuberance of youth.

"I really want to win. That's why I need your help."

She pulled out another twenty and handed one to each of them. They slipped the money into their swim trunks faster than a blind beggar could pocket a dollar on a busy street.

Then they listened to her plan.

A few minutes later, the blond boy raced down the beach toward the river, screaming, his arms flailing above his head. When he got closer to the cops, his incoherent screams turned to pleas for help.

"Help! Help! My friend is drowning!" He motioned wildly at the cops. "He's not waking up. Please! Hurry!"

The cops, trained to be helpful, left their post and chased after the kid.

As soon as they arrived and had their backs turned to her, Brianna left her hiding place behind a tall potted tree and darted across the low river and down the beach. Her robe blew open as she ran, the hood falling back as she used every ounce of adrenaline to speed along the beach.

She'd instructed the brown-haired boy to lie on his side at the edge of the pool, pretending to sleep. When the cops—who she told them were her friends—shook him, he'd spit out some water he'd been holding in his mouth, as if he'd been drowning. She said her friends could never know they'd been set up. It had to be a secret. The secret had cost her another twenty dollars.

Brianna knew that when the cops were assured the boy was okay, they'd go back to their post. She estimated she had three minutes tops to run down the beach. Her years of jogging to stay in shape were finally going to do more than keep her thighs trim.

She pumped her arms and legs, running faster than she'd ever run in her life. She'd wrapped the strap of her shoulder bag around her chest like a messenger bag. As she ran, the pouch bounced against her back.

When she reached the BonitaMar's beach stairs, she bounded up to the pool area and ducked into a copse of trees, looking around as she caught her breath. She would have liked to keep running, but stealth was more important now than speed. Since two cops had been posted on the beach, she had to assume there would be more all over the resort.

Rather than wash the sand off her feet in the beach shower, as guests were supposed to do, she drug her dirty feet in the kids' pool, one after the other, then pulled her sandals out of her bag and slipped them on. Keeping to the shadows, she walked toward the far side of the resort, where she thought Jorge had been attacked.

When Brianna was almost there, she sidled around a pool bar, keeping her back against the concrete wall. Peeking around the edge of the building, she took a moment to scan the area. No cops, no guests. Just geckos and birds.

She was about to slink around the corner when a hand clamped around her mouth, pulling her back against a solid male body.

She tried to scream, but the sound was muffled by the man's large hand.

"Shh," he whispered in her ear. "Do not struggle."

Brianna stilled, her frantic brain trying to compute an escape plan.

"Brianna, it's me." He turned her around to look at him.

"Marcio," she breathed, falling against him in a body hug. "I thought you were in the hospital."

"I was." He winced. "Be gentle. I still have broken bones."

"Sorry." She pulled away. "What are you doing here?"

He brushed a few strands of hair out of her face. "I came here to save you."

She frowned. "I didn't know I needed saving."

He pulled her to him and kissed her, a gentle meeting of their lips.

She pulled away. "Marcio, what are you doing?"

He sighed. "I'd hoped you'd figure it out for yourself when I kissed you." He stared at her. "I am not Marcio. I am Lorenzo."

She jerked back. "How can that be? I found your body."

"You found Marcio's body."

She blinked. "But he was dressed in your clothes."

"Yes, I know." Marcio caressed her left cheek with his fingertips. "I will explain that to you, but first I know who killed my brother."

"Ana Maria Lopes," she said, beating him to it.

He nodded, a smile curving onto his chiseled face. "When I rejected her, she tried to get even."

"But she killed the wrong brother."

He traced the top of her breasts with his fingertips. "Yes. After our amazing dinner, I went home and went to bed. My guess is she must have called the apartment, wanting to see me. When Marcio saw I was asleep, he must have put on my clothes and pretended to be me. We used to do that all the time as kids and even a few times as adults."

"Why didn't you tell me earlier?"

He kissed again, trailing kisses down her neck. "I wanted to tell you, but I had to be certain that you did not kill my brother."

She pulled back so she could look at him, touching his face with the reverence of someone who had been given a second chance. "I understand," she whispered, before leaning in to kiss him again.

"Brianna, I have ached for you." His voice ragged, he kissed her mouth, her cheeks, her eyelids. He put his hands inside her coverup, touching every curve of her body.

She moaned as he kissed her neck. "I thought you were dead."

"Brianna, step away from him," a female voice commanded.

Startled, Brianna whipped her head around. "Ana Maria. What are you doing here?"

"Brianna, I barely recognized you as a blond." Ana Maria stood five feet away, leveling a long-barrel revolver at Lorenzo. "I figured you were behind that whole prostitute farce earlier."

Lorenzo frowned. "You two know each other?"

"I was going to be on her show," Ana Maria said, her gun hand steady, her voice strong. "Please, Brianna, don't make me tell you again. Step away from Marcio."

Brianna took a step away from Lorenzo, expecting Ana Maria to point the gun back and forth between them. "Sorry about that whole prostitute thing, Ana Maria. I needed to rattle your cage."

Ana Maria kept the gun trained on Lorenzo.

Brianna inched farther away. "Why are you doing this? Why are you trying to kill the Silva brothers?"

Ana Maria looked confused. "Why am I doing this? You don't get it, do you?"

Brianna took another step away. "Get what?"

"I'm saving you from Marcio." Her voice cracked. "You don't see it yet, but he's a snake…a vile, disgusting reptile masquerading as a man."

"Ana Maria." Brianna's voice was soft, soothing. "Marcio is dead. This is Lorenzo. You killed the wrong brother."

"I killed…" Her voice trailed off, almost like a question.

Lorenzo lunged for the gun, but before he could reach it, Ana Maria had regained her composure. She pointed the gun at Lorenzo's head, her eyes sparkling with the hardness of steel. "You're not fast enough, Marcio. You never were."

He froze in place, putting his hands up.

"Ana Maria, no one else needs to die." Brianna took a step toward her.

"Brianna, I don't know what crap Marcio has been feeding you, but I did not kill Lorenzo." She gestured with the gun. "He did."

Brianna's head swiveled toward Lorenzo. He rolled his eyes to indicate she was crazy.

"Why would Lorenzo kill his twin brother?" Brianna asked.

Ana Maria snapped the fingers on her free hand. "Keep up, gringa. Lorenzo didn't kill Marcio. It's the other way around. Marcio killed Lorenzo."

Brianna looked from Ana Maria to Lorenzo. "Ana Maria, Lorenzo is standing right in front of you."

"No, gringa, you're the one who has it wrong." She was talking to Brianna, but her eyes were locked on Lorenzo. "Let me start at the beginning, so there is no confusion. I had a younger sister, Lula, a beautiful girl who competed in several pageants and was on her way to becoming Miss Panama. Perhaps even Miss Universe."

Brianna turned to Lorenzo. He looked bored. He clearly had heard this story before.

"Lula met Marcio, and within a week, she'd fallen madly in love, as only eighteen-year-old girls can do. Marcio seduced her, but once he'd had his fun, he threw her away like yesterday's garbage."

"Is that why you killed my brother?" Lorenzo asked, eerily calm.

Ana Maria glared at him. "I didn't kill your brother, you psychopath. I went to him for help when Lula committed suicide." She gasped, trying not to cry. "You killed him because you knew he'd hold you responsible for Lula's death."

"Ana Maria, put the gun down." Brianna's voice was steady. "I'm sorry about what happened to Lula, but Marcio is dead."

Ana Maria shook her head. "No, you're wrong. Lorenzo is dead, and Marcio is trying to impersonate him." She glanced at Brianna. "You don't believe me? Ask him something only Lorenzo would know."

"This has gone on long enough," Lorenzo said. "Put the gun down and let us discuss this like rational adults. You came to me once for help. I still want to help, but I cannot do that with a gun pointed at me."

"Lorenzo, let's humor her." Brianna turned toward him again. "Where was Carpaccio invented?"

He looked at her and smiled. "In Italy, of course."

She smiled back at him. "Yes, at La Campana, the oldest restaurant in Rome."

Lorenzo nodded. "We should go there sometime."

Brianna's world spun. Lorenzo would have remembered the story about Carpaccio being invented at Harry's Bar in Venice. They'd talked about it on their first date. They'd both been there.

Brianna took a step away. "Ana Maria, I'm so sorry."

"Sorry for what?"

"For humiliating you in the courtyard…and for not believing you…"

Ana Maria glanced at her. As soon as her eyes left Marcio, he lunged at her, knocking the gun to the ground.

She scrambled for it, but even injured he was stronger, faster. He grabbed the gun and turned it on Ana Maria. "You stupid bitch. You should have left it alone."

He brought his arm back and swung hard, hitting her on the head with the gun. The crack of the impact sounded like a car crash as metal hit bone. Ana Maria instantly crumpled to the ground.

Brianna went for the gun, but Marcio pivoted, reaching for the gun with his right hand as he pushed her to the ground with his left. Once she was down, he stood over her and pointed the gun at her heart.

He made a tsk sound as he shook his head. "Brianna, Brianna, Brianna. Why could you not just play along? I had such high hopes for us."

She looked up at him. "You killed Lorenzo? But why? He was your brother. Your twin."

He shrugged. "It was inevitable. We competed for everything our entire lives. As boys, we competed for the love and attention of our mamá. As young men, we competed in our fútbol careers." He spat on the ground, barely missing Brianna's head, the only sign that he was winded. "Things got worse when Lorenzo was picked up by Barcelona."

She furrowed her brow. "Barcelona?"

He glared at her. "You Americans do not get it. In Europe and Latin America, we live and breathe fútbol. Barcelona is the best team in the world. It was my dream to play for them, but Lorenzo took my spot." He smiled, lunacy in his dark eyes. "I had to pay another player to end Lorenzo's career. I thought I would get my chance, but then Mamá came to his rescue, as always, and made me keep my promise to stop playing fútbol at the same time as he did."

Brianna tried to keep the revulsion out of her voice. "You paid someone to injure Lorenzo so you could take his place. How could you do that?"

"I told you. Lorenzo stole what should have been mine." He knelt over her, one foot on either side of her torso, relaxing the gun by her face. "We left Spain and came to Panama. Things were good for a while, but then Lula committed suicide. When I saw them talking that day at the BonitaMar, I knew I had to kill him. Plus, that was the day you showed up. The woman we both wanted."

Brianna shook her head back and forth, trying to make the craziness stop. "But you and I never met before Lorenzo was killed."

"It does not matter. When I saw you with him that day on the verandah, I knew I had to have you." He caressed her cheek with the barrel of the gun. "But you could not keep your mouth shut. Now you have forced me to destroy the one thing in life that could have brought me such happiness."

Brianna's eyes widened as panic set in. "What are you going to do? Kill me?"

He sighed, a heavy sound. "The cops will think Ana Maria killed you. I tried to save you, but in the struggle, the gun went off. After she killed you, I was afraid for my life, and I had no choice but to kill her too."

Brianna's eyes darted around, searching for some way to stop him. "Tell me how you did it. How you killed Lorenzo."

He smiled. "That part was easy. I told him you wanted to meet him, that you had a surprise planned. I drove him to our project next door, where we keep a little skiff. No one knows about it because we do not have a crew there yet. I had a picnic basket and blankets waiting, so he thought you had planned an evening rendezvous when we took the boat to the little beach. He never questioned the basket of food after you just had a big meal. The dumb sop did not ask questions; he just smiled from one ear to the other as he kept rattling on about you. Brianna this, Brianna that. I got tired of listening, so I told him to have a drink while I went to get you."

"Why would he have waited in the cave alone?"

"My dear, he was setting up a candlelight picnic for you. I thought of everything, even the candles. After he died, I went back to get everything and decided to leave the bottle of Disaronno as a—how do you say?—a red herring."

She squeezed her eyes shut. "I don't understand."

"The day you met Lorenzo, I asked my friend in security who you were. He told me and gave me a key to your room. I went in there just to find out more about you. I didn't intend to set you up for his murder. When I saw the bottle of amaretto, I just took it, thinking it would be the perfect way to get him to take the cyanide, because Disaronno tastes like almonds.

I hadn't planned to frame you. In fact, after he died, I went out of my way to prove you were innocent."

"How?"

"I put Ana Maria's hair under Lorenzo's bed and put a feather from her apartment in the wheel well of his car. I thought a small accident would make me look innocent and her look guilty. I had not planned on the two Mack trucks making the accident so bad, but it turned out to be a good thing. No one suspects that I am the one who killed my brother."

Brianna looked up at him, the pieces falling into place. "You left the hotel before I interviewed Ana Maria so your accident would distract me. You knew that if I talked to her, I would uncover the truth about her sister's suicide."

"You understand me so well." He used his free hand to stroke her hair. "After you are gone, I will mourn you just as I mourn the loss of my brother. You could have been my one true love."

He stood in one fluid movement, pointing the gun at her again. "Goodbye, Brianna. Give my regards to Lorenzo."

Before he could pull the trigger, he fell to the ground.

Brianna blew out the breath she'd been holding. "Took you long enough."

Chapter 72

Detective Bethancourt threw down the kayak oar he had used to knock Marcio unconscious. "I wanted to get his confession on tape while he could still talk." Wiping the sweat off his brow with his forearm, he picked up his phone, which had been hiding in the shadows while Marcio had confessed to killing his brother.

He motioned, and a dozen cops swarmed the area. "Cuff him before he wakes up," he said, pointing at Marcio.

Several medics brought a gurney for Ana Maria and got her vital signs before whisking her away to an ambulance.

Brianna scooted into a sitting position, resting her arms on her knees. She tried to pull her robe closed, but the zipper had ripped. "You took a chance, you know. When you hit him with the oar, the gun could have gone off."

"I didn't leave it up to chance." Detective Bethancourt peeled off his blazer. "The gun had no ammunition."

Brianna tried to get up but fell back down again. "How could you possibly have known that?"

He reached into his pocket and pulled out a handful of bullets. "Because I was the one who took them out of Ana Maria's gun." He put out his hand to help her. "Take my hand. Let me help you up."

She grabbed his hand, popping up like a jack-in-the-box.

"When I figured out she was in the middle of this, I followed her and saw the gun in her purse. I had one of my men distract her while I took the bullets out."

He patted her on the shoulder, an awkward gesture. "Miss Morgan, I owe you an apology."

"An apology from the great Detective Bethancourt." She pretended to look around. "Wait, let me get my cameraman. I need to get this on film."

He chuckled in that "aw shucks" way that was uniquely his. "I deserved that. Truth is, I thought you did it from the start. I know brothers have been killing each other since Cain and Abel, but I didn't see it. Like

273

everyone else in this city, I was star struck. Those boys had everything going for them: success, money, looks." He looked her up and down. "Beautiful women."

Brianna tried to pull her robe closed again. "Detective, you and I are a lot alike. We spend our lives trying to see through the layers of lies that people bundle themselves in. Even so, I didn't see this coming. I'm still trying to grasp how one brother could kill his twin."

"I'll probably never understand it. I'd do anything for my brother, give him the shirt off my back." He chuckled again. "Or at least my sweaty blazer."

Brianna smiled faintly. "Marcio's jealousy must have been eating him from the inside out."

Hearing someone running, they both turned to see who was coming at them full speed in the dark. Detective Bethancourt drew his gun, preparing for the worst.

Chapter 73

Moses appeared from the bushes, winded from his long run, his limbs flapping in the breeze. "Brianna, you're safe."

She looked from Moses to Detective Bethancourt and back again to Moses. "Do I know you?"

"I work for him," Moses said, pointing toward Detective Bethancourt. "He wanted me to find you because he thought you killed Lorenzo Silva."

Without warning, he lurched toward Brianna, embracing her in a hug. "I knew you didn't do it. I didn't know it at first, but when I figured out that Marcio killed his brother, I knew you were in danger."

Detective Bethancourt tried to suppress a smile. "Moses is a rookie. By the time he has a few dozen cases under his belt, he'll stop getting attached. But you're one of the first." He shrugged. "Moses spent so much time with you, he feels like he knows you. I suppose you'll have a friend for life."

Brianna grinned and stuck out her hand. "Moses, it's a pleasure to meet you."

Blushing, Moses extended his hand. "If you ever need anything, let me know."

"Ditto," she said.

"Something wasn't right from the beginning," Moses said, picking at the stud in his jeans pocket. "I kept going through the security video of the night of the murder. That's when I put it together: I was seeing both brothers at the same time. While you were with Lorenzo having dinner, Marcio went into your room and came out with a heavy plastic bag."

She snapped her fingers. "That must have been when he took my bottle of Disaronno."

Moses's head bobbled up and down. "That's what I thought. When I got to the security office here today, I input photos of both of you into my facial-recognition program to search through the CCTV video feed. When Marcio's face popped up, I went back and watched the footage. That's when I saw him take down a guy with a Taser and drag him into a storeroom."

Detective Bethancourt chimed in. "He called me, and we came down to investigate. We'd just gotten that guy untied when we heard your voice."

She nodded at the oar. "That's where you picked up your weapon of choice."

Detective Bethancourt nodded.

Brianna looked around. "Where's the guy you untied?"

"Is he a friend of yours?"

"Could be. Was he wearing a Guayabera shirt and a Panama hat?"

"That's him."

"His name is Jorge. Isabella Silva hired him to find Lorenzo's killer. When she finds out Marcio killed Lorenzo, she'll be devastated." Brianna took another sip of her water. "Is Jorge okay?"

"He's recovering from a nasty Taser burn, but he'll be okay. My officers are taking his statement. They should be done soon."

Moses kicked the ground. "What are you going to do now, Brianna? Now that we've caught the killer."

She smiled. "I never got my vacation. After the summit ends, I might—"

A gunshot rang out, puncturing through the tranquility of the waves lapping on shore. Then another shot and another.

Chapter 74

When I think about my time in Panama, I remember the sparkling blue ocean and the smell of jasmine in the air. I've locked away the fear of prison and the smell of death. One day I might take it out and examine it, but for now I choose to remember Panama's beauty. — Brianna Morgan

Brianna grabbed her bag and ran toward the sound, Detective Bethancourt and Moses were already ten yards in front of her. Halfway there, she detoured to the towel hut, where she had stuffed her suit. Dumping the dirty towel tub over, she pawed through the pool towels until she found the towel she had wrapped her suit jacket in.

After shedding her coverup, she picked up her crumpled suit and continued running in her bathing suit toward the sounds of screams. When she arrived at the edge of the chaotic scene, she pulled her suit jacket over her bathing suit and scanned the crowd. She spotted Mike, his camera light focused on the center of the melee, capturing video of the chaos.

She pushed through the crowd. When she reached Mike, she pulled the microphone out of his utility belt.

"What happened, Mike?"

"Brianna, I'm so glad you're okay." He gave her a quick bear hug then pulled away. "Three shots fired. Three people down. That's all I know. I got here just before you did."

She pulled her phone out and punched in Babs number in Dallas, feeling the surge of adrenaline that always accompanied an unfolding story. When her producer answered she skipped the hellos. "Babs, we have a shooter in Panama. I want to go live."

As she listened, she pulled a lipstick out of her bag and smeared some on. Juggling the phone between her ears, she fluffed her hair. "Roger that." She clicked her phone off. "Live in fifteen seconds, Mike."

She buttoned her suit jacket as she walked in front of the camera. She didn't bother to put on her pants, as the video wouldn't show below her waist. It was more important to be first than to worry about what the other spectators saw.

Brianna held the microphone in front of her mouth as Mike counted down, her mouth breaking into a smile.

This was her life, and she had it back.

Epilogue

Three days later, Brianna checked out at the front desk of the BonitaMar Hotel. She wheeled her suitcase toward the front door, where a taxi waited to take her to the airport. She stopped before stepping outside, glancing down at her new Jimmy Choo stilettos, a trophy from Panama.

She had evaded the cops, cleared her name, and scooped the entire world on the BonitaMar shooting, which turned out to be a disillusioned investor who'd lost his fortune and blamed the banks. In the space of a few days, she'd had two segments go viral—her coverage of the hotel shooting and her in-depth story regarding the Silva brothers. Her agent was leveraging her infamy and negotiating with the network to take The Morgan Report to a coveted prime time evening slot.

She'd paid El Pie the money she owed him, and she'd said her goodbyes to Detective Bethancourt.

She was about to walk out the front doors of the hotel when the concierge rushed up to her. "Miss Morgan, someone left this envelope for you. I promised to give it to you in person."

Brianna thanked him and took it, looking at her name written in old-fashioned script on the envelope. A woman's writing.

She opened the envelope and pulled out a letter from on thick cotton stationery.

My dearest Brianna,

What a journey we have had. Both my boys loved you, but I am now a mother without sons, for one is dead and the other is in jail.

My new purpose in life is to ensure that Marcio is set free. For better or worse, you and I are connected in his fate. I should not blame you, but how can I not? You were the catalyst for my deepest pain. If he goes to prison, you must share the burden of my suffering.

In my heart, I know this is not goodbye, but rather hasta pronto, as I will see you again soon.

Sincerely yours,
Isabella Silva

Author's Note

If you have enjoyed this book, please consider leaving a short review on Amazon. I would appreciate it more than you will ever know.

Although this is a work of fiction, some of the places are really part of the Panama that I have grown to love. For example, Casa Bonita is an actual luxury residential condo building in Playa Bonita Resort just outside of Panama City. In fact, the apartment where Marcio and Lorenzo lived, Casa Bonita 24o, is an apartment that can be rented for your next vacation. If you would like to stay here, you can go to ChoosePanama.com and look at the apartments for rent. This is a penthouse, and if you would prefer something smaller and less expensive, there are many great options in the building that are also available on the same website.

If you are interested in learning more about Panama as a place to vacation, invest, or retire, please go to ChoosePanama.com and request a free copy of my non-fiction book, *Panama Uncorked*. This is an easy-to-read guide that will give you a good perspective about why this Gringa chose to make Panama her new home.

Panama does indeed have a Johns Hopkins affiliated hospital called Pacifica Salud, a Bio Museum designed by Frank Gehry, and an elegant restaurant on Taboga Island called La Vista, although I took some fictional liberties about where you get on the ferry.

I have started working on Brianna Morgan's second book, *The Cyprus Affair*. If you would like to be notified about its release, please go to MelissaDarnay.com and sign up on my email list.

If you are part of a book club and would like me to join you for a Skype call at your book club meeting, just ask. I try to accommodate each and every request. Just go to MelissaDarnay.com and click on the *Books* link.

Acknowledgments

I would like to thank my great friend Debbie Richardson for encouraging me to write fiction again after a long hiatus. She and I originally met in our neighborhood book club, and then deepened our friendship in a writer's group. Debbie gave me the spark I needed to start writing for one hour per day. Over time, those precious hours became this novel. Debbie is also that friend who helped me get ready to move from Dallas to Panama, packing my office and co-hosting garage sales with me. We should all be so lucky to have a friend like her in our lives!

I would also like to thank the handsome Brazilian men in my life—my Brazilian sweetheart Kleriston Muricy, his brother Moses Muricy, and their cousin Marcio Muricy. Kleriston gave me a second chance at love after my previous husband was killed in a car crash. Kleriston selflessly encouraged me to spend my limited free time writing without making any demands on me.

The inspiration for my character Marcio Silva came after I spent time with my cousin-in-law who is much more handsome in real life than any man has a right to be. I was intrigued by the fact that he has an identical twin and they are both fitness buffs. I wondered what it would have been like for a woman to date one of these beautiful brothers and how their natural rivalry would have impacted a budding new relationship.

I would also like to thank my brother-in-law Moses Muricy, who inspired his namesake character, Moses Souza. The real-life Moses originally asked to be one of the characters in my book, and he proved to be one most fun for me to write. I hope I brought to life the quirky brilliance that makes the flesh-and-blood Moses so endearing. Expect to see Moses Souza appear in future books as a regular supporting character.

If you would like to see what these three men look like in real life, please go to my book page at MelissaDarnay.com.

I hope you have enjoyed taking this journey with me.

If you would be so kind as to leave a nice review on Amazon while you have a glass of wine and dream of Panama, I would appreciate it.

Until next time, Cheers!

Book Club Questions

1. How is it different to use someone the way Brianna did versus a woman marrying a man she doesn't love for financial security? Or a person staying in a job they hate so they can pay their bills?
2. Have you ever loved and hated someone at the same time? Which was stronger, the love or the hate?
3. Have you ever been consumed with such an intense jealousy that you did something you later regretted?
4. While reading this book, did you judge Brianna harshly for the way she used people in order to survive?
5. If your life fell apart and you were on the run from the police, what would you be willing to do to stay out of jail? How would you get cash? Who would you ask for help?
6. If you were on the run—from the police or from a bad situation—and had to change your looks, how would you do it?
7. How would things have been different if Brianna had left Panama as soon as she found Lorenzo's body?
8. Isabella Silva's love for her sons was absolute. Do you think she was right to protect Marcio the way that she did at the end?
9. Which character did you empathize with the most? Why?
10. Who was your favorite secondary character? Why?
11. What did you think about the Swiss banker, Roger Baumann? Did it bother you to think of him as a serial philanderer? Or did you accept that as one of the typical character traits of an ultra-successful man?
12. Did this book make you curious about visiting Panama? Why or why not?

Made in the USA
Columbia, SC
24 December 2021

52382685R00171